PRAISE FOR THE
STEEL BROTHERS SAGA

*"Hold onto the reins:
this red-hot Steel story is one wild ride."*
~ A Love So True

"A spellbinding read from a
New York Times *bestselling author!"*
~ BookBub

*"I'm in complete awe of this author. She has gone and
delivered an epic, all-consuming, addicting, insanely
intense story that's had me holding my breath, my
heart pounding and my mind reeling."*
~ The Sassy Nerd

"Absolutely UNPUTDOWNABLE!"
~ Bookalicious Babes

FREED

FREED

STEEL BROTHERS SAGA
BOOK EIGHTEEN

HELEN HARDT

WATERHOUSE PRESS

For my editor, Scott Saunders.
Thank you for your brilliant guidance
and for your enthusiasm for the Steels.
This series is so much better with your input!

PROLOGUE

Ashley

I park the car, grab the backpack and Penny's leash, and walk to the Syrah vineyards. The harvesting tools sit at the foot of one of the rows. About half of the Syrah has been harvested. I walk to the little shed Dale showed me that first night.

Of course the shed is locked. I didn't expect it to be open. I don't need Dale's tent and sleeping bag. I won't be here long.

But I need to be here. I need to be here with Penny. And with Dale.

I look toward the mountains, where the sun set an hour ago. Dale is somewhere up there. Alone.

He didn't even take his dog.

"Let's sit, girl." I plunk onto the ground.

If I sit, if I touch this ground that he finds so hallowed, maybe I'll understand why he left. Maybe I'll understand that thing inside him that he can't share with me.

Maybe...

Penny lies down next to me, and her body against mine is a warm comfort. I rub my arms to ease the chill.

Dale told me to bring a jacket that first night. Why didn't I bring one tonight? The weather was warm today, but nights are a different story. At least I'm wearing long sleeves.

I grab the backpack and open it. I pull out a bottle of

water and pour some into a bowl for Penny. She eagerly takes a drink. I take a drink from the bottle myself, letting the water coat my dry throat.

I won't cry.

I've cried enough tears for Dale Steel.

I gave him all of me. My body, my heart, my soul.

I take another drink and then look up at the sky. So many stars! If possible, I think more are visible tonight than the first night here with Dale.

Except that I was so consumed by Dale that night… His enthralling red-wine voice. His blond perfection. His dark countenance.

I hardly noticed the stars.

Dale still consumes me, but at least I can see the stars now. They're bright and dazzling, and they seem to twinkle. Ha! There's truth in that song from my childhood, "Twinkle, Twinkle Little Star."

"You like those stars, Pen?"

She's not looking at the stars, of course. Her eyes are closed, her head resting on my thigh. Such a sweet pup.

She loves her daddy. If I let her, would she lead me to Dale? How far into the mountains has he gone? I've no doubt Penny could find him, but I won't put her through that. Who knows how long it would take? I'm not exactly a backwoods type of girl.

I sigh and pull the bottle of wine I packed out of the backpack. "Let's have a toast," I say to Penny.

I uncork the bottle and pour a glass.

"Something's missing." I pull the votive candle out of the pack. "Candlelight would be nice, don't you think?"

Yeah, I'm talking to a dog. She seems to understand me

though. She licks my hand at the mention of candlelight. I take that as agreement.

I strike a match and light the votive inside its crystal holder. Lovely. The candlelight flickers through the glass, casting diamonds on the ground and vines.

"If only I had a cigarette now," I say to Penny. Then I force out a laugh. I don't smoke. I've never smoked. Though I wouldn't say no to a joint right about now. I gave that up years ago, but sometimes a little herb helps when your world is imploding.

This is a lovely place. Peaceful and tranquil, especially at night, when no one else is around. I understand why Dale finds solace here. What I don't understand is why he won't let me provide what he needs.

"What do you have that I don't?" I ask the vines.

I stop then and I actually listen. As if I truly think they might answer me.

The only response I get is a soft breeze that makes me rub at my upper arms once more.

I sit for a few more minutes, waiting for the vines to say to me what they say to Dale when he's here. To reveal those secrets that give him peace.

To reveal Dale to me.

But as they did the last time I came here, the vines stay silent. They keep Dale's secrets.

I love him. I love him so damned much.

But I don't know how to be with him. Clearly I'm not fulfilling his needs.

"Fuck this." I stand, knocking over the votive holder. "Shit." I quickly pick it up and blow out the candle. Then I let it cool for a few minutes before I throw it into the backpack. I pour my undrunk wine onto the ground, recork the bottle, and pack everything up.

"Let's get out of here," I say to Penny. "I don't know what I was thinking."

I take hold of Penny's leash and lead her back to the car.

Where we drive back to Dale's . . . alone.

CHAPTER ONE

Dale

My second night alone in the wilderness, I awaken in the early morning, chills racking my body.

I wanted aloneness—complete aloneness—but at the moment, I wish I'd brought Penny along. While this may not be a three-dog night, it's definitely a one-dog night.

I scramble out of my zero-degree bag and grab my flask of Peach Street. I love my wine, but backpacking and camping alone in the mountains necessitates something a little stronger for the occasional cold snap.

I unscrew the lid and take a drink.

Warm spice and smoke coat my throat. Yes, that's better.

But then—

Everything races back.

My birth father. He's dead now—gone on to a better place, if such a place actually exists. I never believed in hell, but I hope now more than ever that a place of eternal damnation exists for Floyd Jolly—a man who sold his two young sons into sexual slavery for five grand.

Five fucking grand.

I shake my head.

Five grand means nothing to me. It's like twenty bucks to the average person. I have more money to my name than I could spend in five lifetimes.

But what if I didn't?

Would I be desperate enough to ...?

I shake my head vehemently as I screw the lid back on my flask. No one is here. No one can see me shaking my head. No one can see the look of utter disgust and nausea on my face or the bitter bile inside me as I think about what my birth father did.

Never.

Never would I be so desperate as to sell another human being—let alone a child of my body—into the horror that Donny and I lived through.

And we were two of the lucky ones.

Most either died during "training" or were sold to the highest bidder, never to be seen or heard from again.

Donny and I were rescued—rescued by Dad and Uncle Ryan.

Not only did Dad rescue us, he then adopted us. Brought us into his family. Made us Steels and heirs to a megafortune.

For so many years, I wondered why he did. Why he, a newlywed with a biological child on the way, would take in two broken little boys.

Only recently did I learn the truth.

Dad went through something similar. He didn't go into detail when he told me, and I'm not sure I want him to. How can I imagine my father—my strong, loving, and generous father— enduring even a tenth of what Donny and I went through?

And when I have to think about Dad's ordeal, I have to think about—

I have to think about the ugliest, most horrific thing I ever did in my young life. I was ten years old, and I—

I shake my head again. More vehemently this time, enough that I almost feel my brain sloshing between my ears. Those thoughts have no place in my world.

I've left them buried so deep for so long...

But now...

Now they're threatening to emerge.

No. Not emerge.

Erupt.

Detonate like a bomb that has lain dormant for eternity, but now the fuse is lit...

I thought I was in control. I let my love for Ashley out, and the love seemed to override the hate.

But the hate for my birth father has awakened the hate for myself.

The hate I bear for something I did all those years ago.

The hate that brings out the darkness in me—the darkness that was always there but is now too much to endure.

Even my love for Ashley can't fix this.

I was a fool to think it ever could.

I let the chills overtake me as I open my flask and take another sip.

It doesn't help this time.

It doesn't help because I don't deserve warmth.

I could leave the security of my tent and start a small fire. That would help.

But I can't.

I deserve the darkness. I deserve the cold.

I don't even deserve the heat of hell.

★ ★ ★

I wake at sunrise. Already, the air has warmed, and I'm no

longer shivering. I scramble out of my sleeping bag, put on a parka and shoes, and leave the tent. I take a quick piss and settle down to build a small fire. I warm my hands for a few minutes above the flame, and then I pull out my French press. I need coffee.

Though I use a drip coffeemaker at home, coffee made in my French press while I'm alone in the mountains tastes better than any coffee in the universe. Even my mother's—the strongest, most flavorful coffee ever—can't compare to the coffee I press myself when I'm alone outside, surrounded by the beauty of the mountains.

But something wants to destroy this beauty.

I sniff. The smell of forest fire. For a moment, I thought the smoggy air was just the fog of morning, but it's not.

Fire.

Colorado has fires every year, so this isn't unexpected.

Except the smell is strong.

Very close.

I've ventured into the mountains, away from home. Away from my vineyards. That's what I needed to deal with my father's confession.

Something percolates in my mind, though—something I don't want to face.

This fire is closer than it should be.

It's close to me.

But it's closer to my vineyards.

I'm not sure how I know this. I'm not a human compass. I just know.

Those vineyards are a part of me, and I know.

"Fuck," I say aloud. I press my coffee hurriedly and pour it into a thermos. So much for my time alone to deal with yet another shitty piece of my life.

I have to leave this place. I quickly put out my fire, which I should never have lit in the first place. Open flames are discouraged during fire season. Sometimes the government issues a burn ban, though they haven't yet this year.

The fire I'm smelling could be the one that changes that.

I pack up my gear as quickly as I can as the scent of the fire grows stronger. To the west, gray smoke rises.

To the west.

Steel Acres is to the west.

The vineyards are to the west.

Ashley is to the west.

I strap my pack to my back and take a long sip of coffee from the thermos.

I will save the day.

Even if I have to walk through fire to do it.

CHAPTER TWO

Ashley

Penny wakes me up at five a.m. by licking my face.

I open my eyes, and though this is my second morning here waking without Dale, it takes a minute to acclimate myself. Right. I'm at Dale's. Taking care of Penny while he's... I have no idea where he is. Camping? The foothills? The mountains?

I know only that he's not here and he's not in the Syrah vineyards, where Penny and I were two evenings ago.

I rise and wrap myself in a robe. After a quick trip to the bathroom, I pad out to the kitchen and let Penny out. Then I prepare her morning meal from the mixture in the refrigerator. Only a day's worth left. What then? In the pantry, I find a bag of high-end kibble. Good. That will work until I can make Penny something tastier and more nutritious.

Which also means a trip to the grocery store in town. Dale didn't say how long he'd be gone, and I have to feed myself. I suppose I can always eat at the main house with Talon and Jade, but...

I sigh. Now what?

It's only five thirty, and I'm wide awake. I let Penny back in, and she gobbles up her food. Dale likes to start at six or seven in the morning, so what the heck? I'll shower, dress, and head to the vineyards. It's still harvest, after all.

* * *

Once I'm ready to go, it's six thirty, and my phone buzzes. It's Ryan Steel.

"Hello," I say into the phone.

"Ashley, it's Ryan. Apparently Dale will be gone a few days."

"I know," I say. "I'm staying at his place and taking care of Penny. Did he tell you what he wants me to be working on?"

"No, he didn't, but don't you worry. There's plenty to do."

"For harvest, yeah."

"Actually," he says, "I'm taking you off harvest for now."

"Oh?" Not that I'm upset by his decision. Harvesting is difficult work, and I still haven't seen a lot of the winemaking process.

Ryan clears his throat. "We're watching a new fire on the western slope. Our northern vineyards are directly in its path."

I gasp. The northern vineyards? The Syrah...

No, not Dale's Syrah.

"We're not worried yet," Ryan says. "We're really good about removing dead vegetation, and we keep fuel breaks up year-round."

Fuel breaks? Right. I know about fuel breaks. I've just never had to think about them, living in the city. I feel hot, and I see red. All red and orange and flaming as I discuss the possibility of Dale's beloved vines going up in smoke.

"This can't happen," I hear myself saying.

"Nothing has happened yet," Ryan says. "This is Colorado. It's not the first season we've had to outwit a fire, and it won't be the last. We bring in the best experts, and we get it done."

I nod and then gulp. "The irrigation system..."

"The drip hoses can ignite," Ryan says, "but it's unlikely. We have thirty feet of defensible space around the vineyards and structures."

I say nothing.

"These vineyards mean as much to me as they do to Dale," Ryan continues. "I won't let anything happen to them."

"So, the harvest . . . ?"

"We're at the midway point, so we're taking a few days off to build up the defensible space. I don't want any workers in the vineyards while this fire is moving toward us. Safety of our people is always my primary concern."

"Yes, of course," I say robotically. "Will this affect production?"

"Not hugely. We may lose a small amount of harvest to rot, but not enough to matter."

I heave a sigh of relief. "Thank goodness. Dale is so looking forward to the old-vine Syrah."

"We all are, Ashley. We all are."

"So . . . what do you want me to do today?"

"Come into the office," he says. "I'm inundated with paperwork, and I could use some help."

Paperwork. Fun. But it's all part of the business. "I'll be right in. I'm ready to leave now."

"Sounds good. Did Dale happen to say where he was going?"

"To the mountains."

"Fuck."

I shudder instinctively. "What?"

"This fire. It started in the foothills above the vineyards. If Dale . . ."

I don't need Ryan to finish the sentence. I already know what he means.

Dale—my Dale—may be in harm's way.

"No," I say. "He knows these mountains. Doesn't he?"

"I don't know. I assume he does. This isn't the first time he's run to the mountains."

I swallow audibly.

"He'll be okay, Ashley. He's a smart man."

But Ryan's tone has an edge to it.

He's not convinced of his words.

Neither am I.

★ ★ ★

I sit in Dale's office.

Because he's not here, I can use his space instead of my cubicle.

Dale's office ...

We've kissed in here. Done more than kiss ...

I shake my head to clear the images.

My senses are dull today. Nothing has any color at all. Employees bustle around the hallways, speaking and laughing, but the sounds have no vibrancy, no hue.

Nothing.

Why are they laughing? Don't they know their boss is in danger?

He's a smart man.

Ryan's words ring in my ears.

Yes, he's smart. A brilliant winemaker. Does that make him a brilliant backpacker? A brilliant fire evader?

Concentrate, Ashley.

Ryan gave me work to do, and I have to do it. I'm an intern. I have a job here.

I gaze back at my computer screen, when—

"Ashley?" A soft knock on the open door.

I recognize the voice. It's Talon, Dale's father.

"Come on in," I say.

He enters and sits down across from my—Dale's—desk. "I thought you should know," he says, "that Dale's birth father died two days ago."

I nod. "He told me."

He wrinkles his forehead. "Do you know where Dale went?"

"I don't. He said he was going to the mountains." Tears jab at my eyes, but I force them back.

Talon nods, and a heavy sigh whooshes out from his throat. "Shit."

"Please tell me he's going to be okay."

"I hope so, Ashley."

"But you're not sure . . . ?" I can't help a desperate edge to my voice.

"We've already got scouts out searching for him."

He'll hate that.

I don't say it though. Talon most likely knows anyway. If there's anyone who knows Dale better than I do, it's his father.

"Please let me know as soon as they find him."

"Of course we will. But, Ashley . . ."

"What?"

"Dale knows how not to be found when he doesn't want to be found."

"But if there's a fire . . ."

Talon sighs again. "Dale's a brilliant man, but even the smartest men on earth can't outrun a forest fire."

My heart sinks.

Talon hands me a sheet of paper. "This just came in from the AP."

I take the paper and scan it.

FIRE ATTACKS WESTERN SLOPE VINEYARDS

The most recent fire to break out in Colorado this fall began on the western slope, igniting remote, rough terrain including juniper and sagebrush outside the small town of Snow Creek.

Several vineyards are in its path, including those owned by Colorado Pike Winery and Steel Acres Vineyards. Grape harvesting has begun, and so far, the fires have had minimal effect. Firefighters hope the recent moisture from thunderstorms will keep the fire from spreading too rapidly.

No evacuations have been ordered, though that could change at any time. Firefighters are blaming a lightning strike for starting the blaze, but fire from campers in the foothills has not been ruled out.

My stomach drops, and I feel sick. Really sick. Like I'm going to explode out of both ends at once, and it's not going to be pretty.

"Ryan says the vineyards... That he..."

"In all likelihood, the vineyards will survive," Talon says. "Some experts feel they form a natural firebreak, but we've seen other vineyards destroyed, so we reject that train of thought. We take precautions far and above."

"Yes, defensible space..." I murmur. If only I knew for sure there was a decent bubble of defensible space around Dale.

"So Ryan already told you."

I nod.

"Then he told you that we've suspended the harvest for a few days to protect our property."

I nod again.

"I've tried calling Dale. Wherever he is, there's either no service or he's turned off his phone."

"He wouldn't," I say. "Would he?"

"There's a lot you don't know about Dale, Ashley." Talon rubs at his temple. "A lot I can't tell you."

"But…we're in love," I blurt out. "If something is bothering him, I need to know."

Talon smiles weakly. "He's in love with you?"

"Yes. He said so. He loves me and I love him."

Talon smiles again. "Thank you, Ashley."

"What for?"

"You just gave me hope."

CHAPTER THREE

Dale

I walk quickly, resisting the urge to run. If I run, I won't keep the pace for long with the heavy pack I carry. Best to walk, but walk fast. Wind gusts around me, stirring up the dry leaves on the ground.

After about two miles, the brush crunches under my hiking boots. Dry. How hadn't I noticed this when I hiked in?

Easy.

I was thinking only of myself. Of my birth father's confession. I noticed nothing about the condition in the woods that reeked of fire hazards.

Damn.

Still, the shortest distance between two points is a straight line. My best bet is to go down the way I came.

I continue walking, twigs and leaves crunching with each step I take. I inhale. The scent of burning brush is stronger here, and the air quality sucks.

Still, I see no flames. I hurry.

Another mile down, and then another. I'm about ten miles out when the wind picks up.

A streak of flame rushes through the dry brush ahead of me.

An ember lands on my forearm, and I brush it away.

Fuck.

I'm walking right to the path of the fire.

I stop. This isn't new to me. I've lived on the western slope most of my life, and we've dealt with fires before. I concentrate on the breeze. Which way is it coming from?

Shit. It's blowing west. Toward the vines.

I need to go upwind—toward the wind—to escape the fire. But if I walk into the wind, I walk away from my vines.

Away from Ashley.

I turn, ready to do what any backpacker knows is the first step of escaping fire, but my feet don't move. They stay stuck, leaves swirling around them, embers still flying.

Go, damn it, I yell inside my head. *Is your life worth those vines?*

I love those damned vines.

They're such a huge part of me.

They *are* me in so many ways.

Move downhill.

Yes, that's something. The hot air masses created by the fire will rise.

Downhill is against the wind.

Downhill is toward the fire.

Uphill will give me better chances, but downhill is toward my vineyards.

Downhill is toward Ashley.

I trudge downhill.

Streaks of fire still spark through the rough terrain, but they're small. I need a natural firebreak—something I can follow all the way down to the ranch property.

There's a small creek nearby. It'll take me a mile out of my way, but the fire can't get across it. I move slightly north to find it.

I gasp when another streak of fire surges by. I jump over this one, still heading toward the creek.

Embers fly around me, one singeing my cheek.

"Damn it!" I run now, backpack be damned. Nothing will keep me from the creek.

Except fire.

More streaks, and before me a wall of flame has risen.

Now what?

Pine trees. Big ones. They're all around me. Some are dead from pine beetles. I need a live one to shelter under, and even that is far from a sure thing.

The creek is out of the question. The fire looms between me and the water.

I turn. Back uphill is my only choice. Uphill, to the east.

Away from the vines.

Away from Ashley.

I race back from where I came, grunting as I trudge upward. Except more streaks of flame ignite under my feet, more—

Ahead, a figure stands. Yellow fireproof coat.

A fireman or a forest ranger. I don't know which. I don't care.

"Help!" I yell.

He turns and runs toward me. "Dale Steel?"

"Yes. I'm Dale Steel."

"Good." He holds a device to his mouth. "Found him, but we're surrounded." *Pause.* "Got it." Then, to me, "Let's go. I'll get you out of here."

"How did this start?" I yell.

"Lightning strike, we think. Maybe a campfire, though."

Campfire?

No, not my campfire. I put it out this morning, and the fire had already begun.

But my fire yesterday morning… My internal GPS whizzes. Where did I camp the night before last? Closer to home. Closer to the vineyards…

I push the thought out of my mind.

Can't go there.

Not that it matters. Right now I'm with an expert, but flames surround us. How does he think he's going to get me out of here?

"Here." He hands me eye gear and an oxygen mask and tank. "Put this on."

I obey, and he helps me get it set up. He sprays his extinguisher over several of the fire streaks and gestures for me to follow him.

The heat is all around me now. My parka is sweltering. My eyes are protected by the mask, and I inhale sweet breaths of oxygen.

Still, the air is thick, and embers land on my parka, burning tiny holes into the fabric.

We trudge and trudge, until finally, we find a natural break.

Exhaustion weighs on me.

The fireman removes his mask. "We're good here for a while. The wind has picked up, and the fire's moving away."

Moving away? Moving toward my grapes, he means. I take off my mask and inhale. The air is still smoky.

"I know," the fireman says, as if reading my mind. "But we need to conserve the O_2 while we can."

I nod.

"You okay? Any burns?"

I shake my head. "I need to go."

"Find a tree."

"I don't mean I have to piss. I need to go. My property is right in the fire's path. I've got to—"

"There's nowhere to go, Steel. We're here until I get word. Take off your pack and stay a while."

"No," I say. "I need to get down. My vineyards are—"

"You're staying here. Your folks paid us a lot of money to find you up here."

"You mean you're not a fireman?"

He shakes his head. "Yes and no. I'm part of a private company that's called in when the government needs help. We're also for hire by anyone else who needs our services."

"Has the government called you in yet for this fire?"

"It's a new fire, so not yet. I expect they will. It looks pretty vicious."

My father. My uncle. They're paying for this babysitter. "Sorry," I say. "I'm out of here."

"Are you crazy? Sit the fuck down."

"You'll have to physically restrain me," I say. "Nothing's keeping me from going."

He grabs my shoulders. "Your family has been notified that you're safe. Do you want to put them through any more worry?"

"My family knows me. I'm a survivor."

"Not if you go walking into a fucking fire," he says. "You're not doing it."

"Try to stop me." I grab the oxygen but leave my pack. I'll need to move quickly, and everything in the pack is replaceable.

"You're crazy. Go then. I'm not going after you. I don't have a death wish."

I nod.

Then I turn.

Ashley.

At the moment, Ashley thinks I'm safe.

What if I don't make it? What will that do to Ashley?

"Fuck it all." I turn back toward the man. "What's your name?"

"Mark Johnson."

"You win, Johnson." I huff. "Is my family safe?"

He nods. "Yeah. They've evacuated the orchards and vineyards. None of the buildings are in harm's way—at least not yet—and the livestock is safe."

They've evacuated the orchards and vineyards.

The vineyards.

My vineyards could be in flames right now. I long to go to them, put out the damned fire myself.

But I'll stay safe.

I'll stay safe for Ashley.

CHAPTER FOUR

Ashley

Talon peeks into Dale's office a few hours later. I haven't gotten anything done. I can't concentrate because of my concern for Dale.

"Just heard," he tells me. "They found Dale. He's safe on high ground."

A burdensome yoke lifts from my shoulders. "When will he come home?"

"No way to know," Talon says. "The fire's not contained yet, but he's with someone who knows how to stay safe."

"Who?"

"A guy with a private firefighting company. There are others in the area working on containment."

"And this person will stay with Dale? Get him to safety?"

Talon nods. "That's what we paid him for."

My breath whooshes out in a heavy sigh. "Thank God."

"This will be tough for him."

"To wait it out?"

"Yes, but that's not the only reason."

I lift my eyebrows. "Oh?"

"Our defenses have been breached, Ashley. The fire has spread to the northern vineyards."

"No!" I clasp my hand to my mouth.

"Firefighters are working, plus other private people we hired. We're hopeful that not too much will be lost."

"What can I do?"

"Pray the wind changes. That's what will help the most."

"Do we need to get out of here?"

"Yeah, that's what else I need to tell you. Get back to the main house. We don't believe this building is in danger, but it's best to be safe."

"I'm staying at Dale's," I say softly. "Taking care of Penny."

"You'll be safe there as well."

"What if..."

"We'll get the fire under control before any of the residential properties are in danger," Talon says. "We have adequate firebreaks around all residential areas."

I nod.

"You okay?" he asks.

No, I'm not okay. The man I love is stuck on a mountain with only a stranger for company while his Syrah vines are compromised.

No, I'm not okay at all.

★ ★ ★

I lie on Dale's bed, Penny at my feet. I've tried watching television, listening to music, and reading. Nothing has helped me get my mind off the fire destroying Dale's Syrah.

I even tried calling my mother. She didn't answer, so I left a voicemail.

Jade is most likely at work in town, where she's safer than she would be here. Yes, Talon told me this was safe, and I believe him. I'm no stranger to fire, living in California since the day I was born. Fires are a part of life there, as they are here, apparently.

I've never been in harm's way, living in the city. Even when we were homeless, we were never touched by fire, though sometimes, when they got close, I could smell them. The scent of burning wood and brush that seemed bright orange but never really had a color.

Penny barks.

"What is it, girl?"

Then I hear it—a knock on the door. I sigh as I rise from the bed and walk out of the master suite. Another knock.

"I'm coming!" I yell.

I look through the peephole.

It's Brock Steel, Dale's cousin.

Dale's extremely good-looking cousin with dark hair and eyes.

Dale's cousin who kissed me my second night here.

I'm starved for anything to get my mind off Dale in danger, so I open the door.

"Hi, Brock."

"Hey, Ashley. Uncle Tal said you're alone here, so I thought you might like some company." He holds up a game of Travel Scrabble.

I can't help a laugh. For some reason, Travel Scrabble while a fire is raging on Steel property is ridiculously funny to me.

"Aren't you supposed to be at work?" I ask.

"I'm home for the same reason you are. Dad wants as many of us as possible out of the office buildings until the fire's contained."

"The livestock?"

"They should be fine. We have firebreaks."

"Like the firebreak that got breached around the northern vineyards?" I can't help asking.

He doesn't reply, just holds up the game again.

"I'll pass on the game," I say, "but come on in."

"Are you sure? An educated woman like you will kick my ass at Scrabble."

I sigh. "What the heck? Sure. Let's play."

He gives Penny a pet on the head. "Hey, girl."

"You want anything?" I ask. "I have to tell you, though, we're out of pretty much everything. Except kibble."

Brock laughs. "*We're* out of pretty much everything?"

We're. I said it.

"I mean Dale, of course. He left me with an empty fridge. I'm dog sitting."

He smiles. "I know. And I also know your heart belongs to my stoic cousin, so I won't try anything."

"I never said—"

"It's so clear, Ashley. Dale's a lucky guy."

I'm the lucky one. I don't say it, though. I can't even think it when I'm not sure if I'll ever see Dale again.

I *will*. I *will* see him again. I must.

But the Syrah . . .

"Good news," Brock says. "I just heard from my dad that the forest service has the fire ten percent contained."

"That means ninety percent not contained," I reply dryly.

"I've lived through many fires in this area," he says. "Once they get even a little containment, it's on the way out."

Maybe he's right. I don't know. Sure, fires happen in California too. I've just never lived through one in a rural area. I was either homeless on the San Francisco urban streets or living in the heart of LA.

I walk to the kitchen. "We have water and OJ. Or wine." I stop at the French doors leading out to the back. It's gray and murky from the smoke. A brownish-orange haze covers the clouds, and light ash falls from the sky.

Brock grips my shoulders from behind. "This isn't anything new, Ashley. We've lived through this many times."

"The vineyards are compromised," I murmur.

"They've been compromised before."

I turn quickly. "They have?"

"Yes, of course. This is the Colorado western slope. Fires are an annual thing. We're coming out of a drought now, so this isn't even the worst we've seen."

"But the Syrah."

He scoffs. "The Syrah will be fine."

"Talon already said it's been breached."

"Like I said, it's not the first time."

"Dale..."

"Dale will get over it," Brock says. "He's done it before."

"Has he?"

Brock nods. "Of course. Five years ago, half the Cab Franc vines were taken out. Dale survived."

"Dale's proud of his Cab Franc."

"He should be. It's a great wine."

I nod. It's a lovely wine. But it's not Syrah. Both Dale's and my favorite. Those vineyards, where Dale escapes to find... What? I have no idea. I've been there. Tried to find what he finds.

He can't lose them.

He'll lose part of himself.

I can't say any of this to Brock. He won't understand.

Mere weeks ago, I didn't understand either. Part of me still doesn't. I understand only that Dale needs those vineyards as much as he needs air.

He can't lose them.

He can't.

CHAPTER FIVE

Dale

"We've got ten percent containment," Johnson says to me, after talking into his device.

I nod.

I have nothing to say. In reality, I know that getting any containment this early in a fire's life is damned amazing.

Miraculous, even. Clearly my family hiring private firefighters has helped a lot. They found me, brought me to safety. I should be grateful, and I am. Sort of.

But until I know the vineyards are safe, I won't be at peace.

Hell, I'm never at peace anyway, certainly not now.

Johnson's satellite phone rings. "Yeah? Sure thing." He hands it to me. "Your father."

I take the phone. "Dad."

"How are you holding up?" Dad asks.

"I'm fine." Physically, anyway.

"Good. I want you to know Ashley is safe at your place."

"Johnson already told me everyone was safe." Still, hearing that Ashley isn't anywhere near harm's way helps.

"I'm sure he did. I just figured you'd want to hear it from me."

"Yeah, it helps." A little, anyway. "Mom?"

"She's in town at work."

"Will she be coming home?"

"Probably. The fire's not anywhere near any of our residences."

A small wave of relief sweeps over me. I want my mother safe. I want Ashley safe. I want everyone safe.

I want my vineyards safe.

Yes, vines aren't people. I know that. People are more important. Still . . .

"Okay. Good," I say to Dad. "Could you call her and ask her to do me a favor?"

"Of course. You don't have service up there?"

"No, and my phone died, anyway. I should get one of these satellite jobs."

"If you're going to continue hiking up to God knows where, yes, you definitely should. What do you need?"

I inhale slowly, my throat hurting from the smoke. "I left in a hurry, and there isn't much food at my house. Please ask her to get some groceries for Ashley. She likes orange juice. And scrambled eggs."

"Of course. I'll call her. She can pick them up before she leaves town."

"Thanks."

"You're welcome."

I clear my throat. "And Dad?"

"Yeah?"

"Tell Mom I love her."

"She knows, son."

"Tell her anyway."

"I will. Take care. I'll check in with Johnson periodically."

"You take care too. Bye." I hand the phone back to Johnson. "Now what?"

He pauses a moment before replying. "Now, we wait."

"For what?"

"To get word that it's safe to move."

"Are we spending the night out here?"

"We might be." He gestures to my pack. "Looks like you're prepared."

"I am. Are you?"

"Always." He motions to a tiny pack.

"You can't possibly have a tent in there."

"I don't. It's a sub-zero bag. I'll be fine." His phone rings. "Johnson here."

I stop listening to his end of the conversation. If necessary, we can both fit inside my one-man tent. It'll be snug, but we'll manage. I'm thirsty from trying to escape the fire. Water. We'll need water. The creek . . .

I begin walking.

"Hold on, Jack." Johnson moves his phone from his ear. "Where do you think you're off to?"

I look over my shoulder. "Water."

He nods and goes back to his conversation.

The creek I was going to follow to get home is about a mile south. The weather is brisk, which is a good thing. Hotter weather means the fire will last longer. I've seen worse in my day. I'm about halfway down when Johnson calls to me. I turn.

"You following me?"

He shakes his head. "Just got word. It's safe to follow the creek down."

"Thank God," I say under my breath. I need to be there for my vines.

The scent of fire is still thick in the air.

Half a mile later, we reach the creek and both fill up our

canteens. Pure Rocky Mountain spring water is the best, and though it eases my dry mouth and throat, it doesn't ease the dryness in my heart. In my soul.

Ashley is safe. My family is safe. That's the most important.

But until I see with my own eyes that my vines are safe . . .

"Ready?" Johnson says.

I nod. "Let's go."

CHAPTER SIX

Ashley

Brock and I set up the game but never start to play Scrabble. We sit on the deck for a few minutes, watching Penny play, until the air is too much. I don't mind the smell of the fires in the distance, but the ash rain and smoke start to bother my eyes after a bit.

"Why aren't you bothered?" I ask Brock when we go inside and sit at the kitchen table.

"I guess we're used to it. This happens pretty much every year."

"Your lands are compromised every year?"

"No, usually not. But we still have to deal with the smell and the thickness of the air. This is a smaller fire, but because it's so close, the effect is the same."

"A smaller fire, huh?"

"Yeah. It will be contained by the end of the day. Tomorrow at the latest."

"How do you know?"

"I've seen a lot of fires in my day. I just know. Trust me."

"I hope you're right. I wish Dale were safely home."

"Dale's fine. The scout found him and will lead him to safety."

I nod. I don't doubt Brock's words, but I won't rest until

he's home safely in my arms.

"Knock knock!"

I startle when the back door opens.

"Hey, Aunt Jade," Brock says.

"Hey, yourself." She sets down two bags of groceries on the counter. "Ashley, Dale asked me to get some provisions for you in town."

"He did?" *Meaning, he's still not planning to come home?*

"Yeah. He said to get eggs and orange juice. I kind of guessed on the rest."

I attempt a smile. She means well, after all, and she only did what Dale asked her to. "Thank you. I'm sure everything's fine."

Jade starts unpacking the bags. "I got a couple cans of food for Penny. Dale likes to make his own and mix it with kibble. I figured this is the next best thing."

"Thank you," I say again.

Jade turns to face me. "He's okay, Ashley."

I gulp. "I know."

"He just…has to leave sometimes. This isn't anything new."

"I've told her the same thing," Brock adds.

"Why?" I gesture with my hands. "Why in the middle of fire season?"

"I worry too. It's a mother's prerogative. I'll never stop worrying about my children, especially my oldest. He's such a loner, but I try to understand. If you're going to be with him, you need to understand too."

"I know that, and I try."

"I know." Jade opens the door to the pantry and places the cans of dog food on a shelf with other canned goods.

Dale has few canned goods, which doesn't surprise me. He's such a gourmet, he probably uses fresh food as much as possible, even for his dog.

Brock rises. "I'm thinking I've overstayed my welcome."

I turn to him. "You haven't."

"Are you and Dale officially together?"

I nod. "For now, at least. But I could sure use a friend."

He sits back down. "I know we're only friends, but the issue is Dale. I know my cousin, and I'm not sure he'd appreciate me being here alone with you."

"We're not alone. Jade's here."

"For a hot minute," Jade says. "I'll leave as soon as I get this stuff put away. But you should stay, Brock. I'm sure Ashley will appreciate the company. Dale will be fine."

"Works for me," Brock says. "I'm still hoping for a Scrabble game."

I sigh. "My head wouldn't be in it."

Jade meets my gaze. "Hey. Listen to me. Dale is Dale. If you're going to love him, you have to love him as he is."

"I do." It's not a lie. Not even close. I love everything about Dale.

"But you want to help him," Jade says.

"Of course! Don't you?"

"God, yes. I've always wanted that. Still do. But finally—and I mean after *decades*—I've realized I can't. Dale needs to help himself first. That's why he spends so much time in the vineyards, and sometimes in the mountains. It helps him where others can't. He finds something there."

I nod. "I know. I've tried to find it too."

"Ashley, I understand you so well. There were times when Dale was a young adult that I walked among those vines searching for what he sees. Searching, so that *I* could be the one to give him what he needed."

How well I understood what she felt during those times. "And did you find anything?"

She shakes her head. "I found the beauty that he sees. I found the solace. But I didn't find anything I could do to take the place of what he finds there, if that makes any sense."

"It makes perfect sense," I say softly.

"I've got a great idea," Jade says.

"What's that?"

"Why don't the two of you come over to the main house? Darla's making swiss steak, and you know she makes enough to feed an army. Talon and I can't possibly eat it all. We'll open up a bottle of wine and think about the good things."

"Darla's swiss steak?" Brock says. "Count me in."

I nod. "Thank you, Jade. I'd like that too."

She touches my forearm lightly. "He'll be okay. Believe in him. If you love him, that's what he needs."

★ ★ ★

Dinner is far from lively, but it's still enjoyable. Even Brock, who's usually the life of the party, is subdued. Darla clears our plates when Talon's phone rings.

"Sorry," he says. "It's Ryan. I don't normally interrupt dinner, but it could be news about the fires."

"Take it," Jade says. "We're done anyway."

"Hey, Ry," Talon says into the phone.

Pause.

Then his face goes white.

No.

No, no, no.

Not Dale. Not my Dale.

Talon nods. "I see." He ends the call.

My hand flies to my mouth.

"Ashley . . ." Jade says softly.

"Dale is fine," Talon says. "He's on his way home. They're walking along Henderson Creek, so it will take some time. He should be home tomorrow."

Jade and I both let out a breath. Apparently we were both thinking the same thing.

"What is it then?" Brock asks.

"It's the vineyards," Talon says. "Before they got the fire contained, it took out the northern half of the Syrah."

CHAPTER SEVEN

Dale

"Fire's contained," Johnson says to me.

"Good."

We're still twelve miles outside Steel property. We definitely took the long route, and I'm tired as a workhorse after a fifteen-hour day.

"I think we bunk here for the night," Johnson goes on. "The air is better here, and the wind is blowing the smoke and ash to the south. We're good."

Is he serious? "Suit yourself. I'm heading back. If I make pace, it's only a few hours until I hit my property. I've been watching the smoke, and it was way too damned close to my vines. I won't rest until I know they got through this unscathed."

"Your family is paying me to keep you safe."

"You'll get paid. And I'll stay safe."

"I can't guarantee your safety if you don't stay with me."

"Then I will personally pay you, since you seem to be so worried about income."

"Fuck off, Steel," Johnson says. "Not all of us are millionaires."

Billionaires, but whatever. I keep walking.

"For Christ's sake," Johnson mumbles. But he follows me.

I won't be stopping until I get where I'm going.

And where I'm going is my vineyards.

Ashley is safe at home.

But the vineyards . . .

They're not safe.

I already know it.

I'm just trying not to think about it so I can keep moving.

Inside my head, I've buried so much. Trudging along— using all my energy physically just to move forward—has kept my brain occupied so I haven't thought about my birth father and his shocking deathbed revelation.

I'll deal with it later.

Tomorrow, as I've heard Ashley say. *I'll deal with it tomorrow.*

I take a step. I take another, and then another.

Each step takes me closer to home.

Closer to my vineyards.

Closer to Ashley.

★ ★ ★

No.

Just no.

Numbness coats every nerve in my body.

"Let's go," Johnson prods.

I fall to the ground in front of the blackness illuminated only by the starlight above me.

My Syrah.

Such a large part of my Syrah.

Gone.

And I feel nothing.

Not a damned thing.

How can this be?

How can it be when all I've done is feel lately? Ever since I fell in love with Ashley and let everything dormant inside me loose?

"I'm on Steel property," I say robotically. "Your job is done. Get the fuck out of here."

"Steel," he says, "you're lucky. Colorado Pike lost a lot more."

Colorado Pike lost a lot more.

I should feel bad. It's a shame. The Pikes are our neighbors to the north. Good people. It sucks for them. I know this, and I should feel for them.

But I feel nothing.

Not a damned thing.

"Get the fuck out of here," I say once more.

He sighs and shakes his head. "Glad I could save your ass. Maybe you shouldn't be such a fucking dick."

"You'll get your precious paycheck, Johnson," I say.

"Oh, yeah. I will, but if you think I do this solely for the paycheck, think again."

"Why do you do it, then?" I ask, still speaking in monotone. "You like to be a hero?"

"I do it because it's the right thing to do. I serve my fellow man. It feels good, Steel, not that you'd know. What the fuck have you ever done for another human being?"

I don't answer, because at this particular moment, I simply don't care.

I've done a lot for others, both with time and money, but would I put my own life on the line to save someone I didn't know? A person I have no feelings for? The way Johnson saved me?

Did he even save me? I could have gotten back on my own. Right?

Maybe not. I needed that oxygen mask for the first quarter of our walk, and I got it from him. Otherwise, I'd have passed out from smoke inhalation, and the fire would have gotten me.

Maybe that would have been the better option.

I shake my head.

No. I'm not suicidal. Not since Donny and I were in captivity.

Not since we . . .

I fall onto the ground, lying on my side, as memories hurtle to the front of my mind.

★ ★ ★

My little brother cries in my arms as blood trickles from him. He doesn't say anything, just cries tears of pain, tears of . . . Of what?

We don't talk anymore. I stopped telling him it would be okay long ago. Even now, when I take the brunt of the abuse, I can't always protect him.

Like this morning, when he was dragged to the corner of the room by three masked men.

Three this time. Usually it's two, sometimes one. Hardly ever three. The only other time it was three, they took me, not Donny.

I begged them to take me this time.

I screamed and kicked and even bit one of them. I cursed them. Told them to fuck me, to try to break me.

Usually it worked.

Not this time.

They dragged my brother to the corner and forced his T-shirt over his head. I averted my gaze, until one of them walked to me and held me down, forcing my head toward the horrific scene before me.

I squeezed my eyes shut, and the bastard punched me in the head.

Still I didn't open them.

He punched me again, again, again, until finally he had to force them open with his fingers.

Forced me to watch my brother get used. Forced me to listen to his screams.

Forced me . . .

Forced me . . .

Forced me . . .

So now, as I hold my brother, I wonder what could be worse than what we've just endured.

And I know the answer.

Nothing.

Nothing could be worse than this.

Not even death.

Donny's sobs finally stop, but still, he clings to me.

"Hey," I say to him, "this won't happen again."

"That's what you always say," he hiccups.

"I mean it this time. We won't let it."

"How?"

"The only way we can." I grab his cheeks, force him to meet my gaze. "We die."

CHAPTER EIGHT

Ashley

Brock leaves after a cup of after-dinner coffee. I stand.

"I suppose I should get back to Dale's. Penny will need to go out."

Jade nods. "I'll come with you. We'll see to Penny, but then I think you should spend the night here."

"I'll be fine."

"I know you will be," she says. "But it's okay not to want to be alone."

"You're very sweet to offer"—I smile weakly—"but I made a promise to Dale that I'd stay at his place and take care of his dog. I can't break that promise."

"Would you like me to stay there with you?" she asks.

I shake my head. "I'll be fine, but thank you for offering. It means a lot to me."

"You're kind of our honorary daughter, Ashley," she says. "Right, Talon?"

"More than you know," Talon agrees. "Because of you, Dale has something to come home to."

"He's always had something to come home to," I say. "He loves you both very much."

"He does. And his brother and sisters," Jade agrees. "But Talon's right. You've given him a reason not to be alone."

"I'm not so sure I have. He left me after his birth father died."

Neither one of them says anything to that at first.

Until, "I was surprised by that," Talon says. "Perhaps Floyd meant more to Dale than he let on."

"I don't know, Tal," Jade says. "It *is* odd, come to think of it."

"Not odd that he left, though," Talon says. "He does that sometimes, and often we have no idea why. But odd that he'd do it during fire season after a man he claims meant nothing to him passed."

I mull over Talon's words.

Knowing what I do about my own father, I certainly feel nothing when I ponder that he's gone forever. Of course, Dale's birth father didn't rape his mother. Just abandoned her and their two children.

Are there degrees of heinousness?

This is too much to think about when all I want to do is get back to Dale's, snuggle with Penny, and lie in bed and hope sleep will come.

"He's still his father," I say. "No disrespect to you, of course."

Talon nods. "None taken. In some ways, blood may be thicker than water."

Jade takes his hand. "You're his father. He'd be lost without you."

"Thank you, blue eyes. I know that. If I died, he'd be a lot worse off. That's what makes me think..."

"What?" Jade asks.

"Floyd wanted to see Dale. He must have told him something that upset him."

"And then he dropped dead?" I say without thinking. "Sorry, that kind of just popped out."

"He knew he didn't have a lot of time," Talon says. "What if there's something he was keeping from Dale and Donny? That he needed them to know?"

"What, though?" Jade says. "He already abandoned them and their mother. What else could he possibly have to say to them?"

"I don't know"—Talon rubs the stubble on his jawline— "but why else would Dale be so distraught over the man's death?"

I have no answer to Talon's question, but something must have happened between Dale and his birth father. Why else would Dale take off the way he did?

"I should go," I say. "Dale may still come home tonight."

Talon nods. "Johnson already called. He wanted to camp for the night, but Dale insisted he was going to keep going."

"Sounds like Dale." Jade smiles.

"He'll want to check on the vines," I say absently. "He'll be home tonight."

Talon takes a sip of his after-dinner bourbon. "He may, but Ashley..."

"Yeah?"

"Don't expect too much out of him when he gets home. He's safe, but the Syrah..."

"I know." I swallow.

Losing even part of the Syrah will kill Dale.

I need to be there for him.

★ ★ ★

I jerk upward in Dale's bed as Penny scrambles out of the room.

Someone's here, but Penny's not barking, so it must be—

I scurry out of bed and wrap a robe over my pajamas. I run out of the room. "Dale?"

He's here.

Walking toward me. More like *stalking* toward me. His blond hair is a mass of tangles around his unshaven face.

His lips are parted.

And his eyes . . .

His eyes are green and . . . feral. Primal. Animalistic.

"Dale . . ." I say again.

"Get back in bed," he says.

"But I—"

"I said get back in bed." His voice is the familiar darkness of Syrah, but this time with a black velvet cloak covering it. He stalks closer to me, and with every inch he closes between us, I tremble.

From fear?

From arousal?

From . . .

From both, but also from something else. Something more.

"Dale, please. I'm so sorry."

"Do I have to repeat myself, Ashley? I've told you twice now to get back in bed. If you don't, I'm going to fuck you up against this wall."

Shudders rack through me. Yes, I want to go back to bed. And yes, I want him to fuck me up against this wall.

Here. Now. Hard and fast.

He's angry. He's exhausted. He's grimy with dirt, and he smells of the woods. Of the fire. Of all that is wild and primitive.

And I swear, I've never wanted him more.

He's an animal, as if he transformed in some way through this experience. I should tell him to shower first. I should say no. I should hold him and comfort him and tell him I love him. That everything will be okay. That I understand the loss he's bearing, and that I'm bearing it too.

But I don't.

I stand, his for the taking.

"I warned you," he growls, cloaking me in red-wine ruggedness.

He grips my shoulders and pushes me against the wall. Then he shoves the robe over my shoulders and to the floor. I stand before him in a white cotton tank and red-and-white checkered pajama bottoms. That's all that separates my naked body from this madman.

He curls his fist around the neckline of my tank top. Again, a growl rumbles from him, and then he yanks the shirt so harshly that it tears. He adds his other hand and rips the fabric in two, exposing my breasts.

"Fuck. Those tits." He squeezes both of them, almost to the point of causing me pain.

I don't cry out.

I don't cry out because he needs me. He needs me to let him do what he desires, and I want more than anything to be here for him. To do whatever small part I can to get him through this horror.

"Dale..."

"Don't talk."

"But I love you. I want you to know that. I'm so thankful you're all right. That the fire—"

"Fuck the fire," he grits out. "The fire has taken all it's going to take from me. Now it's my turn to do some taking." He bends down and pulls one of my nipples between his lips, not gently.

Again, I don't cry out. I'm determined. I'll do what he needs, and if that includes taking me hard, taking me violently, I'll let it happen.

He groans against my breast, sucking my nipple into a hard berry. I'm already wet, and though I want to squirm against the tickle in my pussy, I don't. I remain still. Still and available for Dale's use.

And he'll use me. I already know what's coming, and I want it as badly as he does.

Possibly more.

Rough sex turns me on, and from the moment I first saw him, I wondered what it would be like with Dale. I didn't let myself think about it then, and even now, our relationship is precarious at best. He's promised me only the next two months, so I'll take what he's willing to give.

If it's dark ... If it's rough ... I'll take it.

I'll revel in it.

And I'll make sure he knows I'm the only woman in the world who can give him what he truly needs.

CHAPTER NINE

Dale

God, her tits. I suck her nipple. I'm going to make it pink. Red. Fucking raw. Without thinking, I close my teeth around it and bite.

She gasps softly. No scream, and damn, I bit hard.

Is she willing? Will she give me what I crave at this moment?

My vineyards, where my darkness dwells... They've been breached, and my darkness has nowhere to go.

Nowhere ... except into Ashley. Ashley, the woman I love. The woman I crave. The woman I'm going to ravish, to ruin ...

I pinch her other nipple between my thumb and forefinger. Rough, yes. Rough and dark, and that's what I want. Ashley cries out this time, but not in pain. It's a sound I recognize. The sound she makes when she's turned on. I inhale deeply. Musk. Tang.

For so long, I've smelled nothing but burning wood and pine needles—the scent of destruction. I inhale again, and Ashley's arousal penetrates through the rest.

She's wet.

She's ready.

And she's mine.

I squeeze those ripe tits again, bite the nipple again.

"God, Dale," she moans through gritted teeth. "God, that's good."

Good? It's better than good. It's fucking unbelievable. I drop the nipple from my mouth and give her a light slap on the breast. The hallway is dark, but already I see her skin reddening from my touch. From my mark.

My mark. Only mine. Never will another man touch what's mine.

I slap her again, harder this time. "Mine," I growl.

"Yours," she echoes softly.

I push her pajama pants over her hips and inhale once more now that no clothing covers her fragrance. Fuck, her sweet musk. Apples and spice and tangy female. The smell of the fire still drifts around me, and damn it if it doesn't make her smell that much better. I'm here to conquer her. I couldn't conquer the fire and save my Syrah, but fuck it all. I'm going to conquer Ashley.

Right here in my hallway.

She steps out of her pajama pants. Completely naked now, except for the tatters of her tank that still hang around her shoulders. She shimmies out of her tank tatters and stands before me, her breasts and nipples red from my rough handling.

Fuck. She hasn't even begun to see rough. To experience rough.

I'm going to do things to her I've only imagined doing. Things I've wanted to try but never had the occasion to.

Things that are inside me, part of me. And now they'll be part of her.

I love her.

I love her so damned much.

Even more, now that she stands here, offering herself to

me. Offering to be the receptacle of my deepest and darkest desires.

I crush my mouth to hers.

She parts her lips instantly, and I devour her, sweeping my tongue into every tiny crevice of her mouth, sliding over her teeth, her gums, the inside of her cheeks. She tastes like sweet cream, almost as delicious as her pussy.

I'll kiss her pussy like this, devour every last millimeter my tongue can reach.

But for now, I plunder her mouth, as if I'm a pirate and she's my treasure.

I kiss her and kiss her and kiss her, until she pushes at my shoulders, breaking the kiss.

Her blue eyes are on fire as she gasps in a breath of air. "Dale..."

I take her in—her beautiful milky body, her rosy breasts and ruddy nipples, her small waist and firm hips. Her shaved pussy and her lean legs.

Everything about her is perfect.

Then I inhale. Her arousal. Her zest. And that note that's uniquely her. A soft floral fragrance. Just Ashley.

I listen.

I listen to her rapid breaths, her soft sighs and moans.

I taste.

Her delicious flavor is still on my tongue, on my lips. Ashley. My Ashley.

I can't wait any longer. I'm still in my soiled flannel shirt, old faded jeans, and hiking boots.

But I'm done waiting.

I unbuckle my belt, unzip my jeans, and free my throbbing cock.

I lift Ashley against the wall until she's at the right height, and I thrust into her hard.

"Fuck," I growl.

She grips me so tightly, gloves me so completely, and for a moment, everything's okay again. I'm inside my woman, and I'm complete.

But everything *isn't* okay. Far from it.

I'll take this moment, though. This precious moment as Ashley gives herself to me.

I pull out slightly and thrust back in.

I'm ready to come already, so I do. I let go. It won't sate me. Won't be enough. Never enough, and especially not tonight.

I thrust into her, touch her innermost parts, and release.

I release everything…except not everything. I'm not even close to done, and though the climax sends me reeling, my mind is far from free from the thoughts that taint it.

The losses I've suffered, and not just today.

I pull out and let her slide down so her feet touch the floor.

I've used her. Really used her.

And I've only just begun.

CHAPTER TEN

Ashley

Dale grabs my hand and leads me back to his bedroom.

I haven't climaxed, but I nearly did, even though he wasn't inside me for long. His rough treatment of my breasts surprised me, but I liked it.

I liked it a lot.

I want more. I want to be ravaged by this virile mountain man—this rugged, feral animal.

He closes the bedroom door and meets my gaze, his green eyes on fire. The red-wine growl rumbles from his chest.

He's a wolf, and I'm his prey.

And I wouldn't have it any other way.

"Get on the bed."

The dark Syrah floats in the air around him as he rasps his commands.

I walk to the bed and sit down.

"On your hands and knees," he says. "Ass in the air. I want to see that pretty behind of yours."

I obey. I don't even consider not obeying. Dale wants to see my ass. I show him my ass.

"Now lower your arms, let your tits touch the bed. I want that ass higher than the rest of you."

I comply.

And—

"Oh!" as he swats my backside with the palm of his hand.

"Such a gorgeous ass, Ashley," he rasps. "I'm going to make it pink like your rosy cheeks."

Slap!

His palm comes down on me again.

Slap!

Again, the other cheek this time.

Slap! Slap! Slap!

The sting is painful but not unbearably so. But with the sting comes a warmth. A warmth unlike anything I've ever experienced. It spreads from my ass through the rest of me as if the blood in my veins has turned to hot lava.

Except the lava isn't orange or red. It's green, the color of Dale's eyes—the eyes that, even though I can't see them at the moment, I know are burning two holes in my flesh.

Two holes of green fire.

"My God, your ass is perfect," Dale says, the dark red of his voice veiling me. "I want to make it red, Ashley. Red and glowing."

Slap!

Slap!

Slap!

Oh, the pain! But oh, the pleasure! It spears through me like a flaming arrow, the sting such a sweet prelude to the warmth and pleasure that morphs from it.

Slap!

Slap!

I brace myself, waiting for the next, when—

The warmth of Dale's lips trails over the cheeks of my ass. He's kissing me. Soothing the pain. Taking care of me.

I sigh in contentment, ready to sink into the depths of the bed, when—

He flicks his tongue over my asshole.

I gasp without meaning to. This isn't anything new to me. I'm experienced sexually. I've had anal sex several times with several partners. Hell, I even let a woman fuck my ass with a strap on once.

Anal is different.

It's also amazing.

Right now, though, just Dale's tongue sliding up my crack is better than the best fucking I've ever had down there.

I don't know if he's after anal tonight, but I do know that if he is, I'll let him do it.

I'll let him do whatever he wants.

I'll let him do whatever he needs.

Because tonight, I already know, is more about his *needs* than his wants.

He's feeling lost, and I'm here to help him find solace.

He spreads my ass cheeks then, and he slides his tongue downward, over the lips of my pussy.

My legs quiver. They're like jelly, and while he commanded that I hold my ass in the air, I'm ready to collapse.

Collapse into a puddle of warm honey all over Dale's bed.

"Fuck, you taste good," he murmurs.

I barely hear him, but his words make it to my ears in a haze of dark red.

Then no more words. Only rapid breaths and the sounds of him eating me, sliding his tongue into my heat and licking and sucking me.

I fist my hands in the comforter, bury my head in the fluffy white pillow. I sink into the depths of pleasure as he takes me on this wild ride. My ass is still tender, and he grabs my cheeks, forcing them farther apart so he can dive deeper into my flesh.

My nerves jump, and all energy in my body seems to channel to my pussy. Only my pussy. It's everything all at once as he nibbles on my clit and takes me down to the ocean floor.

The climax is swift and powerful and unlike any other.

Where I normally soar, now I sink, and in the sinking, I feel something new and exciting and filled with more passion and emotion than I ever imagined.

As I land softly at the bottom, shades and hues of every color in the rainbow swirl around me slowly, as if I'm submerged in water.

I throb. I cry out. I shudder and shiver and tremble.

Waves of pleasure ripple through me, and when I'm finally forced back to reality, my pussy is being massaged.

Massaged by Dale's long thick fingers slowly moving in and out, milking the last drops of orgasm from my used body.

I can't help myself. I collapse onto the bed, my ass no longer in the air.

Still he slides his fingers in and out of me slowly, rhythmically, beautifully.

I close my eyes, unfist my hands.

Relax, relax, relax . . .

Ready for sleep. It's the middle of the night, after all.

Until—

"Ah!"

Dale's palm comes down on my ass again.

"No sleep for you tonight, baby," he says. "I'm not done with you yet."

CHAPTER ELEVEN

Dale

Deep inside, hidden like the rest of things I forbid myself to think about, is the yearning I've always had.

It was never enough to make me do anything about it, but with Ashley... Sweet, beautiful Ashley with that delectable ass...

I needed to spank her. Make that ass red like a cherry and warm like her countenance.

Fuck, I'm so hard.

But I need more.

I need to make her come again. And then again. I need to make her pass out from pleasure. And then, when her body is limp and sated and used up, I want to fuck her hard again. Harder than I fucked her against the wall in the hallway.

Harder than I've ever fucked before.

I need it.

I need it more than air.

I need it to silence the demons inside me. To silence the thoughts running rampant through my mind.

And even more, I need it to forget.

To forget the horror of the past two days.

The horror of part of my life.

My Syrah. My beautiful Syrah.

Lost to a fucking fire that should never have started.

Lightning strike, they said. Possibly a campfire.

Not *my* campfire. I couldn't live with myself if I'd started the fire.

If I'd started the fire, I'd be dead.

Perish the thought.

Death is not an option. For a hot minute, when I was a kid, I thought it was the only option.

Now? I want to live. Even with the demons crawling around inside me raring to get out, I want to live.

I want to live for my parents, my siblings, for Ashley.

I want to live for my vines, my art.

This passion I'm feeling, this ache for sex...

It's proof.

Proof that I'm alive.

My vines may have perished, but *I* live.

And I'll continue to live with all the pain.

Because the pain is me. We can't be separated.

Quickly, I get rid of my clothes and boots. I should shower. Ashley doesn't deserve a dirty lover.

But the woods, the fire—it all made me this way. I'm hungry for her. I'm hungry like a grizzly hunting its next meal. I'm hungry like a wolf sensing a female in heat.

I'm hungry in all ways for this woman. My woman. My Ashley.

"Spread your legs," I order.

She obeys me, her pussy swollen and wet from her orgasm. I'm going to give her another. Then another.

I'm going to eat her until there's nothing left of her, and then I'm going to stuff her full of my cock again and again.

And when I'm done...

I'm going to begin again.

I dive into her heat.

She's still wet—wet and slick and delicious, as always. I enjoyed my foray into her ass, and I'll go back there, but not tonight. Not without talking to her first. Tonight I don't want to talk.

I want to *do*.

Just do.

I lick and eat and bury my face in her cream. When she grabs my head, fists handfuls of my hair, my desire is fueled even further. I need her, need to bury myself in her.

If I bury myself deep enough, can I slay my demons?

No, but I can at least hide from them for a short while.

I nip at her clit as she wails. Then, when I shove two fingers inside her, she contracts around me, coming.

"Dale," she cries. "My God, Dale!"

Her voice. It's a symphony to me, and though I don't see it in color as she sees mine, nothing has ever been more beautiful to me. More musical to me.

I continue, forcing orgasm after orgasm out of her.

She's so responsive. So hot.

One more. And then another.

"Keep coming," I order. "Come until you can't take it anymore."

"Yes. I'm coming. Fuck, I'm coming!"

Another climax rolls through her. Another. Another.

Until—

"Stop. Can't . . ." she whimpers.

"You can," I say. "You will."

I finger fuck her faster, suck harder on her clit, determined to keep pulling out climaxes.

"Can't…"

"You *can*," I growl against her pussy.

One more. Just one more, and then I can fuck her.

One more, Ashley.

But she lies limp. I've drained her. Drained her of all her pleasure.

Now it's time to take mine.

I'm hard as a steel beam as I crawl upward over her body, hover for a moment, letting the head of my cock slide against her slick folds.

Then I thrust.

I burn through her, completing her body with my own.

Even though she's wet and used up, she's still tight as a virgin. Her walls encase my cock, and I hold it there for a few seconds, reveling in our completeness.

But my cock has a mind of its own, and soon I pull out and plunge back in.

Again, again, again…

A fast fuck. A hard fuck.

A fuck that takes what I ache for.

I don't last long.

After five strokes, my balls are tingling, itching to let go.

I don't resist.

I don't resist because I know I'll be ready to go again soon.

Always ready to go again with Ashley.

The climax blazes through me, sending my nerves skittering and my flesh tingling.

All of me. All of me in all of Ashley.

I hold myself inside her, letting the waves crash through me, letting my mind be silent, if only for these few precious moments.

The silence. The golden silence of only pure emotion without words or thoughts—born of a climax inside the woman I love.

This is peace.

If only it were everlasting.

When my release finally subsides, I roll onto my back, my soiled hair slick with sweat and falling into my eyes.

Ashley lies quietly, her eyes closed.

She's used.

So very beautifully used.

What time is it, anyway? Well after midnight, I imagine.

I should get up. Shower. Wash the burn smell off my skin and out of my hair. My hands are dirty, black under my nails.

I touched Ashley with these dirty hands. Put these soiled fingers inside her perfection.

She deserved better.

What's done is done . . . except I'm not done.

For now, though, I'll let her sleep.

In the morning, she's mine again.

And I'll start over.

CHAPTER TWELVE

Ashley

I wake to Penny's nose nuzzling my cheek. Sunlight streams in through the windows in Dale's bedroom. I jerk upward.

It's late!

Dale lies next to me, naked and uncovered. His hair is tangled and knotted. His skin covered in soot.

I'm covered in soot from him.

I hardly care.

I touch his unshaven cheek, only lightly so as not to wake him. He needs to sleep. If he sleeps the day away, it still won't be enough.

I sneak out of bed as quietly as I can and don a robe before heading to the kitchen to let Penny out while I get her breakfast ready.

Speaking of breakfast, I'm famished. Dale took me for quite a ride last night, and I can't begin to imagine all the calories I burned. I'm craving carbs. No bacon and eggs for me today. Toast. Toast with some spiced peach jam. I grab the jar out of the fridge and throw two slices of white bread in the toaster.

It's a brisk morning, but still, I take my plate of toast outside. The sun is shining through a haze of orange.

The fire may be contained, but it's still burning. I grab

my phone out of the pocket of the robe to check the weather forecast. Showers this afternoon.

Good. Rain is good. That will help put out the last of the fire.

I check a news feed on my phone to see what's happening. This fire is small compared to most, which is why they were able to get containment so quickly. Another good thing.

Except it wasn't small enough to stay away from Dale's Syrah.

How much was harvested before the fire? Enough for Dale to create his old-vine wine?

I hope so. I hope with all my heart.

I polish off my toast, grab Penny's empty bowl, and head back inside. Does Ryan have work for me today? I feel like a bum for sleeping in so late. It's nearly eight o'clock.

I text him quickly.

His response is immediate.

Stay home. Take care of Dale today.

Good enough. Normally I'd balk at not working, but today? After what Dale's been through? I need to be with him.

One problem.

He's going to wake up eventually, and he may decide he needs to be alone again.

In which case, I'll let him be alone.

I can't try to hold Dale. If I squeeze my fist around a handful of sand, some of it escapes. If I hold it in the palm of my hand without squeezing so hard, it stays put.

Dale isn't like a handful of sand, though.

No matter how much leeway I give him, he'll leave if he wants to be alone. I can't make him *want* to be with me.

I have no doubt of his love, but I have even less doubt of

that need inside him to be alone at times.

I have to let him be the man he is.

I need a shower, but I don't want to wake Dale, so I sneak into the master bath, grab my supplies, and head into one of the guest rooms to take care of things. Once clean and fresh, I head back to the kitchen to tidy up the breakfast mess. The drip coffeemaker beckons. Should I start a pot for Dale?

No. I want him to sleep.

I take my phone into the family room to check emails, when it buzzes.

Hmm. I don't recognize the number.

"Hello?"

"Ashley?" A man's voice. It's familiar.

"Yeah?"

"Hey, it's Brendan."

It takes me a second to remember Brendan Murphy, even though we shared a bottle of Château Latour a few days ago. A lifetime seems to have passed since then.

"How are you?" I ask.

"I'm good. I called to see how you're doing. I heard about the fire taking out some of the Steel vines."

"Yeah. It sucks."

"You're actually lucky. The Pikes took most of the damage."

Right. Colorado Pike Winery owns the land north of Steel Vineyards. They're a smaller ranch, but they concentrate only on wine, and they produce more wine than the Steels. And they don't have Ryan and Dale. Their wines are good, but they don't have that special something that the Steel wines possess. Not that any of that matters. It's a shame they lost so much.

"I understand," I say. "I doubt that will be much

consolation to Dale and Ryan."

"Maybe not, but there's always someone who has it worse than you do."

His comment puts me on edge. "Did you call to chew me out, Brendan?"

"You think that was getting chewed out?" He chuckles.

He's right. "Of course not. I'm sorry. It's just that Dale's a mess."

"I'm sure. He's a lucky man, though."

"I doubt he sees it that way at the moment."

"If he doesn't, he should."

I scoff. "Why is that?"

"Because he has you, Ashley."

I smile. After I asked the question, I expected a smartass comment about Dale's financial situation. I deserved no less. Instead, I get something nice. Brendan's words are sweet, and he means well. Sure, he has a little crush on me, but he knows where my heart lies.

"Have you checked in with Ava?" I ask.

Brendan also has a little crush on Dale's cousin, the baker.

"A few minutes ago. The bakery's up and running. The air is a little smoky here in town, but we're all okay."

"I'm glad to hear that."

My phone beeps in my ear. "Hold on a minute, okay?"

"Sure," he says.

Jade is calling, so I quickly put Brendan on hold. "Hi, Jade."

"Hi, Ashley. I'm checking on Dale."

"He's asleep. Worn out."

"But he's okay?"

That's another question, but, "Yes, he's okay." At least

physically. He proved that last night.

"All right. Good. We need you both to come to the main house for dinner tonight. Big family meeting to deal with the fallout from the fires."

"If it's a family meeting—"

"You're family, Ashley. You're working with Dale and Ryan, and you're Diana's friend. We want you there. Could you tell Dale when he wakes up?"

"Sure. I have someone on the other line..."

"No problem. That's all I have for now. Take care of my son. Please."

"I will. Bye, Jade." I go back to Brendan. "Sorry about that."

"Everything okay?"

"Yeah. Big family meeting tonight at Talon and Jade's."

"Ugh," he says. "I hate family meetings."

"I've never been to one."

"My mom and dad have them from time to time. I have to run. If you need anything, please let me know."

I smile into the phone. "That's kind of you."

"Hey, anything for a friend. Take it easy."

"You too, Brendan. Bye." I shove my phone into the back pocket of my jeans, and—

"Ashley."

Dale stands in the kitchen, his gaze burning into me. He wears nothing but a pair of jeans. His hair is still tangled and messy, makeshift dreadlocks forming from the dirt and soot. His flesh is still covered with streaks of gray and brown.

"Good morning," I say. "Let me start some coffee for you."

He shakes his head.

"You should still be in bed, then. You're exhausted, Dale."

"Phone woke me up."

"Someone called you?"

"No, a text. The bell woke me."

"I'm sorry."

"My dad says there's a family meeting tonight."

"Yeah, I just got off the phone with your mom. She wanted me to tell you."

"She and Dad must have gotten their signals crossed."

"Maybe," I say.

"I need you to be there," he says.

"Of course. Whatever you need. I'll go with you. Your mom already invited me anyway."

He shakes his head, his tangled hair brushing his shoulders. "No, that's not what I mean. I need you to be there because I won't be."

I widen my eyes. Not that his words surprise me. He's going to run off again. Part of me already knew that was coming.

"Don't," I say, my throat closing against the sobs that want to erupt. "Please."

"I don't have a choice."

"You do, Dale. You always have a choice."

"You don't know what you're talking about."

I walk toward him. "I do. I understand. Your Syrah vineyards were harmed."

"Not harmed, Ashley. Burned."

"Not all of them, and you don't know that they won't come back."

"I know the harvest is lost."

"Only half of it. Plus, most of it has already been harvested."

He rakes his fingers through his blond mane of hair, catching them on a tangle. He tugs, his lips turning down in a frown. "You don't get it."

"Maybe not. Maybe I don't know what you're feeling, but Colorado Pike—"

"Fuck the Pikes," he roars.

I love him. I love Dale so much, but this comment rubs me the wrong way. "Fuck the Pikes? Really? That's self-absorption on your part. They lost way more than you did in this fire."

"Did they?"

"Haven't you seen the news? Didn't the guy who found you tell you?"

"It was still happening when he found me," Dale says.

"Turn on the fucking news, then. Check your phone. They lost three quarters of *all* their vines, Dale."

"Then they didn't adequately prepare."

"Firebreaks aren't guarantees. If they were, you wouldn't have lost what you did. Think about that. You lost half of one varietal. That's it."

"You don't know me at all," he says in a monotone. "You don't now, and you never will."

I whip my hands to my hips. "I know you've suffered a loss. It's a loss to me too. I know what those vines mean to you. I know better than anyone. But they're *things*, Dale. Just things."

Then a thought pops into my mind. He just lost his birth father as well, and though I don't know what the man meant to Dale, I do know it sent him on a trek into the mountains to deal with something alone.

I open my mouth to say as much, but he beats me to it.

"You don't know what you're talking about, so stop it, Ashley. Just stop it."

"I was going to apologize," I say. "You just lost your father. Birth father, I mean. He's not a thing. I'm sorry, Dale. I wasn't thinking."

He scoffs. "Floyd Jolly didn't mean shit to me."

"Then why did you—"

He rakes his hand through his locks once more, snagging his fingers again. "You'll never understand. No one will ever understand."

"You're right," I tell him. "No one will because you don't give anyone a chance. Talk to me, Dale. Tell me what's going on. Let me help you."

"Fuck you," he roars.

"Yeah? Well, fuck you too!" I advance toward him. "You're not the only one who's ever been hurt. You may think you are, but you're not. I'm sorry, Dale. I'm so fucking sorry about the Syrah. I'm sorry about whatever happened with your birth father. I'm sorry for every horrible thing that's ever happened to you. I am. Truly. But until you let someone crash through that wall you've built around yourself, you're never going to heal. I'm going back to your parents' house."

He grips my shoulders. "You're not going anywhere."

"Oh, yeah? You want to watch me?" I pull away, but his grip is too strong. "Let go of me!"

"No," he says.

"You want me to scream? I swear I'll scream so loud your parents will hear me."

"They're a half mile away," he says. "No one will hear you, Ashley."

"Fuck you!" I whip my head toward his hand on my right shoulder and sink my teeth into the space between his thumb and index finger.

He releases me. "What the fuck?"

"I'm out of here. I love you, Dale, but until you let me in, we have nothing." I grab my purse off the kitchen table and walk out the back door.

"Fine," he says. "Get the fuck out of here, and don't bother coming back!"

The tears come then, welling in the bottom of my eyes. I sniff them back. I have to make it to the main house. Penny pants at my heels.

I pet her soft head. "Bye, sweetie. I love you." Then I open the gate and head up the pathway to the main house.

Shit. The tears come. I can't stop them with all the willpower I possess. I rummage through the purse hanging off my shoulder and find a tissue. Only one, but it will have to do. I blow my nose, soiling the tissue in record time. A heavy sigh leaves my throat.

And I walk.

I walk away.

Away from the man I love.

CHAPTER THIRTEEN

Dale

I can't let myself feel anything. Just like last night, when I saw my vines.

I'm a master at swallowing up emotion. Swallowing up pain.

She's gone. I knew there was no future. Not with someone as wonderful as Ashley White. She's all light where I'm all dark.

She deserves sunshine and puppies and rainbows.

All I offer is darkness.

I walk back to my bedroom and into the master bath.

My reflection startles me.

I knew I was dirty, but even I wasn't prepared for what I see.

I look like a caveman, my hair a mass of knots. Even a small twig is tangled in some of my strands. My face is ruddy, my lips chapped. My eyes bloodshot and heavy-lidded. Streaks of black ash cover my cheeks, and my hands are disgusting.

This is what I forced upon Ashley last night.

She didn't hesitate to take me as I was.

She didn't say no.

She didn't stop me.

She let me do what I needed to. Kiss her, bite her nipples, slap her ass.

Fuck her hard and fuck her fast.

She gave me what I yearned for.

Yes, I gave her a dozen orgasms, but I did that for me as well.

It was all about me last night.

Self-absorption. The word she used to describe me this morning.

She was right to yell at me for the comment about the Pikes. To walk out. I'm being self-absorbed. I've always been self-absorbed, unwilling to share my pain with people who want to help me bear the burden of it.

Never.

Never will I share my pain with Ashley.

Never will I taint her with the demons that lurk inside me.

Never.

I turn on the shower, even now resistant to cleaning my body. Right now, physically, I resemble myself on the inside. A mess. Dirty. Smelly. Dark and tainted.

If I don't shower, the world will see me as I truly am.

Perhaps it's time.

Still, though, I shed my jeans and step into the shower. I turn the steam faucet and drop a few drips of peppermint essential oil onto the shower floor.

I'm congested from breathing smoke. My throat is parched and aching.

I stand under one of the dual showerheads, letting the nearly scalding water rain on my head. I close my eyes. Inhale. The steam is rising. Soon it will fill the shower, and the brisk peppermint will help clear my sinuses.

Soon.

But even now I resist.

Part of me wants to stay dirty. Stay unclean.

Stay . . .

★ ★ ★

The water from the showers is lukewarm, but at least it's water. Donny and I stand naked with several other boys, some younger and some older than we are.

I grab my little brother's hand and pull him away from the gazes of the others. I shield him with my body as we stand under the light water pressure. We're dirty. We stink. The acrid smell of body odor and shit surrounds us, the water bringing it out more at first.

I hold my breath. Still, I feel the nausea creeping up my throat.

"I'm going to be sick, Dale," Donny says.

"Swallow," I tell him. "Swallow it down. Swallow it all down."

He gulps loudly. "It's not working." Then he heaves. But nothing comes out of him. His little stomach is empty.

Dry heaves. They hurt. I know because last winter I had a bad stomach bug, and I couldn't keep anything down. Still, I heaved, my stomach cramping worse each time.

"Easy," I say to him. "Swallow it back. You can do it, Donny."

He tries, contorting his little face, but he ultimately fails and heaves again.

Another boy vomits all over the shower floor.

I hold back my own puke. I have to be strong for Donny.

There's no soap. Just the lukewarm water to wash the stink from our bodies.

About five minutes later, the water stops.

"Get out, all of you," a masked man says.

They all wear masks. Black ski masks.

I've never been skiing. I always wanted to learn, but Mom never took us. Never had the time or the money. "Skiing is too expensive," she always said.

The men give us each a tattered towel to dry off and then a gray T-shirt.

"Where's our pants?" one small child asks.

"You don't need pants anymore, shithead," a masked man says.

Donny opens his mouth, but I gesture him not to say anything.

I already know what he was going to say.

Why don't we need pants?

I know the answer, and I'm sick just thinking about it.

I'll give my little brother a few more minutes of childhood before he discovers the answer to the question himself.

CHAPTER FOURTEEN

Ashley

I walk in the back door to the main house. Darla is in the kitchen making lunch.

"Miss Ashley, will you be joining us for—" She gasps, taking a good look at me. "My goodness! Are you all right?"

I nod. If I try to say anything, the tears will come back. I did the best I could to gulp them down before entering.

"Miss Jade!" Darla calls.

"No, Darla, I'm—"

Then the tears come.

They roll down my cheeks, and sobs get locked in my throat.

Jade hurries in. "What is it, Darla? Is everything o—" She rushes to me when she sees me. "Ashley, honey, what's going on?"

But no words come. I sink into Jade's open arms and sob into her shoulder.

"I'll make some tea." Darla turns back to the stove.

"Thanks, Darla," Jade says. "Bring the tea down to the family room."

As much as I want to cry into Jade's arms, I manage to gulp back the sobs. Jade leads me down the small stairway into the family room. She sits down on the leather couch and pats the seat beside her.

"I don't want to talk about it," I say.

"I know. Just sit."

We sit silently for about five minutes until Darla arrives with the teapot, two cups, and a box of selected teas. Jade opens it and hands it to me. "What kind do you like?"

Though I don't drink coffee, I do like tea every now and then. Today seems as good a time as any to indulge. I take the English Breakfast.

Jade smiles. "I'm surprised. I took you for an herbal tea person."

I sniffle, and she hands me a box of tissues.

I pull one out and blow into it unceremoniously. "I'm done now."

"It's okay." She takes an Earl Grey bag for herself.

I rip open the foil packet, dunk my tea bag into the hot water, and watch the brown swirls move slowly in intricate patterns.

"You don't have to talk," Jade says, "but I know this has to do with my son."

I nod, still mesmerized by the steeping tea.

"He doesn't always know what's good for him."

"I don't understand." I continue to dunk my tea bag rhythmically. "I mean, I do understand about the Syrah. I totally get it. But his birth father . . ."

"I know," she says. "Sometimes things affect us differently than we think they will. Dale didn't think he cared about Floyd, but maybe he did."

"It doesn't make sense. Because I understand about birth fathers. I had one too, and he was a horrible person."

"Did you know him?"

I shake my head. "He died when I was young."

"What if he hadn't?" Jade asks. "How would you feel if he came to you today, after abandoning you your whole life?"

"I don't think I'd care."

"Really?"

"Really." I clear my throat. "I only found out recently—in fact, I try not to think about it—but my birth father raped my mother."

"Oh, Ashley . . ."

"I'm the product of that rape." I twist my lips, still dunking the bag. The water has turned a light brown now. "I don't know how she can even look at me. And all those years, she knew and I didn't. She cared for me, made sure no one ever hurt me."

"She loves you."

"But she didn't ask for me. I was forced on her."

Jade smiles. "I'm so sorry for what she went through, but by having you, she can at least understand that the rape led to something good."

I nod. "I guess I never thought of it that way."

"You'll understand when you have a child of your own."

With that last comment, I'm ready to dissolve into sobs again. A child of my own. I'm in love with Dale, but we'll never have a child together. We won't *be* together.

A baby, though . . . A baby boy with Dale's green eyes. He'd be blond, of course, since both of us are blond.

And he'd be beautiful. Just like his daddy.

It's a nice fantasy, but that's all it is. A fantasy.

"I still don't understand," I say. "I have no feelings for my father, and I don't think I would if he showed up from the dead tomorrow. Floyd may not have raped Dale's mother, but he did abandon all three of them. He's no saint."

"He's not," Jade agrees. "Dale knows that."

"I wish I could help him. I just don't know how."

"Sometimes all you have to do is offer your support."

Jade is right. I love Dale, and he needs me. So what did I do? I walked out on him. He told me I wasn't going anywhere, and I went anyway.

"I have to go back," I say.

She nods. "Finish your tea first. Give Dale a chance to cool off."

"I'm afraid, though."

"Of what?"

"That he won't be there when I get back."

"I can understand why you'd think that, but he'll be there. He just got home after two days in the mountains. After surviving a fire. He'll be there, and he needs you."

I shake my head. "He doesn't. He told me not to go, but when I did, he told me not to come back."

Jade waves her hands dismissively. "If I had a dollar for every time Talon told me to leave when we were just beginning—" She laughs. "Well, we have a lot of money now, but I'd have several dollars more."

I can't help chuckling as well.

"Listen," she says. "I'd like to go over there and read my son the riot act for being a dick, but we both know that's not what he needs. Especially not from me."

"Then it's up to me," I say.

"He needs you, Ashley. He may say he doesn't. He may even believe it, but he's wrong."

I finally remove the tea bag and set it on my saucer. "He said he wouldn't be at the family meeting tonight."

"He will be," Jade says. "He's never missed one. Even

Donny and Dee are driving home as we speak. Everyone will be there. Bree's coming home from school. So are my nieces—Gina, Angle, and Sage."

"You all really take care of each other, don't you?"

She smiles. "We're a family. That's what family does."

"I never had a family," I say. "Other than my mom."

"And you took care of each other."

I nod. "I suppose we did. And do."

"Of course you do. She's lucky to have you, no matter how you came into the world."

I set my cup and saucer, tea undrunk, on the coffee table. "I should go, then."

She nods. "Go back to Dale's. He's calmed down by now."

"He won't open up to me."

"Maybe not today. Maybe not tomorrow. Eventually he will. Until then, just be there for him. Show him the world isn't all chaos and horror."

Chaos and horror?

Strong words. Chaos, maybe. But *horror*?

I suppose losing half the Syrah is horror to Dale.

"Okay." I take a quick sip of my tea. Its warmth soothes my throat, which hurts from gulping back sobs. "Thank you for the tea and the talk."

"Anytime," Jade says. "And Ashley?"

"Yeah?"

"Be strong. Dale is so strong—stronger than he gives himself credit for—but right now, he needs *your* strength."

CHAPTER FIFTEEN

Dale

My body and hair are squeaky clean. My jeans and shirt are freshly laundered. The soiled clothes are in the washer.

Still, I feel dirty.

Like my reflection earlier that showed on the outside what I am on the inside.

Did I really tell Ashley not to bother coming back?

I did. I regret it, yes, but in all honesty, she's better off not coming back.

It's time for me to think about her instead of myself. It's time for me to stop being self-absorbed.

So my father sold me into slavery when I was ten. So half of my Syrah vines are lost.

God knows I've been through worse.

All thanks to the man who sired me.

"Fuck!" I say out loud, grabbing at my wet strands of hair.

I've been through so much worse than losing my beautiful vines. All of which could have been avoided but for Floyd Jolly. "Fuck it all!"

"Yes," says the voice that's sweeter than honey. "Fuck it all."

I turn. Ashley is in the kitchen, having let herself in. Penny pants at her heels.

"You're back," I say.

"I am." She walks toward me. "And I'm not going anywhere."

"Even though I told you not to bother coming back?"

"*Especially* because you told me not to bother coming back."

I scoff. "You're the one who left."

"I did. It was a mistake, and I own it."

"Why did you, then?"

"Because you told me not to. Because you were being a dick." She shakes her head. "No. Dick is too tame a word. You were being a prick, Dale. An asshole. A—"

I hold up my hand to stop her words. "I get it."

"Now," she says, "none of that negates what you've been through. Getting caught in a fire that destroyed something you love so dearly. And then the death of your father."

"*Not* my father," I say adamantly.

"Okay. *Not* your father. I get that. But his death affected you. It's obvious."

I scoff. "I'm glad the fucker's dead."

She cocks her head and wrinkles her forehead. "Oh? Then why—"

"I'm not talking about my birth father. I'm never talking about him again."

"All right. We don't have to talk, Dale. Not now, anyway. But I'm here when you're ready."

"Trust me, Ashley. I'll *never* be ready."

She smiles. "That's fine too, then. No pressure. But there is one thing…"

"Of course there is. What?"

She smiles triumphantly. "You promised me these two

months, until the end of my internship, that we could be together."

I shake my head. "A lot has happened since I made that promise."

"I don't recall the promise having any conditions."

"Ash . . ."

"You love me."

I can't deny it. "I do."

"And I love you. Nothing has changed."

"Are you fucking kidding me? *Everything* has changed."

"You lost part of the Syrah."

"That's huge to me."

"I know." She closes the distance between us, looking up to meet my gaze, only a couple inches separating our bodies. "It's huge to me too."

"Not the same."

"You're thinking I don't have the relationship with those vines like you do, and you're right. When I say it's huge to me too, I mean because it's huge to *you*. Anything that's important to you is also important to me, because I love you."

Fuck. "You're not making this easy."

In fact, telling her not to bother coming back was the most difficult thing I've ever done. I told her she wasn't going anywhere. It was her decision to leave.

"Dale . . ." She parts her lips. They're glossy and pink, so ready for a kiss . . . "Very few things in life are ever easy."

Don't I know it. Nothing is easy. Nothing has *ever* been easy.

"But the things that matter most, that are worth the most," she continues, "*shouldn't* be easy. If they're too easy, we take them for granted. It's human nature."

I stare into her vivid blue eyes. They're bloodshot, and her eyelids are swollen. She's been crying, and I only now notice.

Self-absorbed.

I *am* self-absorbed. My sweet Ashley was crying, and I wasn't there to help her.

Damn it. She was crying over *me*.

I trail a finger from her temple down over her cheek, tracing the path her tears must have followed. She closes her eyes at my touch.

"Hey," I say.

She opens her eyes.

"I'm sorry. For making you cry."

"You didn't," she says. "It was all me. I have control over how things affect me."

"But I—"

She turns her head slightly, and her lips graze the palm of my hand. "You do affect me, Dale. I love you, so it's impossible for you not to. But I made the choice to leave when you told me not to go. I shouldn't have. I'm not a quitter, and I'm here to make sure you're not one either."

"I've never quit anything," I say. True words.

"Haven't you? You already said you're not going to the family meeting tonight."

"Maybe I changed my mind."

She smiles. "I hope so. Did you know Donny and Dee are driving home right now?"

I shake my head.

"Bree too. And your other cousins are coming home from school. Apparently everyone will be here. This is *that* big of a deal."

"Of course it's a big deal."

FREED

"My point," she says, "is that you should be there."

"Didn't I just say that maybe I changed my mind?"

She closes the last few inches between us and wraps her arms around my neck. "Did you?"

"No. A family meeting is the last thing I want to do tonight."

"This isn't just your loss, Dale. It's Ryan's. It's Talon's. It's everyone's. The fire hit the orchard too. Did you know that?"

Fuck. No, I didn't. I really *am* self-absorbed. "I'm sorry. Is my dad okay?"

"I don't know, but he's strong."

"Damn." I rake my fingers through my still-damp hair.

"My point is that it affects everyone, not just you."

"I know that."

"Do you? Because I think you do, at least objectively. Subjectively is a different matter."

"Yeah, yeah, yeah." Nothing I haven't heard from Aunt Mel a million times over the years.

"Yeah, yeah, yeah," Ashley mocks me. "Maybe it's time to think about someone other than yourself."

I can't fault her logic. She's right. The fact is that I'm *not* self-absorbed. Not really. Sure, I take things hard sometimes. Who wouldn't, with my background? But in the end, I always put those I love before myself.

Except not always.

Not that one time ...

That lone memory that I've buried so deep in hopes that it never surfaces.

But already, I feel the walls around it crumbling ...

Crumbling, because of the emotion I've allowed inside.

The emotion Ashley emboldened in me.

The love.
And with the love comes ...
Everything.

CHAPTER SIXTEEN

Ashley

Dale slams his mouth on mine.

No warning.

Not that I need a warning. I'm always ready to kiss Dale. To be with him in love and in lust.

But now? Right after I told him he should think of someone other than himself?

His response is to kiss me?

Oddly, it's not one of his angry kisses. It's hard and passionate for sure, but I feel no rage.

Our lips slide together, our tongues tangle, our teeth clash. Hard, passionate, and full of desire.

Then he's tearing at my clothes, his hands everywhere all at once. My shirt is gone, and then my bra. Then my jeans are midway down my thighs.

He lifts me and sets me on the granite countertop. I gasp at the cold on my ass.

Before I can think again, his cock is free and he's thrusting into me. I'm wet, of course. I'm always wet with Dale. One look from him has me squirming.

It's a fast and hard fuck, but still, not an angry fuck.

He slides one hand between my legs and massages my clit—

"Oh!"

After last night, I wasn't sure I had any more climaxes in me, but that's all it takes. I'm flying into orgasm, my blood boiling and racing through my veins, setting my whole body ablaze.

"Yes!" I cry. "Fuck, yes!"

"That's right, Ashley. Come. For me. Only for me."

He thrusts.

He thrusts.

He thrusts once more.

Then—

"Fuck," he says through gritted teeth. "Fuck, I love you."

His release is quick and smooth, and he stays inside me as my own subsides.

He pulls out, grabs a clean towel out of a drawer, and hands it to me while he zips himself up.

Am I supposed to say something? We've had fucks like this before, but they always had a precipitant. This time?

I'm not sure.

Perhaps he *is* angry. Angry that I said he was self-absorbed.

But I feel no rage from him.

And with Dale, rage is usually pretty darned apparent.

I slide off the counter and pull my jeans up.

"Shame to cover up that ass," Dale says huskily.

And the red-wine cloak of his voice is back. It's always there now, so much a part of me that I don't notice it as often.

Am I taking it for granted?

Am I taking Dale for granted?

No. He's promised me nothing beyond these two months.

But he *did* promise me these two months, and I'm holding him to it.

"Does this mean you're keeping your promise?" I ask boldly.

He sighs. "I never break a promise, Ashley."

I smile, but he doesn't return the gesture. His green eyes look . . . haunted in some way, as if he's thinking about a promise he once broke.

I touch his cheek, rubbing my fingertips over the short stubble. "This is *now*, Dale. All we need to worry about is this moment."

"This one," he says, "and the next one, and the one after that. Times infinity."

I smile. "You're always so . . ."

"What?"

"So . . . *Dale*. So very Dale."

He quirks his lips, but he doesn't look angry. "And that means . . . ?"

"It means life sucks sometimes, babe. It just all-out sucks. But if we live in the moment, take a breath and look at the beauty of the world, we can get through it. And it's never as hard as it seems."

He pulls me against him, so closely are we melded that I feel the beat of his heart against the top of my chest.

He wants to believe me. I feel it. I also feel that he *doesn't* believe me.

And he never will.

★ ★ ★

It's a fairly warm night, and Darla, with Talon's help, is grilling burgers. Dale's cousin Ava brought over a huge supply of buns, and I helped Jade and Darla cut onions, tomatoes, and homemade pickles earlier.

"Ashley!" Diana scrambles out the French doors and onto the deck. She grabs me in a hug.

Such a hugging family, but I don't mind it so much now.

"So good to see you," Dee says once she lets go of me.

"You too. How's Denver?"

"It's great, really. You were right about going. I'm glad I did. But..." She glances over at Dale, who's talking to his brother in a corner.

"You're worried about Dale," I finish for her.

"Yeah. Those vines..."

"They mean everything to him," I finish again. "He'll be okay."

She nods. "I'm glad he has you."

I raise my eyebrows. I haven't told Dee about Dale and me.

"Mom filled me in," she says. "I hope you don't mind."

"Of course not. I would have told you myself, but..."

"I understand. Dale is very private."

"He is."

"I'd ask how my big brother compares to your other exploits," she says, "but I'm pretty sure I don't want to know."

My other exploits.

Wow. I haven't given *my other exploits* a lot of thought since Dale catapulted into my life.

I'm experienced. *Really* experienced.

And Dale... He knows what he's doing sexually but not romantically. He's hardly experienced.

I smile as the memory of him spanking me slides into my mind. That was fucking hot.

"I don't kiss and tell, anyway," I say.

"The hell you don't! I seem to recall you telling me about an orgy—"

"Shh!" I warn.

Dale is out of earshot, but I don't want anyone else overhearing—

Too late. Brock saunters up to us, holding a martini glass, his dark eyes gleaming. "What's this I hear about an orgy?"

Just kill me. Kill me now.

"Better not be anything you're involved in, Dee," he continues.

"Not that it's any of your business, baby cousin," Dee says, "but I can't say I've ever had the pleasure."

He turns to me, smiling slyly. "Now why am I not surprised?"

"This is so not happening," I say.

"Crap," Dee says. "I shouldn't have said anything."

"At least not so loudly," I agree.

"I promise not to breathe a word of it"—Brocks waggles his eyebrows—"on the condition that you tell me all about it. Every last detail."

"Sure, I'll do that." I shake my head and roll my eyes. "Sometime around the fifth of never."

"Then I might just get that talking feeling," he says teasingly. "I haven't talked to Dale in a while. We have a lot to catch up on."

"Quit being a dick," Dee says.

"I'm just teasing," Brock replies with a laugh.

I'm not sure I believe him. "It was nothing. Just a little too much drinking one night at a party, and all the women took off their shirts. Nothing really happened."

Other than I fucked two men at once and then had a

threesome with another and a woman. But I'm keeping that to myself. Other than that, my stimulation was purely visual, and boy, was there a lot to see.

Brock licks his lips. "Please tell me you all sucked each other's tits."

"Didn't happen," I say. Though it did.

"Maybe felt each other up a little?" Brock asks hopefully.

"Nope." Except, yep.

"Leave her alone, Brock," Dee says. "It's obvious she's dopey in love with Dale."

Brock takes a sip of his dirty martini. "Doesn't mean she didn't have her fun before she met him."

"Oh my God." I will myself not to pull out a fistful of Brock's thick hair. "Just stop this. Now."

He steps back in mock surrender. "Okay, okay. I hope Dale knows how lucky he is."

"He does," Dee answers for me.

If lucky means a woman who's infinitely more experienced than he is. But romantically, we're both novices. I've had a few relationships here and there, but never anything serious. I know I've had a lot more sex than he has.

Still... that spanking...

He wanted to get rough.

I've always shied away from any kind of kink. Wasn't my thing, or so I thought.

Apparently I was wrong.

It's definitely my thing now, but only with Dale.

Actually... I never want anything except with Dale. Damn. I want way more than these two months.

I want a lifetime with him. By his side, working together, making great wines.

And all he's promised me is two months.

I'm so fucked.

CHAPTER SEVENTEEN

Dale

My brother is home. He's laughing with Henry and Ava at the moment, while dueling forces keep my mind churning. I stand with them, but I'm not involved in the conversation. They laugh and chat while I stand and burn inside. And not in a good way.

First, my birth father's revelation. I originally decided not to tell Donny, but now I'm caught. He has the right to know. On the other hand, Donny has succeeded in erasing that part of his life from his mind. Who am I to bring it all screaming back?

Second, Brock. Brock and Ashley. My womanizing cousin is coming on strong, and it's pissing me off to no end.

Uncle Joe, Brad, and his girlfriend are in the heated pool. Heat isn't necessary for Uncle Joe, though. The man would swim in ice-cold water. He's a born fish. So is Brock, but instead of prancing around in his Speedo, he's homing in on Ashley.

Fuck. It. All.

"What do you think, Dale?"

I jerk at my brother's voice. "Think about what?"

"Thanksgiving this year," Donny says. "It falls on Uncle Ryan and Aunt Ruby's anniversary."

"Gina and I want to do something spectacular," Ava chimes in. "We were thinking a big party at the winery. Aunt Marj and

I will handle the cooking. Turkey and all the trimmings, of course, and I'll supply the bread."

"Seriously?" I say. "You want to party when we've lost half the Syrah?"

"We all feel your loss, bro," Donny says, "but most of it was harvested. We'll still have—"

"What do you mean *we*, Don?" I ask, not nicely. "Those vines are mine, not yours. You don't give a rat's ass about any of my work."

"Wait just a minute," Donny says.

"Easy," Henry pipes in. "We all know how much the Syrah means to you, Dale, and we're all glad you're okay and that you don't have any effects from being caught in the fire. But none of that takes away from Uncle Ry and Aunt Ruby's celebration. This is the first year for the old-vine Syrah."

"Make that the only year," I say. "The vines are gone."

"*Half* the vines are gone," Donny says. "And they could come back."

"There's no guarantee," I say.

"Damn, Dale. Why is the glass always half empty with you? You lost half, yeah. But you still *have* half. As for the loss, of course there's no guarantee they'll come back. Life doesn't give you any guarantees. For God's sake, you and I know that better than anyone."

Big brick to my gut. Donny's right, but he doesn't know the half of it.

No one gets a guarantee in life, least of all Donny and me. And I . . .

I could have done so much better all those years ago. I saved him as best I could. Always told them to take me instead of him, and most of the time, they did.

I was determined. Strong and determined.

But in the end, I was not unbreakable.

I shake my head. I can't think about this now. Let them have their Thanksgiving anniversary party. Let them pretend everything's okay.

Let them...

"Dale?" Donny says. "You going to answer me or what?"

"What was the question?"

Donny shakes his head. "Never mind. Let it go, bro. You've got to let it go."

Let it go.

So easy for my little brother. He can pretend nothing ever happened to us. He can get through the fog of life without the handicaps I possess.

My vines. I need my vines. But if I go to the vineyards, I'll be greeted by ash and soot. Maybe the winery. The harvested grapes are there. The young wine is fermenting.

Still, that will give me no peace.

Not that I ever have peace, but I come close with my Syrah.

That's over now.

Then warm fingers entwine with mine.

Ashley stands next to me. "Hey," she says.

I turn my head. "Where did you come from?"

"My mother always says I came from heaven." She smiles.

Ava, Henry, and Donny laugh. I resist the urge to smile. Why? Why do I resist?

"I'm happy for you two," Ava says.

"Me too," Donny says.

Ashley squeezes my hand.

"It's complicated," finally comes out of my mouth.

Ashley's grip on my hand weakens. I've disappointed her. That's the last thing I want, but it was always inevitable. I disappoint those closest to me.

I disappointed the most important person in my life once before, so many years ago.

It's what I do.

"What's complicated about it?" Ava asks. "It's a relationship."

"That's what makes it complicated," I say.

"It doesn't have to be," Ava continues.

I love Ava, and she means well, but she doesn't know the half of what Donny and I went through. We never told Diana, Bree, and the cousins. The adults all decided for Donny and me at the time, and now . . . Well, now it would just be punitive to tell them. They'd all feel terrible, and not one of us wants that.

"I keep trying to tell him that," Ashley agrees.

Ava smiles at me through her lip piercing. "You got this."

I'm not sure if she's talking to me or to Ashley. Doesn't matter. I don't "got this." Two months. I'll give Ashley her two months.

Which means she won't be here for the big Ryan and Ruby Thanksgiving extravaganza.

And a little part of me dies inside at the thought.

CHAPTER EIGHTEEN

Ashley

It's complicated.

Aren't all relationships complicated? *Shouldn't* they be? If they were easy, everyone would be in one. There'd be no breakups. No divorce.

If they were easy, they wouldn't be worth anything.

I sigh inwardly. Getting Dale to understand that concept *won't* be easy, but I'll face the challenge. He's worth it. He's worth everything.

I squeeze his hand once more. "Want to get something to eat?"

"I'm not hungry."

"I am."

"All right. Excuse us, I guess." He leads me over to the table where Darla has set up dinner.

I fill a plate with a burger and all the fixings. Brendan Murphy pops into my head. He made burgers the night we shared the Château Latour.

"Come on," I urge Dale. "You have to eat something. You're probably still weak from being caught in the fire."

He stiffens.

Damn. I had to go and mention the fire.

"I'm sorry," I say softly, "but you do need to eat. And drink.

Water, not wine."

He sighs. "You're right." He takes a plate and piles two burgers on a bun.

"A double, huh?" I smile.

"You told me I had to eat." He grabs a bottle of water and holds it up. "And water."

I nod and take another bottle. "I'll join you."

"Why? You can have alcohol."

"Maybe I don't want any."

"Suit yourself." He leads me to an unoccupied table.

"You don't want to join anyone?" I ask.

"If I did, I would have joined them."

I nod and sit down next to him. This is classic Dale. The loner. At least I get to be with him.

"So when does the big family meeting start?" I ask.

"Usually after everyone has eaten. Dad and my uncles will lead it."

"Not Aunt Marjorie?"

"She doesn't work for the company. Uncle Bryce does."

"Oh. Right. Got it." I take a bite of my burger. Juice runs down my chin, and I whisk it away with my napkin. "Wow. Juicy."

"Best burgers ever," he says, taking a bite.

"They're even better than Brendan's," I say, and then I want to flog myself.

Why the hell did I offer that? It just popped out.

Dale goes rigid next to me. Then, after he swallows, "Murphy served you burgers with Château Latour?"

Right. Dale's a gourmet cook. Brendan decidedly is not. "He did. They actually went really well with it."

"Steel Chateaubriand for two would have gone better."

"True."

Brendan Murphy probably didn't have a Steel tenderloin at his disposal. Probably couldn't afford it anyway. But I keep this tidbit to myself.

"Was the wine any good?" Dale asks.

"Of course it was. It's a Latour."

He nods, stuffing another bite of burger into his mouth. He swallows. "My favorite is Château Lascombes."

I raise my eyebrows. "A second cru? Really?"

"That surprises you," he says.

"A little. I mean, premier cru is premier cru."

"First growth doesn't necessarily mean better. Besides, there's a certain subjectivity to wine tasting, as you know."

"I know. It's just..."

"You thought a Steel would want a premier cru, right?"

"Well...yeah."

"I want what tastes the best to me, and that's Château Lascombes."

I smile at him. "Fair enough. I've actually never tried Château Lascombes. We tried all the premiers crus in one of my tasting labs, but only some of the seconds."

"I have several bottles in the cellar," he says. "You want to taste it now?"

"Right now? Before the meeting?"

"Sure. Why not?"

"Because... Because I want to enjoy it with you. Take the time it deserves. Not when we're here with everyone."

He pauses, and for a hot minute, I wonder if he's going to reply at all.

Finally, "I understand. And I agree."

I smile again and reach forward to touch his cheek. Its

warmth flows through my arm and makes it tingle. Just a simple touch, and I'm ready to melt.

We finish our burgers without talking. No one joins us at our table. If I didn't know better, I'd think a neon sign were flashing above us, saying *Leave Us Alone.*

Then I realize.

That neon sign *is* there.

It's Dale. He's still an island. Still a loner. Still needs his space.

And he's let me in.

Just a little, but it's a start.

At this gathering of his huge family, only I am in his bubble. I like that. I like it a lot.

Still, a person needs people. Maybe someday Dale will come to terms with that.

In the meantime? I'm glad he's decided he needs me. At least for now.

★ ★ ★

Talon and Ryan, along with two others who I recognize as Jonah Steel and Bryce Simpson, head to the deck, where they stand above the rest of us. Ryan clinks a spoon on his wineglass.

I almost expect them to be microphoned, but I already know Ryan has a big and booming voice.

Once everyone is attentive, Ryan begins. "Tal and I will take the lead since it's the vineyards and the orchard that have taken the brunt of the damage from the fire. I think it's only right, of course, to think about the Pikes and what they've lost. We were damned lucky to only lose a fraction of what they did, and we're thankful. We've offered to help them in any way we can."

Murmurs of approval flow around us, but Dale is noticeably quiet.

"Unfortunately, our Syrah vines took the worst of it. Tal's Fuji orchard took a hit as well. But there is a lot of good news."

Dale's lips form a straight line. Apparently he isn't in the mood to hear any good news.

"This was the year we were going to produce our first old-vine Syrah. We can still do that with what we've already harvested. Of course it will be a smaller production. That's not necessarily a bad thing, economically. Supply and demand and all. Tal?"

"Right," Talon agrees. "And our Fuji production this year was bigger than ever, so the loss will be minimal economically. It's crucial to remember, in times like these, that people are more important than things. Though my trees and Ryan's vines are living things, people are the most important, and we're happy that all of us are healthy and accounted for. Dale was in the mountains when the fire came, and thanks to our great firefighters, he came home safely."

Cheers and hoots and hollers follow.

Dale looks around, and his lips curve up slightly, but it's forced. His family is thrilled that he's safe, and he knows that. He wants to appease them, smile, show them he's happy that they're happy.

But still, it's forced.

Those vines may not be people, but to Dale, they are, in a way.

They're something he's close to. Something that gives him solace.

And he'll mourn them as he'll mourn his birth father.

Already I know this.

"So here's the situation," Talon continues. "We're looking to furlough some staffers due to decreased production and harvest. This isn't something we like to do, and because it's been a good year up until now, they'll be receiving full pay and benefits."

More murmurs and some claps.

"Those that live in the residences on the Steel property will be able to stay as long as needed. If they find other work, they're welcome to go if they'd rather. We hope they'll choose to stay. Turnover costs money, and we pride ourselves on finding the best people to work our land and take care of our business. I'm going to hand it over to Bryce now."

Bryce Simpson, tall with silver hair and beautiful blue eyes, is the image of Henry in thirty years. "Financially, we're doing fine," he says. "Yes, there will be a loss this year, but you all know that this ranch is far from the Steels' only enterprise. Other investments are doing great, and Melanie, congratulations on your latest book release."

Jonah's wife—and Dale's therapist—waves. "Thanks, Bryce. Jonah promised me he wouldn't bring that up when there's so much else going on."

Jonah laughs. "I kept my promise. I didn't bring it up. I told Bryce to."

Laughter all around.

"So the point is," Bryce continues, "we're doing great, as always. Yes, we'll have to make a few adjustments, but it's nothing we can't handle. As Ryan said, we're furloughing some of the orchard and vineyard employees, but they'll be compensated. Any of you who are interested in looking at numbers, feel free to come by my office, and I'll explain everything to you. But for now, this isn't anything to worry about. We'll be able to fulfill our contracts. We may have less fruit to sell to smaller businesses, but our large contracts will be fulfilled."

Brock stands then. "I hate it when small businesses take it in the shorts. Sure, we'll be okay, but what about the Pikes? What about the mom-and-pop shops who depend on our fruit?"

"We've got it covered," Bryce answers. "Like Ry said, we're going to offer our help to the Pikes, and we can offer small business grants and loans through the foundation, right, Brad?"

Brock's older brother stands then, and if it's possible, Bradley Steel is even better looking than Brock. His features are almost feminine, except they're not, if that makes sense. He's male model material, with silky black hair and long-lashed hazel eyes.

"Yeah, Henry and I have already been talking internally about what the foundation can do to help."

I touch Dale's forearm. "I thought the foundation supported human trafficking and mental illness."

"It does," he whispers back. "Those are its two main focuses, but they do other stuff as well. We take care of our community."

"That's really nice." I smile.

Dale doesn't return my smile, though. He's still rigid and sullen.

All the talk from his father and uncles about what good shape the ranch is in didn't affect him at all.

Because to him, the Syrah vines are everything.

And not for the first time, I wonder . . .

Does he love those vines more than he loves me?

CHAPTER NINETEEN

Dale

My father and uncles keep talking, but I stop listening.

Yes, I get it.

We're lucky. Damned lucky. The Pikes took the worst of it, and I feel for them. I do. Truly.

But...

I sigh. No one will understand. Even Uncle Ryan stands up there and tries to tell me that my vines are merely things. Things that can be replaced. People can't be replaced.

Funny thing is that I agree with him. In theory. Even in practice.

Doesn't make this any easier, though.

Ashley sits next to me, so beautiful and lovely, her smile a beacon in the darkness. The stars shine above, and she rubs her bare arms to warm them.

I'm wearing long sleeves, and though the air is still smoggy from the fire and we're in a beautiful Indian summer, she's a California girl. She's chilly.

"Come here." I pull her into my lap and wrap my arms around her.

She darts her gaze around at the others, all seated at surrounding tables in the backyard. "Dale..."

"What?"

HELEN HARDT

"Here?"

"You're cold. I'm helping you stay warm. Everyone knows about us anyway, thanks to my mother."

Yeah, my voice has a definite edge. I'm not angry with my mother so much as... I'm not sure, really. She just irks me sometimes. If Dad had done the same thing, I wouldn't be irked.

Fuck. Why am I even like this?

Except I know why.

It's not the abuse I endured as a child.

It's not the fire and the loss of the vineyards.

It's not even my father's confession, though all those things play a role.

It's something else.

That sinister memory that threatens to surface the more I allow my emotions to control me.

And Ashley...

She brings out emotion in me like no one ever has.

It dawns on me then.

Why my mother irks me. Why I never allowed myself to get close to her.

Because I know how much I loved my birth mother. Losing her, especially after the abduction and torture, nearly broke me.

I couldn't get close to another mother. Couldn't set myself up for that again.

Why?

Why now?

Why, after years of therapy, do I just now realize this?

Jade Steel deserves better, and now that I've opened up this can of worms—aka emotion—perhaps I can give it to her.

What the hell? I'm all in now, anyway.

I'll never be able to bury the feelings I possess for Ashley. She fits perfectly in my arms, and even though my groin is tightening as she sits on my lap, I feel so much more than lust and even love for her.

I feel whole.

A wholeness I've never felt before. Never allowed myself to feel.

A wholeness I don't deserve.

Dad and my uncles are still talking and answering questions, but I stopped listening a while ago. I already know how this affects me. I already know that financially, the Steels will never be affected. We have more fortune than we could spend in ten lifetimes. Our children, grandchildren, and great-grandchildren are already set for life.

That isn't the purpose of the meeting.

The purpose is *family*. To reinforce the fact that we're all in this together.

I breathe in deeply. I will try. I will try to remember that my family is here for me. That my loss is not mine to bear alone. That I can get through this with the woman I love at my side.

I will *try*.

Try to accept my family's support even though they don't understand what those vines mean to me. Even though they can never understand...

I lean forward and press a kiss to Ashley's shoulder. She turns and meets my gaze, smiling.

I will try...

She's not letting me off the hook for the two months I promised her.

I shouldn't let myself off the hook either.

I love her. She makes me feel things I never thought I had any business feeling.

I still have no business feeling them, but...

I will *try*...

I will try to be all that she deserves.

And God help me if I fail.

★ ★ ★

My brother corners me once the meeting has ended. "I'm happy for you," he says.

I wrinkle my forehead. "Why? My vines just went up in flames."

"I know, and I'm sorry. I was talking about Ashley."

"Oh." I can't help smiling slightly.

"I talked to Dee. She says Ashley's great, and she must be if she brought you to your knees. Never thought I'd see the day." He shakes his head and chuckles.

"I'm not exactly on my knees here," I retort.

"Easy, man. I didn't mean anything by it. You deserve happiness, Dale."

"Do I?" So much he doesn't know.

"You always have. You're the only one who never thought you did."

Again, so much he doesn't know. I say only, "If you say so."

"I say so. I've always said so."

"Things seem a lot easier for you," I say.

He shakes his head again. "Are you kidding me? Do you think I don't have nightmares? Do you think I don't have memories?"

"Do you?"

"Of course I do. I'm a human being, just as you are. The only difference is I've made an effort—and it's a big effort sometimes, trust me—not to let the past rule my life."

My brother is strong, no doubt. But he's also a different personality than I am. He's an extrovert to my introvert. He needs to be around others. Others give him energy, and with that energy, he's able to fight the demons harder.

And of course, his demons are different. He doesn't have the darkest demon that haunts my soul. He'll never have it, and I'm glad of it. I don't wish it on anyone, especially not my own brother.

"You're a good man, Dale," he says. "She's lucky to have you."

"Is she?"

He grips my shoulder. "She is. She knows it. The rest of us know it. You just have to believe it yourself."

I scoff softly.

"I'm serious, man. The only thing holding you back is you." Donny releases my shoulder. "You want to go into town and have a drink?"

"At Murphy's?"

"You know another bar in town?" He laughs.

"I'll pass."

"Suit yourself. I want to talk to some of the locals. Haven't seen them in a while."

"I'm sure Brock and Henry can accommodate you."

"I'm sure they can, but I'd rather have a drink with my big brother."

I sigh. "Fine. Let's go."

"Tell Ashley," he says. "Bring her along."

I spy Ashley talking with Dee and Bree. "All right. Be right back."

CHAPTER TWENTY

Ashley

I'm determined not to play pool at Murphy's. Brendan, who apparently isn't working tonight, joins Brock and Henry at a table. I sit at the bar with Dale, sipping a glass of Ruby. None of the older Steels joined us, but nearly all the younger ones did. Only Angie and Sage are missing, as they had plans to get together with some girlfriends from their high school class.

Ava joins the others at the pool table. Does she know Brendan has a super crush on her? He's eleven years her senior, but Dale and I are ten years apart. Being with him feels as natural as air to me.

"Hey, Dale!" Brock calls out. "You're the one to beat. Come play."

Dale looks over his shoulder. "No thanks. Not tonight."

"If you want to play, go ahead," I tell him. "I promise I won't play."

"Not in the mood." He takes a sip of wine.

He's still hurting. How I wish I could ease his pain. Then he turns to me. "Ash?"

"Yeah?"

"I need your help with something."

"Sure. Of course. Anything."

"Tell me about your mom."

I widen my eyes. "What about her?"

"You're close to her, right?"

"Yeah. Definitely. I mean, she has issues with my whole oenology interest. She thinks I should have gone into something a little more stable."

He nods. "But other than that?"

"Yeah, we're close. Why?"

"And the fact that . . ." he hedges.

I swallow and then bite my lips slightly. "The fact that my father raped her? Is that what you're getting at?"

"Yeah. I'm sorry to bring it up."

"It's okay. I only found out about that recently, as you know, and I've always felt, from the very beginning, how much my mother loves me and what I mean to her. She never let it make a difference."

"Good. That's good. She must be a strong woman."

"Absolutely. She's been through hell. She got us off the streets by herself."

He nods again. "Tell me, then. How do you show her that you love her?"

I open my mouth and then close it. How do I answer that question? "I'm not sure," I finally say. "She just knows."

"Do you tell her?"

"Sometimes, but it's not like we fawn all over each other and say it every day."

"Then how does she know?"

I swallow a sip of wine. "She just does. What's this about, Dale?"

He sighs. "I haven't been fair to my mother."

"How so?"

"I never let her get close to me."

"She understands. It's hard for you."

"It is, but I had kind of an epiphany tonight about why that is."

"Why, then?"

"Crap," he says.

"Not following . . ."

"I didn't mean to say that. My emotions . . . I keep them . . ."

I can't help a soft chuckle. "You keep your emotions at bay. That's not really a surprise to anyone, Dale."

He smiles slightly. "You've made a difference there."

"I'm glad."

"I'm letting myself feel something fully for the first time. It scares me."

"Why would that scare you?"

He clams up then. Takes several sips of his wine. Finally, "I didn't mean to say all of that."

"That you're feeling something fully? That's a good thing."

"Something about you . . ." He sets his empty wineglass on the wooden bar.

"What about me?"

"You make me want to spill my guts, and trust me, Ashley. No one wants that."

I touch his forearm. "What if *I* want that?"

He sighs heavily. "You don't."

"Who are you to say what I want?"

"Ashley"—he whisks away from my touch—"if I let everything out, we all lose."

Chills skitter over my flesh.

I've always known Dale is hiding something, but for the first time, I realize the magnitude of it.

What he's hiding isn't just some run-of-the-mill secret.

It's huge. It's why the wall he's built around himself is nearly impossible to penetrate.

But I . . .

I penetrated it.

He let me in.

And whatever is in there?

It's downright frightening.

I'm scared.

Not so much of Dale, but of what's buried inside him.

Trust me, Ashley. No one wants that.

I'm all in now.

I love this man, no matter what he's hiding. He needs to know that. I reach forward and cup his cheek, scraping my fingertips over his blond stubble. "It's okay. Whatever it is, it's okay."

He brushes my hand away.

"If we love each other," I say, "it will always be okay. I love you."

Silence.

"And . . ." I prod.

"It goes without saying, Ashley. I love you. I will always love you. That's no longer an option."

I swallow my heart. "Do you want it to be an option?"

He scoffs softly. "For your sake, yes, I wish it were."

"For *my* sake?"

"My sweet, beautiful love"—he cups my cheek this time—"if you could see what's inside me, you'd go running as far away as you could."

CHAPTER TWENTY-ONE

Dale

Ashley covers my hand with her own, so we're both holding on to her warm cheek.

"Try me," she says indignantly.

God, if she only knew what she was asking.

I shake my head slowly. "I'll never put you through that."

"I love you," she says.

"I know. I love you too."

"Then there's nothing we can't get through, Dale."

I shake my head again. "I know you believe that, sweetheart."

Her cheeks pink at my use of the endearment. I've never called her sweetheart before. I've never called anyone sweetheart before.

"Of course I believe that. It's true, Dale. Our love will get us through anything."

"You're so innocent," I say.

She scoffs then. A big and sarcastic scoff. "Innocent? Hardly. You know my background. And if you want to know how innocent I am sexually? The answer is that I'm not. I've done it all, Dale. Every last thing."

A spear of jealousy anchors itself in my heart.

I don't want to know about her sexual past, but she opened the door.

"Oh?"

"Yeah. Ask Brock. He knows."

The spear of jealousy embeds itself deeper. "What?" I say through clenched teeth.

"I told him earlier tonight." She draws in a breath, as if considering what she's about to say. Then, "I once took part in an orgy."

That spear of jealousy? It's now a blade of fire burning through my entrails.

"You *what*?" Again through clenched teeth.

"I did. And that's not all. I've been with more than one man at a time. I've been with a woman. I've been—"

I shut her up the only way I know how—by crushing my mouth onto hers.

Fuck it all.

I still want her. Still love her. I don't care how much sex she's had. From now on, though, her only sex will be with me.

Except that . . .

Except that . . .

She deserves so much better than to be drawn into my chaos.

"Why don't you two get a room?"

I break the kiss with a loud smack. Brock is laughing jovially, Henry, Donny, and the others egging him on.

I glare at them.

"Ease up," Donny says, smiling. "You know my big brother can't take a joke."

Then they laugh again.

All of them.

Even Ashley joins in.

It's all in fun. I know this.

But underneath I hear a mocking jeer. A laugh once so frequent that I got used to it.

★ ★ ★

They're laughing again.

Laughing as they drag me out of the room.

Laughing and jeering as they take me away from my little brother.

I kick. I paw. I bite.

I'm rewarded with a punch to the nose. The pain splinters through me as blood gushes. Everything they do to me is painful, but no matter how often they punch my nose, I never get used to the sharp jab and spurting blood.

Scary, how I can get used to the other things.

The unspeakable things.

I learned when and when not to fight it.

I fight the most when I'm protecting Donny.

When they use me, I try to escape somewhere else in my mind. To a place that makes me happy.

I never find such a place, but still I try.

At least I can lie there until it's over. Yeah, it hurts each time. Yeah, sometimes there's blood. Going to the bathroom afterward is murder.

Until it all became part of the daily routine.

The daily routine . . .

Until this day.

They take me.

Take me away from my brother, which they almost never do. Usually, we're forced to watch as the other gets violated, and it's usually me.

This time.

I should have known.

This time, they're going to do something so horrible they don't want my brother to see it.

And they laugh.

They laugh like the maniacs they are.

And I brace myself.

But even I, after all I've been through, can't imagine the horrors that await.

★ ★ ★

"Dale!" Ashley shakes my shoulder. "Dale!"

I return to reality with a jolt. "What?"

"You were a million miles away for a minute. Brock was just teasing."

I look over at Brock and the others. They're involved in their pool game once again. Ashley and I are nothing more than a couple flies on the wall that merited their attention infrequently.

"I wish you hadn't told me," I say.

"Told you what?"

"About . . . everything. The orgy. All the sex."

"It was impulsive," she admits. "I shouldn't have, at least not here, but do you love me any less?"

"Of course not. I just . . . I don't like to think of you with anyone else."

"You've been with others."

"Not nearly as many as you." No truer words.

She twists her lips. "I'm not going to apologize to you for my past."

"I'm not asking you to."

"Aren't you?"

"No. Not really. I'm just wondering . . . why."

She smiles. "I like sex. It's a huge sensory experience for me because of my synesthesia."

"So if not for the synesthesia, you wouldn't be so experienced?"

"What kind of question is that?" she demands. "I'm me. Ashley. And *Ashley* has synesthesia. *Ashley* likes sex. *Ashley* is in love with *you*."

"What if we'd met before now?"

She crosses her arms. "Dale, what is this about? Are you doubting my love for you?"

Yeah. Yeah, I am, though I don't say it aloud. Of course I doubt her love for me. I'm a fucked-up mess. One day, when she realizes she can't live with the chaos, she'll leave.

Which is why I won't commit to more than two months. That way, I'll be the one to end it. If she ended it, I'd die.

Her phone buzzes on the bar. "Just a sec." She picks it up. "It's my mom. Do you mind?"

I shake my head. "Of course not. Go ahead."

Her mom. Who loves her and whom she loves. This conversation started about our mothers. I wanted to understand how to be a better son to my own mother. Boy, have we gone on a detour.

"Hey, Mom," she says.

I signal the barkeep for a refill on my wine.

Why don't you two get a room?

Not a bad idea at all. I pull my phone out of my pocket and speed dial the hotel down the street.

Get a room.

Damned good idea.

CHAPTER TWENTY-TWO

Ashley

"Hold on," I say to my mom. "I'm at a bar, and it's kind of loud in here. I'm going to step outside." I gesture to Dale where I'm going and then head outside onto the sidewalk. "Sorry about that."

"No problem," Mom says. "I have some exciting news!"

"Oh? What's going on?"

"We're coming to visit you!"

I jerk in surprise. "You are?"

"Yes! I got some time off work, and we're coming to Colorado."

This is weird. Mom never takes time off work. She says her clients need her to be beautiful.

"Wait a minute. What do you mean *we*?"

"That's the other part of the news, Ashley. I'm getting married!"

My stomach drops. Married? She wasn't dating anyone when I left. Was she?

I'm not sure how much time passes before Mom says, "Aren't you going to say anything?"

"Uh ... who exactly are you marrying?"

"His name is Dennis. I know you're going to love him."

"And you've known him *how* long?"

"A couple months."

"You were dating him before I left?"

"I was."

"Why didn't you tell me?"

"There was no reason to at the time. We were just starting to see each other."

Okay, makes sense. I guess. "Are you sure, Mom? You've never..."

"Never what?"

"You never seemed to have any interest in marriage before now."

"I wasn't interested before now. I had you. You were my priority, but now you're almost done with your doctorate. You'll be working, taking care of yourself, so I can think about myself and what makes *me* happy."

"Mom, I never meant for you—"

"This isn't a guilt trip, Ash. I *wanted* to make you a priority. If you'd gone into a trade, like I suggested, I could have..."

I could have done something for myself before now.

Those are the words she isn't saying.

"Mom..."

"That's not what I mean, and you know it." Her tone is sincere. "I'm thrilled you're doing something you love. Something you have passion for. That means more than going into some trade just for money and security."

"Are you saying you were wrong to push me in that direction?" I can't help asking.

She laughs softly. "I don't think I was wrong. I was being sensible. But I don't think you were wrong for following your heart, either. It's really all just opinion. Your happiness has always been the most important thing to me, and if this wine stuff—"

"Oenology, Mom."

"Ee-nology . . . makes you happy, then it makes me happy too. Besides, if I'd started dating before now, I never would have met Dennis."

"He must be something special," I say.

"He is. I'm super excited for you to meet him."

Super excited. My mom sounds like a schoolgirl with a crush. Her voice is bright pink with energy and puppy love. So unlike her. She's always been so mature. So responsible. So determined to give me the life she thought I deserved. Living on the street was hell for her. Far worse than it was for me. I didn't know any better, but she . . . She thought it was her fault.

I never did.

She was just Mom. My constant, whom I loved and I knew loved me.

Funny. Dale was asking me about my mom—about my love for her, how I showed it. This will be a good thing, Mom coming to Colorado. Dale can see our relationship firsthand. Maybe it will help him heal his relationship with Jade the way he wants to.

"When are you coming?" I ask.

"We're driving Dennis's RV," she says, "and we're leaving tomorrow."

"RV?"

"Yes, isn't that perfect? We have our hotel with us, so we don't have to bother you for lodging."

Nice gesture. The Steels have plenty of room, but it's certainly not my place to ask them to house my mother and her new boyfriend. Er . . . fiancé.

"When's the big day?" I ask.

"We're stopping in Las Vegas on the way to Colorado," she

says, "and we'd both love it if you could be there."

Shoot. I'd hate to miss my mother's wedding, but, "I'm in the middle of an internship, Mom. Part of the vineyards were just destroyed in a fire. I can't ask to leave right now."

"Oh, Ashley, I'm so sorry! Is everyone all right?"

"Yes, everyone is unscathed." Physically, at least, though I don't say this. It will just invite questions. "Some employees are getting laid off, but the Steels are paying them. They're great people."

"I'm sure they are." She pauses a second. "Which is why I'm positive they'll let you attend your mother's wedding."

This isn't like my mom. She has the work ethic of a Fortune 500 CEO. She must really want me there.

"Would you consider postponing the wedding?" I ask. "You can come for a visit, and then I can meet this man before he's my stepfather."

"Oh, honey ... We can't. The plans are already in motion. Besides, I'm just so excited!"

Giddy is more like it. Although I don't know this man from Adam, if he makes my mother this happy, I can't be displeased. Still, I hate the idea of her rushing into something.

"All right, Mom. Call me tomorrow. I love you."

"Love you too, honey. Bye!"

I walk back into the bar.

Dale sits, his second wineglass still full. Unless he downed it in the ten minutes I was gone and this is his third.

But that's not like Dale. He's not a heavy drinker.

Then an idea sparks in my head.

My mother's getting married ... Dale is my immediate superior at the winery and can give me a few days off ...

Maybe a trip to Las Vegas is just what Dale needs.

Doesn't hurt to ask, anyway.

"Hey, you," I say, after giving him a quick peck on the cheek.

"How's your mom?" he asks.

"Good. Better than good, actually. She's ... She's getting married."

His eyebrows rise. "Oh?"

"Yeah. Apparently she's been dating this guy for a few months, but she didn't tell me about him until now. They're going to Vegas in his RV and then coming here for a visit afterward."

"So I'll get to meet your mom, then."

"Absolutely. But I was thinking ..."

"What?"

"What if we went to Las Vegas for the wedding? Just you and me. It would be a nice escape for a few days, you know?"

"Escape from what?"

Really? He wants to go there? "You know exactly what. You've been through some shit, Dale. The fire. Your vines."

"I can't just leave. Not now. Harvest is nearly done, and we're going to put the grapes—"

I gesture him to stop. "You're right. I'm sorry I brought it up."

"You can go, though," he says. "You shouldn't miss your mother's wedding."

I shake my head. "I made a commitment to this internship. I'll stay the course."

"But it's your mom's wedding."

"To a guy I've never met. No, you're right, Dale. Neither of us should go."

"Ash ..."

"It's okay. I totally understand."

"You're not going to miss your mom's wedding because of me. You're going. Your internship will still be here when you get back."

I'm stuck now. I want to attend my mother's wedding. I don't want to leave Dale or the internship.

He still says he's only giving me these two months, and I don't want to waste a single day.

On the other hand . . . this is my mother's wedding. My mother—the one person who was there for me my whole life.

I must be there.

And . . .

Maybe Dale needs to be without me.

What's the old adage?

If you love something, set it free. If it comes back, it's yours. If it doesn't, it never was.

Damn.

Damn, damn, damn.

I'll go.

I'll set Dale free, if only for a few days—a few days after a huge loss. Sounds horrid, but it's the one way I'll know for sure if he truly loves me more than anything. Even the vines he lost.

And I'll pray like hell he comes back to me.

CHAPTER TWENTY-THREE

Dale

Ashley changed her mind.

"You did the right thing," Uncle Ry says to me the next afternoon. "You had to let her go. It's her mom's wedding."

"But the internship . . ."

"Can wait. Aren't you the one who said we didn't need an intern?"

"I was right. We don't."

He laughs. "You seem to need *her*, though."

I don't reply. Everyone knows, thanks to my mother, and those who didn't do since I pulled her onto my lap at the meeting last night and then shoved my tongue down her throat at Murphy's.

No secret, and to be honest? I'm okay with that. My family is probably happy to see me in any kind of a relationship other than with botanicals.

And above all, I do want my family happy.

I want Ashley happy.

And I'm deathly afraid that being with me would eventually make her extremely *un*happy.

I can't live with that.

So I let her go.

And I'll see if she comes back.

Sure, I gave her a guilt trip about leaving the internship, but that was for me. I didn't want her to leave. She'll be back in a few days, but already my world is colorless without her. Funny. She's the one with synesthesia, but she's given my world so much color.

The love she brought out in me ... It's made me so happy. Happy enough that I've been able to tamp down the darkness.

Now she's gone, and ...

The darkness is coming.

Already I feel it.

Already the chaos tries to consume me. I'll fight it. I always have, but this is the first time I've had to while my emotions have been let out.

"You know you want to," Uncle Ry is saying.

I jerk out of my mind. "Want to what?"

"Go to Vegas. Be with Ashley."

"What?"

"Have you been listening to me at all, Dale? I said you should go to Las Vegas. You know you want to."

I thread my fingers through my long hair. "I never said that."

"You didn't have to. It's all there. In your eyes, whenever her name is mentioned."

"You're imagining things. I'm happy for her. It's her mother's wedding, for God's sake."

"And she'll be back in a few days."

"Right." I clear my throat. "She'll be back in a few days."

But what will *I* be like when she returns? I can throw myself into my work. Winemaking is my passion. I can help complete the harvest. I love being outdoors. I can take to the mountains until she gets home. It's still fire season, of course, but I know how to protect myself. Or I can ...

Go to Las Vegas.

Be with Ashley.

The winemaking will wait. It's only a few days. I'm using it as an excuse, and Uncle Ry knows it.

I know it too.

"Just go," he says. "Please. For all of our sakes."

That gets a slight chuckle out of me. "I'm fine, Uncle Ry. Really."

"Dale, you're *not* fine. You're grieving for what you've lost in the Syrah vineyards. That's okay. Grieve. But let us all help you, and the person you need now more than any of us is Ashley."

"I won't ruin her mother's wedding."

"Of course you won't. Ashley wants you there."

"I mean ... Fuck. I'm a mess, and you know it."

"Sure you are. We *all* are. Maybe you more than the rest of us because the Syrah means so much to you."

Yeah. Me more than the rest of them for reasons they don't even know. Reasons that spear into me even more than losing some of my vines.

"Just go," Ryan says again. "A few days won't make a difference here. You know that as well as I do."

"She's on a flight. She may have already landed."

"So get on a flight yourself. Or you can be there in seven hours if you start driving."

"I don't know where she is. Where she's staying. Where the wedding will be."

He scoffs, shaking his head. "She has a phone. Call her."

But I won't call her. I want to surprise her. I smile at the thought. Surprising the woman I love.

The thought makes me happy. Makes me think I actually can do this. Have a relationship for more than two months.

Have a lifetime . . .

A lifetime with such a remarkable woman. A woman who completes me in a way I never thought possible.

A woman who might just be able to chase the demons away for good.

I stand. "I'm going."

"Good for you. I'll drive you to the airport in Grand Junction, and you can get on the next flight out."

I shake my head. "I'm leaving now. I'll take the truck."

"The truck? Don't be ridiculous. Go home. Take one of the cars."

"Nope. I'm leaving now, before I change my mind."

"You need to pack."

"All I need to do is call Mom to take care of Penny."

"You might want something other than jeans for a wedding." Ryan snickers.

I sigh. "For God's sake. Fine." I grab my key fob. "I'll call you when I have details. I'll be back in a few days."

"Good enough. And Dale?"

I look over my shoulder. "Yeah?"

"Go get her, man."

★ ★ ★

Uncle Ryan was right. I'm much more comfortable in my Mercedes. It's nearing midnight, and I'm ten minutes outside the Las Vegas strip. Uncle Ry's assistant got me Ashley's hotel information. The Rio. Her mother, Willow White, is due to arrive tomorrow, and the wedding . . . The assistant couldn't find a reservation at a chapel, but I'll see Ashley before then.

It's late, but I already have Ashley's room number. I reserved a suite at the Cosmopolitan. We'll move there tomorrow.

Will she be happy to see me? I have to assume so, since she invited me to come in the first place.

But...

I pull into the Rio and hand off my keys to the valet.

I enter the glitzy hotel and look around for the elevators. Looks like I'll have to walk through part of the casino to get to where I need to go. Not a problem. I'm hardly a gam—

My heart jolts so hard I swear I can see it trying to escape my chest.

Ashley sits at a blackjack table, flanked by two handsome businessmen—one black-haired and bronze-skinned, the other blond and tanned—in suits. Expensive suits. Just because I only wear them when necessary doesn't mean I can't tell fine clothes from cheap ones.

Fuck. It. All.

She's laughing, but I don't hear her, of course. The din of the casino—bells, laughter, screams of joy—overshadows everything.

Everything is black and white. Only Ashley vibrates with color—her blond hair, red lips, pink shirt cut low to expose the tiny bit of cleavage she has. Is that a push-up bra? Why is she wearing a push-up bra?

Anger heaves into me. Or is it jealous rage?

I don't know what the hell it is. I know only that my Ashley is flirting with two men who are probably younger than I am.

I had sex with two men at once.

Her confession from last night. Rather, two nights ago, as

it's after midnight now.

This is so not happening.

I stalk toward her despite the crowds. People cower and make way for me, as if I'm a giant plowing through their Lilliputian environment.

Apparently it's obvious I mean business.

I come up behind her.

"Ashley," I say gruffly.

She turns, and—

"Oh my God! Dale!" She jumps off her stool and throws her arms around my neck. "What are you doing here? You know what? I don't care. It doesn't matter. I'm just so glad you're here." She presses her lips to mine in a quick kiss.

"You're up, darlin'," the dark-haired suited man says.

I say nothing, though I feel a growl deep in my chest. Does Ashley hear it? Is it wine red? Or is it black, the way I feel?

She turns. "Oh! Right." She scrambles back onto her stool and makes the gesture to stay. "Dale, this is Carlos and Mike. They're from Texas."

Like I care. "Cash out," I say. "We're leaving."

"But I'm on a winning streak. Carlos says never to leave a table when—"

Do I look like I care what Carlos has to say?

Carlos—I assume—meets my gaze and holds out his hand. "Carlos Cruz."

I take his hand under duress and grip it hard. *Hands off. She's mine.*

The blond holds out his hand next. "Mike Hammond. And you are?"

"Dale Steel. Ashley's boyfriend."

Man, that sounds stupid. I'm thirty-five years old. Too old

to be simply a boyfriend. This bites.

So your idea of a threesome is off the table.

"Carlos and Mike are here for an oil and gas convention," Ashley says. "They just happened to find me at the slot machines and asked if I wanted to learn blackjack."

Just happened to find her. Right.

"They've given me some great pointers." Ashley holds up a little card. "This tells you what to do each time to maximize your odds of winning."

Great pointers, huh? Those cards are available in every gift shop in Vegas. *Nice touch, guys.* You found a woman who's never gambled before—never been to Vegas before—and you've made yourselves look like you know what the hell you're doing.

Game over.

"Ash," I say, "let's go."

"But—"

"Now." Through gritted teeth this time.

"Hey, man," Mike says. "The lady's doin' great. She shouldn't stop now."

I lift one eyebrow. "The lady is leaving. Now."

Ashley moves from her stool once more. "I can't leave now," she whispers. "The guys have been buying me drinks. I don't want to be rude."

"Buying you drinks, huh?"

"Yeah."

"While you're playing?"

"Yeah."

I can't help myself. I burst into laughter. "Sweet Ashley, drinks are free while you're playing. The house *wants* you drinking."

"But they ordered..."

"You'd know this if you'd ever been to Las Vegas before."

"So they haven't bought me any drinks . . ."

"Did you see either of them start a tab?"

"Well, no, but . . ."

I laugh again.

"Stop it, Dale." She gives me a swat on my upper arm. "Just stop it. I'm not *that* innocent."

I shake my head. "Innocent? Hardly. Not after what I learned last night."

Her cheeks redden.

I've pissed her off.

Good. She pissed me off. She gets to Vegas, and the first thing she does is hook up with two Texans who convince her they know blackjack with a betting-odds card anyone can find and trick her into thinking they're buying her drinks.

"I guess I've fucked up your plans for a threesome," I continue. "I'm out of here."

"Really, Dale?" she says. "You really want to go there? I was thrilled to see you. I jumped out of my chair. You really want to accuse me of anything untoward with those two? They're not even my type!"

"They have dicks, don't they?"

She shakes her head. "Fuck you." She turns and flounces back to the table.

I want to follow her. Instead, I watch her. I watch her sit back down between the Texans—one dark and one light. I imagine her as the prime beef between sourdough and pumpernickel.

And I'm mad.

I'm mad as hell.

CHAPTER TWENTY-FOUR

Ashley

Who does Dale Steel think he is?

I smile charmingly at Mike and then at Carlos and nod to the dealer. "I'm in."

Except my heart is no longer in the game. I was having fun. So what if this card I'm holding can be bought anywhere? So what if Mike and Carlos weren't actually buying me drinks? It's not like I was planning to go to bed with them. It never entered my mind.

Fuck Dale Steel.

After the next hand, I grab my chips. "I'm out, guys," I tell Carlos and Mike. "Thanks for a fun evening."

"You're not leaving yet, are you?" Carlos says in his voice dripping with caramel color.

"Yeah. I have to go see him."

"He left you here with us," Mike cajoles in his joyful bright-red voice. "Let us show you a good time."

Flirty Ashley kicks in then, and I smile. "What kind of a good time?"

"How about drinks in our suite?" Carlos offers.

Yeah, that's the good time they have in mind. Not that I'm slightly surprised.

"Sorry, guys. I'm taken."

"By a guy who left you here with us," Mike says again.

I breathe in. Funny. If not for Dale, I'd totally be into these two, despite the fact that they tried to convince me they were blackjack experts who were buying me drinks. Sex was always about what I could gain, and if the guys got what they wanted as well, where was the harm?

No more, though.

I'm now a one-man woman.

Even if that man is being a jackass.

He came for me, though. He came here after he nearly died in a fire and lost half his Syrah crop. He made the effort.

"It was great meeting you guys," I say. "Look around. This place is flooded with eligible women. You won't be alone tonight. I guarantee it."

I flounce away, smiling to myself.

They're both incredibly good-looking. They won't be alone for long. I never labored under any delusion that I was special to them. I was just having fun. I had no intention of going to bed with Carlos or Mike or both. But I did flirt with them audaciously. Maybe it's time I stop doing that.

I love Dale. I only want Dale.

Even when he's an ass.

I walk through the casino, but it's nearly impossible to find anyone in this haystack of people. It's a miracle he found me at the blackjack table.

To the lobby, then. I wait in a short line to ask whether Dale has registered. He hasn't.

I sigh. Up to my room, then. It's nearly two a.m., and my mom and Dennis arrive tomorrow morning. I need to get some sleep.

After riding up the elevator, I walk to my room and tap

the keycard to the door.

I open it, and—

"It's about time."

The cloak of red wine fills the room.

Dale's voice.

Dale is here.

But I'm not letting him off the hook that easily.

"How did you get in here?" I demand.

"Steel privilege," he snarks.

Of course. He paid someone off. Easy enough when you're richer than God.

"This is my room," I say. "You have no right—"

His lips are on mine, then. He's kissing me, and this time it's his trademark kiss of rage. He's angry. Mad as a hornet because I dared to spend the evening with two men who taught me some stuff about blackjack.

I didn't abuse his trust. Neither of them touched me, other than the brushing of a finger when they handed me drinks.

But he doesn't know that. He doesn't think about that. He's filled with rage.

As much as I love this kiss, want this kiss, I push him away, breaking it.

"This isn't happening," I say.

"Want to bet?" He chuckles at his own joke.

"Yeah, I'll bet the house. I'll bet the entire Steel fortune. Because I know you, Dale. I know you're an honorable man, and you'll do nothing without my consent. I hereby do not consent to anything. Not until you tell me what the hell that was about down there."

"Fine," he says. "I drove five hundred miles to see you and find you sandwiched between two Texans. *That's* what this is about."

My lips tremble. "I wasn't sandwiched."

"Flanked, then. Use whatever word you want. It's all a euphemism for threesome, anyway."

"That's it, then. You're bothered by the fact that I've had a threesome."

He says nothing.

"What I did before I knew you has nothing to do with us. With how I feel about you."

"Then what was tonight about?"

"I sat between them at a blackjack table," I say defiantly. "I didn't fuck them."

"They wanted to."

"So what? Lots of women want to fuck you too. That doesn't mean they get to."

"Maybe, but I don't encourage them."

"You think I encouraged Carlos and Mike?"

"For God's sake, Ashley, of course you did. With all your experience, surely you know men by now. They're always looking for a pretty girl to fuck. Show one spark of interest, and they think you're game."

"I was interested in learning blackjack, not in fucking them." I shake my head. "This is crazy. I honestly thought you were different from most men. I honestly thought . . ."

"What?" he demands. "What did you think?"

"I thought we had a chance, Dale. Don't you get it? I like sex, okay? I like it a lot, and I've had a lot of it. But I never got serious with anyone I had sex with because it was only sex on both sides. But you . . . It's different with you. It means more. It's not just physical. It's . . . It's . . ."

"What is it, exactly?"

"It's emotional. I love you, Dale. I love you so much. And

I ... Damn! I just want things to be the way they were."

I stop then. The way they were? Nothing has really changed. It's never been perfect with Dale. Perfect would be a relationship without an end in sight, not one confined to two months.

"Things change, Ash," he says finally. "The fire ..."

"I know, babe, and I'm so sorry." I walk toward him tentatively. "But—"

"Please." He gestures with his hands as he interrupts me. "Don't tell me how good I have it. Don't lecture me on Steel privilege. Don't tell me the Pikes got hit worse. And don't tell me I'm self-absorbed. I can't take it right now."

I drop my mouth open. I have no words.

"There are things about me—things I hide deep inside— that will never change. That I'll never heal from. Things that have nothing to do with the fire or the Syrah."

I reach toward him, but he backs away, shaking his head.

"Don't ask me to open up. I can't."

Jade's voice haunts me from within. *Don't push.*

What don't I know? Something before the adoption. It has to be. But what?

Something terrible. Worse than growing up without a home? Worse than going to bed cold and hungry? Worse than ... Worse than being raped and left pregnant?

My God, I can't go there. Not Dale. Not my Dale.

"All I want is to be here for you," I say softly. "Anything else is up to you."

CHAPTER TWENTY-FIVE

Dale

Surprising.

Ashley doesn't ask me to elaborate.

Not that I would, but why doesn't she ask?

She claims to love me yet doesn't ask about my background?

Odd.

Do I trust in her love?

Do I trust she had no intention of hooking up with the Texans?

She smiled and jumped off her chair when I showed up. She threw herself into my arms.

Yes, she was happy to see me.

And as usual, I ruined it.

I can't ruin this anymore. It's not a matter of trusting Ashley. In my heart, I know she'd never be unfaithful to me. Sure, seeing her between two men who clearly wanted to get into her pants pissed me off, but not because I doubt her.

Because I doubt *myself*.

I doubt my own ability to make her happy. To be what she deserves. Hell, I don't just doubt. I fucking *know*. I know she deserves a hell of a lot better than what I'm capable of giving.

I sigh.

FREED

Maybe it's time to put that to bed.

I trust her, so I need to trust myself.

Give myself the gift that she's given me. Complete trust.

There's a reason I haven't made a bigger commitment, and it's not because my love for her isn't enough.

My love for her is infinite. All-consuming. Never-ceasing.

It's my love for myself that fails.

Ashley called me self-absorbed recently, and she was right.

But self-absorption is far from self-love.

I need less of the former and more of the latter.

It's time to start now.

Ashley deserves all of me.

And so do I.

But I . . .

No. I will not go there. Not tonight. Tonight, I'm going to love Ashley enough to love myself.

I cup her soft cheek, thumbing her satin flesh. "I love you."

"I know," she says softly. "I love you too."

"I want to be the man you deserve."

"You *are*, Dale. The only one who doesn't know that is *you*."

Amazing how she knows exactly what I'm thinking sometimes.

"I want to take you somewhere tomorrow," I say.

"Of course. But I need to be back in time for my mother's wedding. It'll be sometime in the evening."

"Of course. We won't go far."

"Then it's a date." She smiles.

And my love for her triples, quadruples. But how can something quadruple if it's already infinite?

Then I remember trig class in high school, how some infinities are larger than others. Makes no sense, logically. I was the guy who simply learned the mathematical rules and applied them. I didn't care whether they made sense.

I get it now. I truly *see*.

"Can we please go to bed now?" Ashley pleads. "I've missed you."

"You've been gone ten hours," I say.

"A minute is too long to be away from you." She wraps her arms around my neck. "I wanted you to come with me. Remember?"

I nod. "And here I am."

"I'm so happy you're here. I can't wait for you to meet my mom. But for now . . ." She eyes the bed, licking her lips.

"It's late," I say.

"Very," she agrees. "Your point is . . . ?"

"I don't have one." Then I kiss her.

She parts her lips for me, and I dive between them. My rage has subsided, and now I let the love flow through every cell of my body, let it take me away to the place I've only found with Ashley.

Oh, the rage will return. I know myself too well.

But I'm determined to see what Ashley sees in me.

I'm determined to be what she deserves.

I deepen the kiss, hold her close to my body—as close as I can—and even though we're both fully clothed, the completeness is real, as if we're already joined physically.

This will work, I think to myself.

I can do this.

I surrender then, in a way I never have.

I let my thoughts go.

I let myself feel.

I let myself simply be.

I allow my emotions to surface. All the way.

I have to accept the dark to embrace the light.

I have to trust myself.

I break the kiss and pull backward a bit, just so I can look into her beautiful blue eyes.

So beautiful, my Ashley. Her light-blond hair falls over her shoulders in a soft curtain. I undress her slowly, relishing each new inch of flesh I expose.

When she stands before me, naked and lovely, I suck in a breath.

"Your turn," she says softly.

She unbuttons my black shirt, parting the sides and smoothing her hands over my chest. Her touch makes me tremble. Seriously shudder.

My cock is hard as a rock, of course, as it always is around her. How many times have I been determined to make love to her slowly? To love her as she deserves?

But what I crave right now, as she undresses me, is to grab that gorgeous curtain of hair, force her head back, and shove my erect cock into her red mouth. Fuck her mouth good and hard, force her to swallow my come and then flip her over, smack her ass until it's red as a maraschino cherry, and then take her from behind.

Then that ass . . .

I've never taken a woman's ass before . . .

No.

Damn it!

Slow.

Determined to go slow.

Slow.

Slow and sweet. What this woman deserves.

She pushes me down onto the bed and then removes my boots one by one.

And it's fucking sexy.

No woman has ever removed my boots before.

She peels my socks from my feet and then kneels between my legs to work my belt.

God, my cock is going to burst.

Faster, Ashley. Faster.

But I don't say it aloud. No. Slowly. Slowly. Going to give her what she deserves.

What she deserves is a hard spanking for sandwiching between those two Texans...

Damn it!

No!

Fuck! How am I supposed to deny my base instincts?

How?

She slides my jeans and underwear over my hips, and my hard dick juts out. Her eyes pop.

I can't help a self-satisfied smile. My dick always impresses her.

"God, you're gorgeous, Dale." She pulls the jeans the last few inches off me.

I'm naked now.

We both are.

Slow, Dale. Go slow.

But the image of Ashley sitting between the Texans won't dissolve from my mind. I grab her, pull her over my lap so that gorgeous ass is at my beckoning. I bring my palm down on its creamy flesh.

"Ow!" she cries. "What's that for?"

"That," I say in a low growl, "is for putting me through hell tonight. Making me think about you fucking those two horny Texans."

"But I wasn't—"

Swat! My palm goes down again, leaving a rosy pink mark on her milky skin.

God, I'm getting harder. She's so beautiful, so . . .

Slap!

Once more.

"Dale!"

"Tell me to stop," I say, "and I'll stop."

I wait a second. Then another.

She says nothing.

Slap!

Slap! Slap! Slap!

Then I slide my fingers through her folds.

Fuck. She's wet. Slick and wet and warm.

She likes this as much as I do. A smile spreads over my lips.

I ease my fingers upward, over her crack, massaging her asshole, her own juices lubricating it.

"Tell me to stop," I say, my voice a husky rasp. "Tell me, or I'm going in."

"Dale, please . . ."

"Please what?"

"Please. Do what you want. I want what you want."

God damn, those words. I'm hot and horny and splitting into pieces.

I nudge the tip of my finger against her asshole, imagining it's the head of my cock.

She gasps when I breach the entrance. I stop for a few seconds, let her get used to the invasion.

Then I slide my finger all the way in.

Such lovely forbidden warmth.

God, how will it feel against my cock?

So much for slow and sweet.

I'm going dark and taboo.

Dark and oh, so taboo.

I pull my finger out and slide it back in.

"Oh . . ." she breathes.

"Feel good, baby?"

"God. Yes. Love it."

Has she done this before? I don't doubt it, given her experience. I won't be the first to breach this ass.

But damn it. I'll be the last.

CHAPTER TWENTY-SIX

Ashley

I love anal. What can I say? It's hot. I tell my girlfriends who say they'll never do it to try it once and then get back to me.

There's little I haven't tried in the bedroom.

Dale knows this now.

But I swear to God, he makes me feel like a virgin.

Everything he does to me is like an awakening. A sexual rebirth.

His finger gliding in and out of my ass has me so wet I can't see straight. I want his cock there. I want it in my pussy. Fuck, I wish he had two cocks.

I'm dripping, and my nipples are so hard I'm sure they might pop off.

"Fuck," he growls. "I can't take this anymore." He flips me over and onto my back on the bed. "Need to be inside you."

He thrusts, filling my pussy, burning a fiery path through every part of me.

"I love you," he grits out. "Love every part of you. Want every part of you."

"It's yours," I breathe, gasping at each thrust that takes me closer and closer to the release I yearn for. "Every part of me is yours."

"Going to make you mine," he says. "Mine and only mine."

I already am. My words float above us and around us, in a soft pink melody to his deep-red harmony.

"Never let you go," he groans. "Can't. Not ever."

No one's asking you to.

His groin hits my clit with each plunge, and this time, this time—

"Yes! I'm coming, Dale!"

My walls contract around him, and with each spasm I ride higher, higher, higher . . .

Every orgasm with Dale is better than the last. Every. Single. One.

I grab his cheeks, look into his gorgeous green eyes. So much I want to say. So much I'm saying inside.

So much he's not yet ready to hear.

But I'll say it.

I'll say it all before our two months are over.

And I'll hope it's enough to matter to him. Enough to make him give me a lifetime.

For that's what I need, what I want, what I crave more than anything else in the world.

A lifetime with this man I love. This man who's shown me I'm more than just sex.

I'm about love. About going all in for what matters to me.

I'm about Dale Steel.

★ ★ ★

Strong arms jiggle me out of my slumber. I open my eyes to the Syrah-colored veil of Dale's voice.

"Time to get up, Ash. I have a surprise for you."

I pop my eyes open farther. "A surprise? What time is it?

My mom gets in sometime this morning. They spent the night at an RV park in Reno."

"It's early. Seven thirty. I ordered breakfast, and you have time for a shower. We have an appointment at nine."

"An appointment? Where?"

"That's the surprise." He smiles. "Come on."

★ ★ ★

After the limo driver drops us off at another hotel, Dale leads me inside, past the lobby and glitzy casino, to the shops.

He stops at—

"Tiffany's!" I gasp.

"Yes."

The door swings open, and an attractive older woman with light-blond hair greets us. "Mr. Steel," she says. "And you must be Ms. White."

I don't answer. I'm not sure I'll ever be able to speak again. What are we doing here?

"Thank you, Iris," Dale says.

"You're quite welcome," Iris says. "I've laid out the items as you asked."

Dale holds my hand, and we both follow Iris to one of the jewelry counters. Sparkling on top of velvet in Tiffany light blue lie no fewer than twenty diamond rings.

Diamond rings.

I can't help gaping. They're all huge. They're all sparkling. They're all beautiful.

I don't let myself think about what this may mean. Surely Dale can't be thinking... I mean, he only committed to two months.

He meets my gaze. "Choose."

I gulp. "Er . . . what?"

"Choose," he says again. "Pick the loveliest one, and it's yours."

"You're . . . What?" I say again.

"I'll leave the two of you alone. Just wave me over if you need me." Iris heads to the front of the store.

We're the only customers so far. Did Iris open just for us? I have no idea.

"Ashley," Dale says, "you're mine."

"I'm yours," I echo.

"So let's get married tonight. With your mom. It'll be a double wedding."

The words float around me in the dark red of his voice. I actually see them—the first time I've seen words in color, like most synesthetes. They break into individual letters, like a word scramble I'm trying to make sense of in my head.

Because it has to be a scramble, right? He didn't just ask me to be his wife. This is all so un-Dale-like.

Clearly I'm still up in the room. In bed. Asleep.

This is all a dream. A lovely dream.

Except that it's not.

Dale drops to a knee, taking both my hands in his. "I never thought I'd say these words to anyone, but I want to marry you. You deserve a lot better than what you'll get with me, but if you love me as I love you, we can make it, Ashley."

My mouth drops open.

It's real. And his words are real. Except they're not his words. They're my own. They're what *I* believe, not what he believes.

I drop to my knees so that our gazes are level. "Are you

sure?" I have to ask.

He smiles and chuckles. "I'm not really sure of anything, but I know I love you. I know I've never felt this way before, and I know I'll never feel this way for anyone else. You're my love, Ashley. I don't ever want to be without you."

"At least you're honest." I reach out and cup his cheek. "I don't want you any other way than who you are, because who you are is the man I'll always love."

"Marry me, then," he says. "We'll find our way through life together."

I melt against him and bury my cheek into his strong shoulder. "I'll marry you, Dale. It's all I've ever wanted."

The letters swirling around me finally form words, and then a sentence.

This is real.

Truly real.

And still kind of unreal.

Do I think Dale is ready for this? No. Even *he* isn't sure. But I have to grab the brass ring while he's offering it.

I love him, and somehow, I'll make him see that he made the right choice.

What led him here?

Seeing me with the Texans last night?

Something else?

I'm ridiculously curious, but I don't ask. If he thinks too much about what he's doing, he may change his mind.

I can't risk that.

He pulls me to my feet, and we face the display of rings. "Choose your favorite. If you don't like any of these, I'll have one designed to your specifications. I want you to be happy, Ashley."

"I'm already happy. They're all beautiful. I'm not sure I can choose."

"Then I'll buy all of them. You can wear a different one each day."

I can't help laughing. "You're being silly."

He pauses a moment, his forehead wrinkling. "Wait just a minute." He heads over to where Iris stands. The two of them whisper together, and then Iris heads to the back.

Dale returns. "Iris is bringing out something you'll love."

"Something else? I love all of these."

"You'll love this one even more."

A few minutes later, Iris appears with a blue Tiffany's velvet box. She hands it to Dale. He opens it, and his eyes widen.

Then he turns so I can see.

I gasp loudly.

It's set in platinum. A large round diamond, three carats at least, and set around it are tiny garnets. Or they could be darker-colored rubies for all I know.

But they're the color.

The color I love.

The color of Dale's voice.

"I should have thought of this before," Dale says. "I told Iris to set out her most beautiful engagement rings. Of course she thought only of diamonds, but a simple diamond will never suffice for you, Ashley. Your favorite stone is the garnet."

He remembered.

Well, of course he did. He gave me his mother's garnet necklace. It's upstairs in my hotel room. I plan to wear it for my mother's wedding this evening.

I will. And I'll wear it when I marry Dale.

"What about your family?" I ask.

"What about them?"

"Don't you want them here?"

"They'll understand. Hell, they'll all be ecstatic, honestly."

I don't doubt his words. Talon and Jade worry about him being alone. Now he won't be. He'll have me.

He slides the ring onto the third finger of my left hand.

It fits perfectly.

CHAPTER TWENTY-SEVEN

Dale

Though I expect to feel apprehension, I'm surprised when I don't.

The bauble is beautiful, but not nearly as ravishing and priceless as the woman wearing it.

I stand and pull her up beside me. "We'll take this one, Iris."

"Perfect," Iris says with a smile. "I'll get the paperwork started, Mr. Steel."

Iris just made a hell of a commission. Of course she's smiling.

Ashley holds her left hand in front of her and stares. Then she looks at me, her eyes questioning.

Are you sure?

I expect the words to come out of her mouth, but they don't.

Good.

At this moment, I'm sure. About as sure as I'll ever be.

Her phone chimes, and she pulls it out of her purse. Her eyes light up. "It's Mom! Hey!" she says into the phone.

I head to Iris at the cash register and complete the purchase of Ashley's ring.

A lump forms in my stomach.

No. Can't go there. This is what I want. This is the best thing in the world for me.

But is it the best thing for her?

Shut up! I nearly say the words aloud. Am I not entitled to happiness? She makes me happy, and damn it, I seem to make her happy.

This is win-win.

"Great news!" Ashley squeals as I shove the receipt for the ring in my pocket. "Mom just pulled in!"

"Are they staying at the Rio?"

She nods. "They're going to check in and then meet us for coffee back at the hotel."

"Us?"

"Of course, silly! You have to meet them sometime."

"Right. I know." This was all my idea, after all. Of course I need to meet her parents before we show up at the wedding chapel and announce we're hijacking their nuptials.

She grabs my hand and pulls me out of Tiffany & Co.

"Bye, Mr. Steel," Iris calls. "And goodbye soon-to-be Mrs. Steel!"

Ashley's cheeks turn that lovely pink I adore. "I can't even believe this is happening, Dale. I'm just so happy."

I squeeze her hand. "I am too, sweetheart."

It's not a lie. Not by a long shot.

So why do I feel like it is?

Probably because I never allow myself to be happy. I don't feel I deserve to be happy.

Fuck it.

I'm going to embrace happiness, just this once.

For as long as it lasts.

We take the limo back to the Rio, walk to the coffee shop

where Ashley's mother and her betrothed will meet us, and my stomach rumbles. I didn't eat much of the breakfast we ordered, as I was nervous as all get-out about my plans.

"Hungry?" I ask Ashley.

"Are you kidding? I may never eat again. My stomach has butterflies flying through it at cosmic speed."

I chuckle. "Cosmic speed?"

"Faster than that even. Just some OJ for me."

"Should we wait for your mom?"

She shakes her head. "Let's go ahead and order."

"Good enough." I place the order for a glass of OJ for her and coffee and a breakfast sandwich for me.

We grab a table in the corner.

No sooner do I take a bite of my sandwich when Ashley jumps out of her chair.

"Mom!" She runs to a man and woman entering the small shop.

Ashley's mother doesn't look much older than Ashley. Her hair is blond—same as Ashley's—and a long braid falls over one shoulder about halfway down her chest. Her cheekbones are high, and her eyes are nearly identical to her daughter's. Her lips are thinner but nicely shaped, and she wears jeans and a black tank top that says *Vegas or Bust* across the front. Her companion is tall and handsome and looks about my age.

Ashley drags her mother hand in hand to where I stand.

"Dale, this is my mom, Willow."

Willow holds out her hand. "Dale, it's so great to meet you! Ashley's told me so much about you."

Interesting. Ashley hasn't told me a lot about her mother as a person. Only about the life they led together, and she wasn't overly open-lipped about that. Not that I blame her. Growing

FREED

up homeless and the child of a rape isn't something I'd talk about either. God knows I never talk about my childhood.

"Nice to meet you too," I reply, taking her hand.

"And this is Dennis James," Ashley says.

Dennis smiles and grabs my hand. "Nice to meet you."

I grasp his hand in a firm shake. "You too. Have a seat, both of you. Ashley and I already placed our order, but what can I get for you?"

"Ashley ordered coffee?" Willow asks in mock surprise.

"Are you kidding, Mom? OJ for me. My mom'll have black coffee, though," Ashley says to me.

"I think I'll live on the edge a little," Willow says. "It's my wedding day, after all. I'll have a vanilla latte."

"Dennis?" I ask.

"The same. Make mine with a double shot."

"Got it. A scone or anything?"

"I'm good," Willow says, as Dennis shakes his head.

I head to the counter to place the order. When I return, Ashley and her mother are talking animatedly, finishing each other's sentences.

Dennis turns to me. "Ever feel like a fish out of water?"

Yeah, like my whole life. But he has no way of knowing that. "I'm sure they've missed each other."

"Ashley is all Willow talks about," Dennis says. "She's so proud of her."

"She's an amazing young woman."

"So is her mother."

I nod. "How did you two meet, exactly?"

"Online, believe it or not. I'd just about given up meeting anyone decent on one of those sites, and then she came along."

I drain the last of my coffee. Now what? I've effectively

run out of things to talk to this man about.

"I understand you're a winemaker," he says.

"You understand correctly."

"Then we have something in common," Dennis says.

"Oh?"

"Yes," he chuckles. "I drink a lot of wine."

Ha! Never heard that one before. "Have you tried any of the Steel Vineyards wines?"

"Can't say I have."

"We'll have to remedy that, then."

"Sounds great. I'd enjoy it."

Silence between us again. Ashley and her mother continue to jabber.

My name is called, and I walk to the counter and bring back the lattes.

"Thank you," Willow says in a sing-songy voice.

"What do I owe you?" Dennis asks.

"Please, it's on me."

"Thank you. That's kind of you." He takes a sip of his latte.

And again . . . silence.

He seems like an okay guy, though.

"I can't get over how young Willow looks," I finally say. "She and Ashley could be sisters."

"She is young," Dennis says. "Didn't Ashley tell you?"

"Her age? No, she didn't."

"She had Ashley when she was fifteen."

I stop my jaw from dropping onto the floor. Fifteen? The poor woman was raped at fifteen? More likely at fourteen, if she had the baby at fifteen.

How did I not know this?

I'm about to marry a woman, and I know next to nothing

about her or her family.

Not that it matters. I love Ashley no matter what. But we've known each other for less than a month.

What the hell am I doing? This is so off-brand for me.

Ashley's twenty-five, which means Willow is forty, only five years older than I am.

"How old are you?" I ask Dennis.

He laughs. "I admit it. I'm a cub, and I have no problem with it. I'm thirty-three."

Again, I stop my jaw from dropping. This guy is two years younger than I am.

"We joke that she's a cougar," Dennis continues. "But you have to admit, she looks amazing for forty."

"She's very striking," I agree.

"It's a match made in heaven," he says. "I never wanted children, and she's not looking to have any more."

"How long have you known each other?"

"About six months, but Willow only just told Ashley. She didn't want her to worry."

"Why would Ashley worry?"

"Ashley's very protective of her mother, apparently," Dennis says. "At least that's what Willow says."

I nod. That's certainly understandable.

"What do you do, Dennis?" I ask.

"I'm a pastry chef."

Good. That's a decent living.

"Where do you work?"

"At Chevalier in LA," he says. "They're getting bought out, though, so I don't know if I'll have a job in a couple months. We're all hoping the new owners don't want to bring in all new people."

"Oh. I hope not."

"I'm not overly worried. I have a good reputation in the area. Something will come up."

Nice. He has a good attitude.

"And Willow does hair?" I say.

He nods, swallowing another sip of latte. "She does. She's great at it, too."

"I'm sure she is."

More silence.

"How old are *you*, Dale?"

Weird question, though I did just ask him how old he was. "Thirty-five."

"Older than I am? You look younger."

"It's probably my hair."

He nods. "Not too many guys our age wear it long like that. Looks good on you, though. I could never do it in my line of work. The hair net's bad enough on short hair."

Ashley and Willow squeal in unison.

"Okay," Dennis laughs. "You got our attention. What's going on?"

"Look at this rock!" Willow shoves Ashley's hand under Dennis's nose. "My baby girl is getting married!"

"My God." Dennis leans back. "I think I might have just gone blind from that glacier."

"Isn't it beautiful?" Ashley says. "Dale knows my favorite gemstone is the garnet."

Willow meets my gaze. "Dale, I have to tell you. As a stylist, I'd love to get my hands on that hair of yours."

"No, Mom. Never," Ashley says. "Dale, don't you dare ever cut that gorgeous hair."

I smile—a bit forced, but I get it out. "Don't worry. If I

haven't cut it by now, I never will."

"How about a deep condition, then?" Willow says. "You can't dangle that glorious mane in front of me and not let me work with it."

"Mom's deep condition treatments are the best," Ashley says. "You really should, Dale."

"I'll go to bat for Willow too," Dennis adds. "Her scalp treatments are heaven."

Really? Is this really happening? What am I supposed to say?

"Maybe," I finally relent. "But this is vacation for you, Willow."

"I don't mean now," she says. "I'm talking about when the two of you come visit Dennis and me in LA."

"Of course." I hope my cheeks aren't red from embarrassment. "I'm sure we'll visit soon."

"Not until my internship is over, of course," Ashley says. "I've already taken too much time off by coming here."

"Isn't this your boss?" Dennis gestures to me.

Ashley laughs. "He is, but Mom will tell you about my work ethic. I learned from the best."

"Ashley . . ." Willow begins.

I get it. Willow hasn't told Dennis about their homeless past. I understand. There's a hell of a lot I haven't told Ashley about my own past, and still, I'm going to marry her.

What can it harm?

I can't let myself think about the answer to that question.

CHAPTER TWENTY-EIGHT

Ashley

Mom and I leave Dale and Dennis at the hotel to go shopping.

I had no idea when I left Colorado that I'd be getting married. I brought along a nice dress to wear to Mom's wedding, but now that it's my wedding as well, I want something special.

"I had no idea the two of you were so serious," Mom says as we peruse shops neither of us can afford.

"I've been serious since the first day I met him," I tell her. "I just didn't know *he* was."

"Love at first sight, huh? Miss I-don't-believe-in-love-at-first-sight? Miss I-love-sex-and-I-offer-no-excuses? Miss I-leave-condoms-on-the-floor-for-my-moth—"

"Okay, okay." I interrupt her with a gesture of my hand. "That all changed when I met Dale. It was love at first sight for me. Honestly, the way I feel now, I can't even remember a time in my life when I didn't love him."

"Ashley, of course you can."

"You know what I mean. Everything about him fills me. It's like I wasn't even *me* before I met him. Isn't that how you feel with Dennis?"

"I love Dennis very much," she says. "But you and I are different people, Ash."

"A woman in love is a woman in love."

"In some ways, but you... You feel things differently. Maybe it's because of your synesthesia." She laughs. "I still remember that day you told me the sound of the gunshot we heard was yellow. I was scared out of my wits, but you were jubilant because you'd never heard a yellow sound before."

I smile. I remember as well. It was the first time I told my mother I heard colors. I never felt the need to tell her before because I assumed she did too.

"I'm huddled with you in that damned tent, worried we won't make it through the night because someone's running through our area with a gun, and you're happy as a clam. You wanted to hear it again."

"The gun didn't fire again."

She shakes her head. "It didn't, thank God. That one was way too close for comfort."

"It was the first one that had a color. The others were always too faint."

"The others came from the gang bangers in the streets at night. I found a place for us that was far away from their territory. Still, we were always in danger, baby. I'll never forgive myself for putting you through that."

"It wasn't your fault."

"No, but..." She shakes her head. "I was your mother. I should have done better."

"You were only a kid yourself."

"Which is why I should have..." She sighs. "Enough! This is a happy day for both of us." She hands me a white satin dress. "For you. You should wear white."

I can't help a belt of laughter. "I've probably had more sex than you have."

She nods. "You're probably right. I was turned off it for a lot of years."

"I know."

She meets my gaze. "I hope it wasn't a mistake to tell you who your father really was."

I brush it off. "I try not to think about it. For the most part, I don't."

"Good." She turns back to the rack. "If you don't want white, how about this one?" She hands me a light-pink sundress.

I touch the silky fabric. "So soft." Then I see the price tag. Five hundred dollars. "Uh ... no."

"You're marrying a Steel."

"And I'm not going to ask him to buy me a wedding dress."

"Five hundred is nothing to him. He must have paid fifty grand for that rock on your hand."

"Mom ..."

"All right. You're right. We'll find something in your price range."

"What are you wearing?" I ask.

"It's an adorable ivory suit," she says. "I found it on clearance at Nordstrom."

"Sounds lovely."

"It is. I couldn't believe my luck." She sighs. "Unfortunately, I don't think we'll find any bargain bins in Las Vegas, unless you want to take a cab outside city limits."

I pull the pink dress off the rack once more. "I suppose I could at least try it on ..."

A salesperson approaches us then. "Can I help you ladies?"

"Yes, thank you. I'd like to try this on, please."

"Of course. Follow me."

Once inside the dressing room, I undress and put on the dress.

"Damn," I say out loud.

"Anything wrong?" the woman asks.

"No." I scoff softly. "It's perfect, actually."

"Wonderful! I have a lovely pair of pumps that will match the color if you're interested."

I bite my lower lip. Shoes. Hadn't thought of that. I brought black pumps to wear with the dress I brought for Mom's wedding, but they won't do.

What the heck?

Tomorrow I'll be a Steel.

Why not live in the moment? I have a credit card with enough of a limit.

"Sure," I say. "Bring them in. Size seven. I'd like to see how they look with the dress."

★ ★ ★

Twelve hundred dollars later, I'm ready to get married.

"I'll do your hair, of course," Mom says.

"Who's doing yours?" I ask.

"I have an appointment at the salon. Of course, I won't be satisfied with what they do, and I'll end up redoing it myself."

"Why pay for it, then?"

"Dennis insisted. It's his gift to me. A salt scrub, massage, mani-pedi, and hair and makeup." She looks at her watch. "In fact, we need to get back to the hotel. The appointment's in an hour. You should join me! I bet they have openings."

"Are you kidding? I nearly maxed out my credit card with the dress and shoes."

"Come on. It'll be fun."

"May I remind you that yours is already paid for?"

"My treat, then."

"Mom, Vegas spas aren't cheap."

She smiles. "You know what? I just don't care today. I want to treat my lovely daughter. Let's go."

"How long will it be?" I ask. "I think Dale wants to take us to dinner."

"I'm booked from one until five," she says.

"Okay, that should be good. When is the appointment at the chapel?"

"Dennis took care of all that. All I know is that the ceremony is at seven."

"We'll probably have to do dinner afterward, then," I say. "I'd better text Dale."

Mom wants to treat me to the spa this afternoon. You okay with that?

Sure. But what do I do with Dennis?

Poor Dale. He's such an introvert.

Tell him you have an appointment or something. You don't have to babysit him.

Okay. Love you.

Love you too.

"Dale's good," I tell Mom. "Let's get a quick bite and then head to the spa."

★ ★ ★

The spa has openings, and I'm suddenly booked for a half day of pampering along with my mother.

"I guess I'll end up redoing both of our hairdos," Mom laughs.

The receptionist nearly drops her jaw. "Are you not happy

with the stylists you're booked with, ma'am?"

I smile to defuse the situation. "You have to excuse my mother. She's a stylist herself. I'm sure whoever is doing our hair will be great."

The receptionist pastes a smile back on her face. "I know you'll both be thrilled. Looks like you're up for salt glows first. Fill out this paperwork, and then your concierges will take you to the locker room and show you the amenities you can avail yourself of while you wait for your therapists."

"Amenities we can avail ourselves of," Mom says, only slightly mocking. "How exciting!"

We take a seat, fill out our paperwork, and I take both our clipboards back to the receptionist. A few moments later, two women in white fetch us and take us to the locker room.

Our lockers are on opposite sides of the room, so Mom and I are separated. I change out of my clothes and into the robe offered. Then I decide to relax in the hot tub for fifteen minutes before my salt glow and massage. I take the glass of cucumber water my concierge poured for me, walk to the hot tub, remove my robe, and immerse myself in the water.

Mom is nowhere to be found, and oddly, I have the large tub to myself.

I close my eyes.

Tonight, I'm marrying the man of my dreams.

In a wedding chapel in Las Vegas.

My mom will be there, and that's all I could ever hope for.

But what about Dale? Will Talon and Jade be upset?

Donny, Diana, and Brianna?

I breathe in the warm steam. Dale doesn't seem concerned, so why should I be?

I'll simply enjoy this afternoon of pampering and revel in

the reality that Dale and I will soon be husband and wife.

I'll have all I could possibly want.

Seems too good to be true.

CHAPTER TWENTY-NINE

Dale

Turns out I don't have to worry about entertaining Dennis, after all. He's a poker player, so once he's settled in the low-stakes poker room, I have the afternoon to myself.

I didn't bring my tux, of course. The idea to marry Ashley came to me after I got here. I did bring a black suit and tie, though, for her mother's wedding. I'll wear that, with my hair pulled back the way my mother likes it.

Though Ashley seems to prefer it down.

Fuck. I hope I'm not making a huge mistake.

It's not like me to be so impulsive.

But I can't deny that the thought of marrying Ashley makes me feel…

Fuck it all. It makes me feel happy. Happier than I've ever felt, to be honest.

I should call Mom and Dad. Donny and the girls. I've thought about it since Ashley left to go shopping with her mom.

But something stops me.

I don't call them, and I know I won't.

If I do, the newness of the moment will be bastardized, somehow. The more I think about what I'm about to do—the more people I tell—the more I may realize how ridiculous the idea truly is.

For it *is* ridiculous.

I've known this woman for a month, and though I'll never doubt my love for her, I doubt my ability to be what she deserves.

"No," I say out loud. "Stop thinking about it."

I have to do something this afternoon before I meet Ashley and the others at the chapel for our double wedding.

I won't let Ashley down.

I'm not much of a gambler, so I decide to take in a matinee. *Drag Queens in Outer Space.*

Should be good for a laugh.

★ ★ ★

Ashley texted me the information for the chapel. She told me she couldn't see me until the wedding. Superstition or some such.

I stand with Dennis in the small foyer, talking to the officiant.

"Have you written your own vows?" he asks.

"Traditional vows for Willow and me," Dennis says.

I've given vows absolutely no thought. "Yeah, traditional is fine."

"Very good. Rings?"

"Got 'em." Dennis pats his pocket.

"Ashley has her engagement ring," I say.

"You need rings for the ceremony," Dennis says.

I know that. Why didn't I think about it? I could have gone back to Tiffany & Co. instead of watching a really bad show this afternoon.

"Not a problem," the officiant says. "We offer a lovely line of rings."

Of course they do.

I choose the most expensive set, though they're white gold, not platinum like Ashley's engagement ring. Big deal. I'll replace them as soon as I can.

"Do you know the lady's size?"

"I do, actually." I pull the receipt for the Tiffany ring out of my pocket. "Six."

"Great. And your size?"

"I have no idea. I've never worn a ring in my life."

"We'll just measure you." He pulls out a device and has me stick my finger through holes until one fits. "Eleven and a half. Excellent."

I crack out the credit card and pay for the rings.

The officiant checks his phone. "Looks like the ladies have arrived, which means you gentlemen need to go into the chapel so you don't see them until they walk down the aisle to you."

Dennis and I follow him into the chapel, which isn't nearly as gaudy as I expect. It's actually nice. Apparently Dennis and Willow opted for a traditional ceremony and not one of the chapel's Elvis-impersonating shindigs. Good.

Oddly, I'm not at all nervous. In fact, I feel eerily calm. I'm standing next to a man who's younger than I am and who's about to marry my fiancée's mother.

Twilight Zone city.

Organ music begins, but I'm not sure where it's coming from.

Traditional, of course. Wagner's "Bridal Chorus."

Here comes the bride, all dressed in white . . .

The words from my childhood. Not sure where I learned them. Dee and Bree, maybe, when they used to play dress-up while I was trying to study for my college boards.

I stand on one side of the officiant while Dennis stands on the other.

Then I turn.

Ashley and her mother, with linked arms, walk toward us.

Willow looks nice, but her daughter totally eclipses her.

I have no idea what she's wearing, what color. All I see is her in total—my angel, my mother's garnet necklace sparkling around her neck, her new ring sparkling on her finger, but nothing sparkling nearly as much as her beautiful blue eyes.

My angel.

My Ashley.

The ceremony passes in a daze.

I repeat the vows the officiant speaks.

And Ashley is my wife.

We're walking down the aisle together . . .

All in a haze.

My God. What have I done?

CHAPTER THIRTY

Ashley

It happened.

I'm Mrs. Dale Steel.

Dale and Ashley Steel.

As if I'm back in middle school, I imagine writing Mr. and Mrs. Dale Steel on the cover of my three-ring binder, complete with ornate calligraphy.

Mom and I talk all during the limo ride to the restaurant for our wedding dinner. Dennis chimes in now and then, but Dale is noticeably silent.

I make it a point not to second-guess him. If he wanted to get out of the wedding, he could have.

He didn't.

So clearly he wants this as much as I do.

I look down at the sparkler on my left hand. So beautiful, but honestly, the plain white band means more to me. It's that ring that Dale slipped on my finger as he wed me. After he promised to love me in sickness and health, for richer or poorer, till death do us part.

My hand rests comfortably in his warm and much larger one.

I squeeze his hand slightly.

He squeezes back.

Good sign. Definitely a good sign.

The limo pulls up at our restaurant, the Linen Room. The driver opens the door, and Dale helps me out. We walk in silence into the place.

"I hear the pastry chef here is excellent," Dennis offers.

"He can't be any better than you, sweetie," Mom says, looking up at him with stars in her eyes.

"I guess we'll all be the judge of that." Dennis laughs.

"Mr. Steel," the maître d' greets Dale. "It's a privilege to serve you tonight. Your table is ready."

He leads us to a lovely table in the back of the restaurant, secluded from the rest of the patrons.

And I remember . . .

I remember the first time Dale took me to a fine restaurant. We never made it past the appetizers . . .

We ended up in a hotel room, making furious love, and . . .

And . . .

He left me there with two hundred dollars.

I breathe in deeply.

That doesn't matter. It's the past. Tonight is the beginning of the future.

"Your server will be with you in a moment, Mr. Steel," the maître d' says. "In the meantime, is there anything I can do for you?"

"A bottle of your best Champagne, please," Dale says.

Cristal. That's what he ordered that night in Grand Junction. Dom Pérignon is probably what the sommelier will bring tonight. It's considered the best.

"Absolutely." The maître d' bows slightly and leaves.

The bow. I can't help a smile. The bowing thing bothers Dale. Will I bow when I'm a sommelier in a place such as this?

Probably.

It's what we're taught to do.

The bubbly arrives within minutes, and after Dale tastes it and pronounces it "fine," the sommelier, presumably, a young woman with short red hair, pours four flutes.

Dale raises his glass. "To my lovely wife," he says softly.

"And to mine," Dennis agrees.

We clink, and I take a sip.

It's crisp and tasty, as usual. A little citrus, a little wood, a little mineral. Perfect on the tongue.

"This is just the most wonderful wedding day I could have asked for," Mom says. "The man of my dreams, and the man of my little girl's dreams."

"Absolutely," I agree wholeheartedly.

Dinner passes in a blur.

I think I order salmon.

I think Dale and Dennis order the chocolate soufflé for four for dessert, and I think my mother says it's not as good as Dennis's.

I think we ride to the Cosmopolitan in the limo after dropping Mom and Dennis back at the Rio.

And I think Dale takes me to a suite. My stuff is already there. He had it all moved.

And I think...

I think...

Then I stop thinking.

I stop thinking because Dale is kissing me, undressing me, taking me to bed for the first time as his wife.

No more thinking.

Only feeling.

Feeling as he peels my new dress from my body.

Feeling as he trails his lips from my mouth to my cheek, my earlobe, my neck, my shoulder . . .

Feeling as he flicks his tongue over one hard nipple and then the other.

Feeling as he sucks the nipple between his lips, bites it lightly . . .

Then not so lightly . . .

Feeling as he lays me on the bed, spreads my legs, and dives between them.

One orgasm.

Then two. Three. Four.

Until finally he flips me over and slides his tongue between my ass cheeks.

And I know it's time.

Time for anal.

Slap!

His hand comes down on my ass.

He growls. "Fuck."

Has he done anal before? Doesn't matter. Already I know it will be the best ever.

"Okay?" he groans, probing my ass with the tip of his finger.

"Whatever you want . . ." I sigh.

"Fuck," he growls again.

Warmth coats my ass. Lube. Lube that he warmed in his hand. I'm still in a haze from my orgasms and from my marriage.

It's all so unreal.

Yet it's real. I'm here. Dale's here. And he's about to take my ass.

"Have you done this before?" I can't help asking.

"Does it matter?"

"No."

Then his warm cock is sliding between my cheeks, stopping at my entrance. I lift my hips in further invitation.

"Ah!" The pain is sharp as he slides in balls deep.

He begins to pull out—

"Wait! Let me get used to it."

Then he pulls out completely.

I look over my shoulder. "What's wrong?"

"Apparently I don't know what I'm doing."

"You're doing fine."

He yanks the band out of his hair, letting it flow over his shoulders. "I didn't even know how to hold your hand at first. What the hell made me think I could make love to you this way?"

I was right. He's never done it before. And I love him all the more.

I wish I could give him something that I've never done before.

"Hey," I say. "I trust you. This is the ultimate gift, and I want to give it to you tonight. Our wedding night."

He scoffs. "You've given it away before, haven't you?"

"Does it matter?"

"Hell, yes, it matters!" He rakes his fingers through his hair, making it a mass of gold around his perfect face.

"So I'm not a virgin," I say. "No surprise there."

"I am," he says. "At least when it comes to this."

I smile. "Not for long. Please, Dale. Let me do this for you."

"Fuck." He rakes his fingers through his mane once more. "Tell me what to do, then. I want it to be good for you."

"You were doing fine."

"You screamed."

"It's anal. It's painful at first."

"But you've done it before."

"It's not like breaking a hymen, Dale. The asshole is always tight." I smile. "Which means it's good for you every time."

"Get on your hands and knees," he snarls.

My nipples tighten, and my pussy throbs. That red-wine voice...

I'll obey that voice until the day I die.

Anything. He can tell me to do anything in that animalistic red-wine voice, and I'll do it.

My God...

"Tell me," he says. "Tell me how to make this good for you."

"Ease in," I say, "past the tight rim. Hold there for a minute, and then slide all the way in."

I let out a breath as he breaches me again. Damn, he's even harder this time. I breathe out again as he slides all the way in.

"Fuck," he growls for the third time. "I need you. I need this."

"Go ahead," I tell him. "Fuck me, Dale. Fuck my ass. Make me yours."

He pulls out and pushes back in, this time the pain lessening. I'm so full. So full of the man I love. And though I've done this before, my heart swells this time.

This isn't simply anal sex.

This is Dale and me and our wedding night.

This is my trust in this man, and his trust in me.

He gave way to me, let me take the lead because this is something I know about.

As hard as that must have been for Dale, he did it.

And we're closer for it.

I breathe out again, relishing in the intrusion. So good. Once the pain is gone, anal is so good.

With Dale, it's perfect.

He slides in and out of my ass, and with each new invasion, I feel renewed. I feel as though we're a part of each other as we never were before.

"Damn it, Ashley. Damn." He thrusts harder.

I push back against him, letting him go in as deeply as possible.

"Fuck. Need to come."

"God, please," I say. "Please come, Dale. Come for me. Come for *us*."

He plunges into me, and the force of his orgasm rumbles against my tightness.

When he finally pulls out, he sighs. "My God . . ."

"Pretty amazing," I say dreamily.

He moves toward the bathroom door. I hear water whoosh out of a faucet. A few minutes later, a warm cloth covers my ass.

He's taking care of me.

My wonderful husband is taking care of me.

He discards the cloth and pushes me over onto my back. Then he lies next to me.

"I want this to work," he says in a serious tone.

"It will," I reply, still reveling in the orgasms and then the anal.

I'm used up. Used up in the most wonderful way.

"I'm serious," Dale says.

"So am I. I love you."

"This will take more than love, Ash."

I ruminate on his words. I've told him before that love is enough. That love will conquer anything.

He's always disagreed.

Apparently he still does.

"What, then?" I ask. "What will it take? Because I'll make damned sure we both do it."

He sighs. "Honesty. Complete honesty between us."

"You know everything about me."

He scoffs softly. "Not everything. Not every single person you've—"

I cover his mouth with my fingers. "Does that matter? Does it have to matter?"

"No," he says after pausing a few seconds. "It doesn't matter."

I heave a sigh of relief. "Good. Because I can't change any of it, Dale, nor would I. My past made me who I am today."

"I can't change my past either, Ashley," he says.

"Right. And I wouldn't want you to, for the same rea—"

"That's the difference between us," he says. "I *would* change parts of my past if I could. And that's something we both have to live with."

CHAPTER THIRTY-ONE

Dale

I have to tell her.

Have to tell her how I came to be adopted into the Steel family.

Will she run away screaming?

It dawns on me, then, why I rushed into marriage after maintaining that I'd never go there. That I couldn't give Ashley more than two months.

I don't want to lose her.

I never want to be without her.

I'm being so selfish.

Sure, she loves me, but when she finds out about all my baggage, she's going to run away as fast as she can.

I won't blame her.

Hell, I'd run away from me too.

"What is it?" she asks.

My past lies dormant within me. I never talk about it. I rarely even think about it. Only in nightmares or daydreams.

Since Ashley arrived in my life, though, I find myself ruminating on the past more and more. Remembering.

Remembering, because if I don't, I'll get myself into something I can no longer control.

Marrying Ashley was a whim. Very unlike me.

Totally unlike me.

But damn, I love her so much.

I should have told her everything before I married her. Should have...

Should have...

"Ashley," I say softly. "There's so much you don't know about me."

She cups my cheek. "I know you're my husband, and I know I love you very much. That's enough."

I don't respond.

"I also know you love me."

"I do," I affirm.

"You can tell me anything. Nothing will change how I feel about you."

I say nothing.

"Dale," she says, "what is it?"

"My past... It's...complicated."

"Whose isn't? You know mine. I'm the child of a rapist. I was homeless when I was a kid."

"And you pulled yourself out of it," I say.

"With a lot of help from my mom."

"I..."

"It's okay," she says. "Whatever it is, it's okay."

"Screw it." I pull her on top of me.

My dick is hard again, and I want to be inside that tight little pussy.

"Dale, I—"

I lift her hips and bring her down onto my erection.

She shrieks.

A good shriek.

"Ride me, baby. Fuck me."

She lifts her hips until the head of my cock is caught between those slick folds. She teases me for a few seconds, rubbing her wetness over me, and then she sinks down.

"Fuck," I growl. "Never enough. Never enough with you."

She closes her eyes, one hand trailing over her left breast, the other descending toward her clit. "You can tell me anything, my love. Anything... God, feels so good."

She continues to fuck me. Up. Down. Up. Down.

Finally, I grip her hips, raising my own and pistoning into her.

Until I implode, each burst from my dick throbbing throughout my body.

"I love you, Ashley," I shout. "I fucking love you!"

"I love you too." She shatters around me, milking spurt after spurt out of me.

When she's done, she collapses against my chest, her soft cheek nuzzled into my neck.

We fall asleep that way.

And for the first time in a long time, I don't have a nightmare.

★ ★ ★

After meeting Willow and Dennis for a quick breakfast, Ashley and I drive home to Colorado, Willow and Dennis following in the RV. They'll stay at my place, since Mom and Dad don't know they're coming. Willow wanted to stay in the RV, but I insisted they stay in the guesthouse.

In seven hours, I'll enter Steel Acres as a married man.

Mom and Dad will be thrilled.

I think.

CHAPTER THIRTY-TWO

Ashley

"Of course we're thrilled!" Jade says. "We'd have liked to have been there, of course, but it's great timing. Everyone's still home from the family meeting. We'll have a reception for all of you tomorrow night."

"You don't have to go to all that trouble, Mrs. Steel," Mom says.

"Please, it's Jade. And you're family now. It's no trouble at all. Marj and I love to plan parties."

"Marj?" Mom asks.

"My sister-in-law. Dale's aunt. She and I are the party planners. I can't wait to tell her."

"Congratulations, son." Talon pulls Dale into a fatherly bear hug. Then he whispers something into his ear.

I'll ask him about that later.

"Dee and Bree are in town for dinner tonight," Jade says. "I'll text them to come home right away. I've got to tell everyone. This is so exciting!"

"Brace yourself," I say to Mom and Dennis. "This family is huge."

"The more the merrier." Mom smiles radiantly. So far, marriage shines on her. I'm so happy that she's happy.

Dennis is a nice guy, from what I've seen. He's nice and

funny and looks at Mom the way Dale looks at me.

Perfect.

"Are you hungry?" Jade asks. "We have plenty. Darla's already gone home, but I make a mean grilled cheese and tomato sandwich."

"We're fine, thank you," Mom says. "We stopped for dinner in Grand Junction."

"Wonderful. Then let me show you to your room."

"They're staying with us," Dale says.

"Nonsense. Our place is a lot bigger. The rooms are a lot bigger."

"Jade," I say, "we didn't give you any notice."

"It's no problem." She winks at me. "Though I understand."

Good. I don't want to put Mom and Dennis into the position of staying with someone they just met.

We say our goodbyes, take Penny, who stayed at the main house while Dale was gone, and drive to Dale's place.

Mom and Dennis get settled, and Dale and I unpack in the master suite.

Wow. I live here now. This is my bedroom.

Dale wanted to say something to me last night. Something about his past.

Don't push.

Jade's warning.

But I'm his wife now.

Still … Does that matter?

I won't push him.

I can't.

★ ★ ★

I work with Ryan and Dale in the winery the next day. The mechanical crushers are crushing the harvested Syrah for the old vine. Production is changed to accommodate half the allotted grapes due to the loss from the fire.

I can't help but think of the old traditional crushing done by barefooted crushers. I've always wondered what that feels like.

"Wouldn't that be fun?" I say to Dale and Ryan.

"It's a lot more work than you think it is," Dale says.

"How do you know? Have you ever done it?"

"Of course not."

"I rest my case."

"Your feet would be permanently dyed purple," Ryan adds.

"Wouldn't bother me," I say indignantly.

"Why are you two here, anyway?" Ryan asks. "Shouldn't you be honeymooning?"

"Ashley insisted," Dale says. "She's determined not to take any more time off from her internship."

"And I suppose you told her that since she's a Steel now, she's no longer bound—"

"Yes, yes, he told me all that," I say. "But I follow through on my commitments. It's a White trait."

"Good enough," Ryan says.

I can't wipe the ridiculous smile off my face. I'm married to the man of my dreams, and we're making wine. We're making wine! I know all about the process. Once the grapes are crushed and the juice is extracted, fermentation will begin. This is where the magic happens. If left alone, the wild yeasts in the air will start fermentation within about twelve hours, but winemakers often intervene by inoculating the must to introduce a strain that will better predict what kind of wine the juice produces. I'm excited to see Dale and Ryan at work here. What will they do? How will they manipulate the fermentation? I pepper them with questions.

"How long will you ferment?" I ask.

"Until all the sugar is converted to alcohol," Dale says. "I want the driest wine possible. It takes about a month, usually."

"Are you using ICV isolates?" I ask.

"Someone's done her homework." Ryan winks at me.

"I *am* almost a doctor of wine, after all," I taunt him. "D254, then?"

"I'm not that predictable," Dale says.

"You're really not using D254?" I ask. "That's the most popular strain to use with Syrah for that lushness in the mouth."

"It is," he agrees, "but I choose to make my wines a little less ordinary."

I can't help smiling at the burst of pride I feel for my husband. He's truly a genius at this. He knows things I can never learn in a classroom. He's in his element here, creating. For a moment, I almost think he's forgotten that this is only half of what he expected to harvest this season.

"I hope you're planning to leave early," Ryan interrupts. "I am, for the big party tonight."

Dale goes rigid.

I've seen this side of him before. Anytime there's a big party. It's not his thing.

Of course, I love parties. I shrug. Opposites attract, they always say.

The whirring of the crushers as they're extracting juice from the Syrah grapes mesmerizes me.

Tomorrow, I'll truly see Dale in action. I'll watch him choose the strains of yeast, and I'll learn the Steel secrets. For this is Dale's wine. Ryan already gave him control over the old-vine Syrah. After this season, Dale will have control over everything after Ryan retires.

I'll be mistress of Steel Vineyards.

Still seems unreal yet very real, if that makes any sense at all.

This is a wonderful day.

And tonight ... we celebrate.

CHAPTER THIRTY-THREE

Dale

They didn't feed us today.

Did they forget?

More likely they're trying some new kind of torture.

Donny and I have been in this room for a week now. At least I think it's a week. There are no windows, so I don't really know how much time has passed.

We've gotten three meals a day up until now. Usually bread and water, but sometimes some meat or eggs. No vegetables, which is fine with Donny. He hates everything green.

They've smacked us around a lot. Donny has a black eye, and I've got bruises everywhere.

That's all they've done.

But I know what's coming.

My little brother doesn't. He's only seven, and he doesn't know what awaits us.

I do.

I've heard about child molestation. Child rape.

Yeah, it can happen to boys too.

It won't happen to Donny, though. Not on my watch.

★ ★ ★

Willow and Dennis are getting along great with everyone in

my family, just like Ashley when she first showed up. Brock, of course, turns on the charm and flirts audaciously with the newly married Willow.

The man has no shame. She's old enough to be his very young mother.

I'm not sure Brock knows how *not* to flirt.

"Thanks a lot for inviting us to your wedding," Donny says sarcastically, flanked by Diana and Brianna.

I move my gaze from Brock to my three siblings. "It was spur of the moment."

"Apparently." Donny claps me on the back. "I'm happy for you, bro. Though I should have been there to give you away." He chuckles.

"You'd have been the best man," Bree laughs. "Dee and I could give him away."

"Hey," I say to Donny, "I wasn't thinking."

"I'd say you were thinking clearly for the first time in a long time," he says.

"I mean, about the best man. You should have been there."

"We'd have all loved to have been there," he says, "but Dale, none of us wanted you to end up alone."

"Ashley's great," Dee says. "I'm so happy for both of you."

"Thanks, sis."

"You love her, right?" Dee hedges.

"What the hell kind of question is that?"

"She's been through some stuff." Dee bites her lower lip.

And I haven't?

I don't say that, because Dee doesn't know.

Donny does, though, and his eyes take on a haunted look.

Every once in a while, he remembers. He thinks about it.

Not nearly as much as I do, though. I'd hate it if he did.

"I love her," I say with conviction.

It's true. No matter what else sits in my way, loving Ashley isn't part of it.

"I have to say," Donny says, "she isn't the type of woman I ever thought you'd go for."

"True!" Bree agrees. "I figured Dale would go for a strong and silent type."

"Then they'd never talk!" Donny laughs at his own joke.

My sisters and brother continue to talk as they always do, while I nod and add a word or two here and there.

Until—

Shit. A tall redhead catches my eye. Brendan Murphy is here.

And he's talking to Ashley.

For God's sake, Dale. She's your wife. There's nothing to worry about.

Still, I excuse myself and stalk toward them.

"Hey, there's my hubby!" Ashley grabs my arm, linking hers through it.

"Congratulations, Dale." Brendan holds out his hand.

"Thanks."

"Thank you for inviting me to the reception."

"I didn't."

"Well, somebody did." He winks at Ashley.

"You invited Brendan?"

"I didn't invite anyone. Your mother did, silly."

"Right."

"My mom and dad are on their way," he says. "Hey, is Ava here yet?"

"Her pink head is probably bobbing around here somewhere," I say. "She always brings the baked goods."

"Awesome. I'll do some mingling, then." Brendan smiles. "You lovebirds behave yourself."

Ashley squeezes my upper arm after Brendan takes off. "Hey, there's something I want to ask you."

"Yeah?"

"Your dad whispered something in your ear when he hugged you last night after we got home."

Don't let the past rule you. Be happy, son.

"He did. He told me to be happy." I deliberately leave out the part about my past. I have to tell her eventually, but our wedding reception certainly isn't the time or place.

"That's all I want," Ashley says. "For us both to be happy."

I trail my index finger over her soft cheek. "Me too. I love you, Ash."

"I love you too, babe." She smiles mischievously. "You ready to party?"

"You should know by now I'm no partier. But you have fun."

"We'll both have fun." She pulls me toward the crowd of people gathered outside in the yard and around the pool area.

"Ash..."

"They're all here for us. We have to make the rounds, Dale."

She's right, of course. I know the drill. God knows I've had to feign extroversion during wine tastings and business conferences. And my mom and Aunt Marj's big parties like this one.

Donny is talking to the middle Pike sister, a friend of Henry's. I'm ready to tell him she's too young for him, but then I realize she's older than Ashley is, so they're only six years apart at most. I robbed the cradle for sure.

But so did Dad. And Uncle Bryce really did.

What does it matter? We love each other.

But we know next to nothing about each other. What kind of parents will we make?

Looking at my huge-ass family, I can't help but think about children. Ashley and I haven't talked about a family. At all. She's young, so it's not something we have to decide tomorrow, but what if she wants kids?

I've never thought I'd be a good father. I'm too messed up inside.

But if Dad's been through something similar... He's a great dad. A really great dad.

I need to talk to him. Alone. And tonight, if possible.

For the next hour, though, Ashley and I make our rounds with the guests, letting them offer congratulations. We do a lot of introductions for Willow and Dennis. The two of them are so bright and talkative that they fit right in.

I spy Brendan with Ava, laughing. Will they become an item? Good thing Ava's pink hair is naturally brown, like her mother's. I'd hate to think of what Murphy's orange and Ava's pink would do to a kid.

The band—yes, Mom and Aunt Marj hired a local rock band, Dragonlock, to perform—is setting up, and somehow Dad and Uncle Ryan get their hands on the mic.

"Hey," Dad says. "Your attention, please."

Most look toward the makeshift stage, where he stands, though some continue to murmur among themselves.

"Thanks to all of you for coming tonight. It's been a rough week here on the western slope, not just for us but especially for our neighbors the Pikes. Frank, Maureen, we're here for you."

Applause.

"But tonight we're coming together to celebrate something wonderful. I'm thrilled to congratulate my oldest, Dale, on his marriage to Ashley White!"

Thunderous applause.

"And we're thrilled to have Ashley's mother, Willow, here tonight, and her brand-new husband, Dennis James. Please give them a Snow Creek welcome!"

And again, applause.

"I'll hand it over to Ryan, who'll propose the official toast with his sparkler. Everyone, be sure to get a glass."

Servers bring around trays of bubbly while Uncle Ry raises his glass.

"Dale is my protégé, as you all know. I'll be retiring at the end of this season, and he'll be the master winemaker here at Steel Vineyards. This season, we welcomed an intern. Ashley is not only an 'almost doctor' of wine, but she also did something we weren't sure anyone could ever do. She captured Dale's heart."

Applause. Fucking huge applause.

Does everyone think I was that incapable of a relationship? Apparently so.

"So raise your glasses to Dale and Ashley! And to Willow and Dennis! We wish you all the happiness in the world!"

Everyone sips in unison, and the murmuring begins again.

Dragonlock warms up.

"Tell me about this band," Ashley says.

"They're pretty good. The lead singer is Jesse Pike of the Pike winery. He's Donny's age and the brother of Callie Pike, who Donny's been hanging on all night. She's twenty-six, went to school with Henry."

"The Pikes, huh? They seem in pretty good spirits."

Ashley's right. The Pikes lost way more than we did, but they're moving forward, with our help. My father and his brothers are so generous. I need to remember that when they're gone. When I'm in charge of the winery, Bree's in charge of the orchard, and my cousins are in charge of the ranch.

"Tell me more about the Pikes," Ashley says.

"They're a big family, like we are," I say, "though their operation is a lot younger."

"Oh?"

"Yeah. Their vines have only been producing for about five years. They bought the old Shane property."

The Shane farm. Boy, I haven't thought about that name in forever.

Anna Shane was a former girlfriend of Uncle Ryan's. That's all I know about her.

"The Shane property?"

"Yeah. We bought it out from under the Shanes a long time ago but then sold it back to them. It's a complicated story that I don't know the details of. Anyway, Frank and Maureen Pike bought it about twenty years ago, when I was a teenager. They do a little beef farming, but they wanted to get into the wine business. It took some time, but they made their dream come true." I sigh. "And now it's gone."

Ashley smiles. "They can get it back."

I nod. "They can. I'm sure they're insured. Still . . ."

She squeezes my hand. "I know."

"Anyway, Jesse's their oldest. Then comes Aurora, called Rory. Then Caroline—Callie—who's Henry's age. And then the baby, Madeline, who goes by Maddie."

"Big family."

"Like I said, almost as big as ours. Frank's sister Lena lives on the property with her husband, Scott Ramsey. They have three grown children—Cage, Jordan, and Rachel."

"Wow. Is wine their biggest business?"

"They were hoping it would be eventually. Now they're back to square one."

"Nothing survived?"

I shake my head. "Nothing of consequence."

"Man." Ashley squeezes my hand again. "I wish there were something we could do."

"We're doing what we can. Henry and Brad have gotten the foundation involved, as you know. With grants and loans, they'll be able to purchase grapes."

"This late in the season?"

I shake my head. "No. But next year, and on and on until their vineyards are producing again."

"Totally sucks," she says.

I sigh.

She's right.

We got lucky as shit, even losing half my Syrah.

Ashley's good for me.

She makes me see beauty where before I saw only ugliness.

The problem is, I'll never be able to do the same for her.

I'll always be a thorn in her side.

CHAPTER THIRTY-FOUR

Ashley

Jesse Pike's band rocks!

He's good-looking, too, with long hair like Dale's, except it's dark instead of blond. Bree is especially mesmerized by him. Her gaze hasn't left him since the band began playing.

Looks like a schoolgirl crush.

Of course I can't get Dale to dance with me, until the band starts to play something slow.

Jesse comes to the mic. "Let's get both sets of newlyweds out here for a dance."

Oddly, I don't have to drag Dale to the floor. I guess he knows he's stuck. He pulls me into his arms and holds me close as we melt together to the music.

Mom and Dennis come to the floor as well, smiling adoringly at each other.

They do seem happy.

I'm happy for them.

But I'm happiest most of all for Dale and me.

This is my dream come true.

When the song is over, we leave the floor to more thunderous applause, and Jesse and his band get back to business. Hard rock with the occasional headbanger.

Good stuff.

Dale excuses himself. "I need to talk to my dad. You okay?"

"I'm fine. I'll catch up some more with Dee."

He kisses me quickly on the lips and heads into the main house.

"Hey, you!" I say to Dee. "Tell me. Is Bree totally in love with Jesse Pike?"

"Bree is totally in love with whoever is giving her attention at the current time." Dee laughs. "But Jesse Pike is a hottie."

"He is that," I agree. "Tell me more about the Pikes."

"Uh . . . you're married to my brother, Ash."

"I'm not interested in dating them. I just feel bad for what they've been through. Plus, I guess they're my neighbors now."

"They're good people," Dee says. "We all went to school together. Jesse and Donny played on the football team together."

"So they were friends?"

"More like rivals. Donny was a wide receiver, and Jesse was the quarterback. They were equally talented, and when Donny got MVP senior year, Jesse was sure it was because the Steels financed the team that year."

"Oh."

"There might be some truth to it," Dee goes on, "but our family never does anything for the glory."

"I know that. That's what Dale says, anyway."

"Dale's right. Our family takes care of the town. We're happy to do it."

"Dee," I say, "since I'm part of the family now, I guess I can ask. Just how rich *are* you?"

She laughs. "Don't you mean, 'just how rich are *we*?'"

My eyes pop into circles.

"My God. I don't think it hit me until right this minute. I honestly didn't marry your brother for his money."

"I know that. If I thought you had, we'd be arguing right now."

I pick my jaw off the floor, while Dee continues.

"The Steels are worth billions. Really only Uncle Joe and Uncle Bryce know at any time how much. Uncle Bryce is the chief financial officer, and Uncle Joe is the CEO. Dad and Uncle Ry stay out of the money end."

"Which means . . ."

"Which means there's so much money they never need to know any exact numbers."

My stomach churns. This is crazy. I'm rich. Rather, my husband is rich, but that means I'm rich too.

"I never imagined," I say.

"It's hard to wrap your head around. Ask my mom about it sometime. She had the same problem when she married Dad."

"So I'll never have to worry about money again."

"Nope."

"Surreal."

"I don't want to sound like a spoiled brat," Dee says, "but I've never worried about money once in my life. I'm sorry you've had to."

"I'm pretty sure I'm in the majority. Most people worry about money at one time or another. Right now, the Pikes are probably worried."

"We'll take care of the Pikes."

"I know that, but doesn't that bother them?"

"Why would it?"

Dee doesn't get it. She grew up around all this. The Pikes are probably feeling like a charity case at the moment. She won't understand, so I push it no further. Instead, "I want you to know that I really love Dale."

"I know that, silly. I've known that since I saw the first look pass between you two the first night we got home."

"Love at first sight, huh?" I say, smiling.

"I never thought it was possible. For Dale, I mean. Well, for you, either."

"I don't think it was for him," I say truthfully. "Though . . . We did kiss that first night when he drove me to see the vineyards."

"Ha! I knew it! That's really unlike Dale."

"It's the real thing, Dee," I say.

"I know that. No one's been able to drag Dale to the altar, and believe me, they've tried."

"Really? He told me he never had a real relationship."

"He didn't. He sure had a lot of women chase him over the years, though. You can count Callie Pike in that number."

My eyes pop open. "Callie Pike? The one who's been monopolizing Donny all night?"

"Yup. She had it bad for Dale for years. She used to come around all the time when we were younger."

"She's too young for Dale."

"She's a year older than you are, Ash."

My cheeks warm.

"Hey, I'm not giving you shit. My parents are ten years apart. It'll work."

"I'm not worried about that. But Callie . . . She's gorgeous."

"She's no prettier than you are."

She is, but I don't say this. It doesn't matter, anyway.

"If Dale were interested in Callie, he'd have done something about it way before now."

"Brendan told me people used to think Dale might be gay."

"It crossed my own mind a few times, but never for more than a minute. He dated every now and then, and sometimes he'd disappear for a week here and there. Women would call here, looking for him. He's just a loner. Until now."

"Oh, he's still very much a loner. It's who he is." I clear my throat. "Dee, how much do you know about Dale's and Donny's lives before they came to the ranch?"

"Not much. I don't ever think about it, honestly. They were here before I was born, and they're my brothers."

"I know that. But how did your parents come to adopt them?"

"Their mother passed away."

"I know that much."

"They needed a home, and—"

"Dee," I say, "your mom was only twenty-five, and she adopted a ten- and seven-year-old while she was pregnant. There has to be a reason."

"When you put it that way . . ." Dee wrinkles her forehead.

"I'm not trying to pry." I laugh. "Okay, I am. But I love your brother, and he never talks about his life before he came here."

"This is going to sound ridiculous, but none of us ever think about it. Like I said, he was here when I got here. He's always been my brother, and I love him."

"Yeah, I get it."

I do. Dee doesn't worry about Dale's life before he became a Steel, because to her, he's always been a Steel.

Perhaps I shouldn't concern myself with it either.

Except that Dale almost told me on our wedding night.

Almost . . .

And his birth father just turned up, only to die within

weeks of meeting his sons.

Something's up with all of that, and I wish I knew what it was.

Not because I'm curious—though I am—but because I want to help Dale through it.

He's hiding something.

Something that I fear may take him from me.

I can't let that happen. Ever.

CHAPTER THIRTY-FIVE

Dale

"Your mother will have a fit if we stay in here too long," Dad says to me, sitting behind the desk in his office.

"I know, but there's some stuff I need to know."

"About...?"

"I'm married now." I shake my head. "Sometimes I can't believe I did this."

"Honestly, Dale, neither can I, but I'm glad you did."

"I've known her for a month. Less than a month, even."

"You know when you know," he says. "That's how it was for your mother and me."

I nod. "I hope it wasn't a mistake."

"Why would you think that?"

"She doesn't know about me, Dad. So I need to ask you..."

"Yeah?"

"Did Mom know about your...past? When you got married."

He inhales swiftly, and for a moment, I'm not sure he's going to answer.

Until, "She did, actually."

My heart drops. Fuck. I should have told Ashley.

"How did you tell her?"

"You and I are two different people," he says. "Don't think

it won't work if she doesn't know."

"I don't want her to know," I say adamantly. "At the same time, I feel she has to know."

Dad chuckles. "I understand exactly."

"How did you tell Mom?"

"It wasn't pretty."

"Okay." I'm determined to find out. "*What* did you tell Mom?"

He sighs. "You're asking what I went through. Do you really want to go there?"

I look inside myself. Do I? "I never told you what I went through."

"You didn't. And I never asked."

"Because you already knew."

"I had a pretty good idea," he says. "There's one thing you suffered through that I didn't, though. My little brother got away."

"What?"

He nods. "Ryan was with me the day I got taken. He got away. For many years, I thought I saved him. That he got away because of me. I kicked the guy holding him. He let Ryan go, and I told him to run."

"I didn't have that chance. I'd have done anything to save Donny."

"I know you would have. I would have done anything to save Ryan."

"You did."

He pauses a moment, stroking his chin. "Actually, I didn't."

"But you just said—"

He gestures me to stop talking. "After we adopted you and Donny, your mother and I sat down with the rest of the family. Your mother was pregnant with Diana, Aunt Mel had just given birth to Brad, and Aunt Ruby announced she was expecting. We wanted a better life for our children. We didn't want any of you to suffer because of our past."

"You couldn't help your past."

He pauses again, seeming to think. Is he regretting taking a step down this path? I don't know.

"No, we couldn't, but we could make sure yours was easier."

"Mine? Did I hear you right?"

"I mean the plural you, Dale. All I could do for you and Donny was to give you love, a home, and the help I didn't get until much later."

I nod. "You told me. Your father didn't get you the help you needed."

"No, he did not."

"Why?"

"It's a long story, one your mother and I hoped to shield you from, but I see maybe it's time you knew. But first . . . about your brother."

"What about him?"

"Not about your brother so much as mine. I thought I'd saved him from my fate. Turned out, I had nothing to do with it."

"How would you know that?"

"I'm going to ask that you keep what I'm about to tell you between you and me. You can tell Ashley if you want to, only because I don't condone secrets between married people. But if you do so, she must keep it confidential between the two of you."

"Wait, wait, wait . . . You don't condone secrets between

married people. So you think I should tell Ashley..."

"I do, but in your own time. That's not what this is about."

I swallow. "You're freaking me out a little, Dad."

"I'm sure I am. Here goes." He inhales. "We didn't find out until we were adults that Ryan is only my half brother."

A brick hits me with a dull thud. Finally, I speak. "Uh... what?"

"He's a Steel, but my mother wasn't *his* mother. Your grandfather had an affair. Well, according to him it wasn't an affair so much as one time with an old flame."

"Why would he do that?"

Dad scoffs. "I gave up trying to figure my father out long ago. He always claimed everything he did was for my mother and the four of us kids."

I can't wrap my mind around what he's telling me. Uncle Ry? Only my half uncle? Of course, not really my uncle at all, if you want to get technical. No *real* Steel blood flows through my veins.

"Let me make this long story short for now, since we're in the middle of your wedding party. All that time, I thought I'd saved Ryan from being abducted and abused, but in reality, he was never in any danger. His birth mother arranged my abduction, and Ryan, who was *her* son, was never supposed to be harmed. He didn't get away because I saved him. He got away because of who he *was*."

"So this woman..." My brain hurts from trying to put all this together.

"The woman was insane," Dad says. "Certifiably insane and obsessed with my father. Apparently an evil genius, as well."

"Evil genius?"

"A very high IQ, and definitely evil."

Dad's words race around in circles in my head. What is he talking about? I open my mouth to speak, but I have no idea what to say.

"It's all related," he says. "I don't have time to get into the specifics, but I suppose it's time you knew ev—"

"Talon!" Mom rushes into the office.

"What is it, blue eyes? Are you all right?"

"I'm fine. Yes. But it's Ashley's new stepfather. He... I don't know. He just dropped his drink and—"

I stand and rush out the door. The big party has broken up, obviously. Ashley. Where is Ashley?

"She left," Brendan says, Ava next to him. "They took your mom's car and headed to Grand Junction. We figured it would take an ambulance too long to get here."

"They're... Wait... what?"

Brendan continues, but his voice is low and distorted, as if everything is in slow motion. "They're rushing Dennis to the hospital in Grand Junction. It's the closest. Dee went with them because she knows the shortcuts to get off Steel property."

"Stop, stop, stop!" I shake my head, trying to put two and two together in a seemingly impossible equation.

People are murmuring among themselves, a white-noise buzz that I can't decipher.

Brianna runs to me. "Dale, thank God. Where were you?"

"In the office with Dad. What's going on?"

"Dennis dropped his drink and started slurring his words. Aunt Mel says—"

Then Aunt Mel is there, beside Bree. "It looks like a stroke, Dale," she says. "But I could be wrong. He's so young."

Aunt Mel is a doctor. She's not wrong.

"I need to go. Which hospital did they go to? Never mind, I'll call Dee on the way."

"Call us," Aunt Mel says. "Please."

I nod, sprint to my house, and hop into my truck.

I dial Dee quickly.

CHAPTER THIRTY-SIX

Ashley

Diana's phone rings.

"Get that, will you?" she says to me.

I nod. "It's Dale. Hey," I say into the phone.

"Baby, are you all right? I'm right behind you. Ask Dee which hospital she's heading toward."

"Yeah. I mean, yeah. I'm fine. We're going to St. Mary's."

"How's Dennis?"

"He's . . . I don't know, Dale. I just don't know."

"Okay. I'll see you at the ER. Tell Dee to drive safely."

"Quickly but safely," I say.

"Right. I love you."

"I love you too." I set Dee's phone down on the console.

Mom is crying in the back seat. Dennis is awake but unresponsive, as if he wants to respond but can't. He's not paralyzed, so maybe Dale's aunt is wrong. Maybe it's not a stroke. But it's something, and whatever it is isn't good. He's clutching at his chest.

"He's coming," I tell Dee. "He was in the office talking to your dad."

She nods. "He's probably only ten minutes or so behind us. Dale knows these roads better than I do. He'll get there quickly."

Thank God. This is crazy. So crazy. The party was great. I was having fun. The band was awesome, and I was getting to know some of the members of my new family better.

Mom was glowing. So happy. She'd finally found her love. And then . . .

Dennis dropped his champagne flute.

"Hey, clumsy," Mom chided him, laughing.

I watched the whole thing from only five feet away.

She bent down and picked up the flute, handing it to him. He reached out, shaking, and took it.

"We'll just call you butterfingers." Mom laughed again.

Dennis didn't crack a smile, and though he tried to hold on to the flute, it fell to the ground once more.

"Dennis?" Mom said.

No smile. No response.

"Dennis, what's the matter?"

Then, "Oh my God. Someone help me!"

That's when I approached them, along with several others.

"Get Melanie!" someone shouted.

It's all a blur after that.

"Come back to me, baby," my mom croons to Dennis in the back seat. "Please."

I'm nauseated. Not just in my belly and my throat. My whole body is nauseated. Every nook and cranny feels sick, as if I'm being poisoned.

My mother's voice is puke brown as she tries to bring her new husband back to her.

Puke brown.

And I know what that means.

It means whatever news we're going to get at the hospital isn't going to be good.

This happened to me once before, back on the streets, when one of our tent neighbors died.

The people trying to help him all sounded pukey and brown. To this day, I don't know what took him. Could have been anything. Maybe pneumonia. Maybe cancer. I was just a kid, and we were homeless. No one knew how or why the man died. No one but us cared.

We finally make it to the ER. Dee hands off the keys to the valet, and I run inside to get a wheelchair. An orderly follows me out, and somehow we manage to get Dennis into the chair.

"What happened here?" someone asks when we get into the ER.

I open my mouth, but nothing comes out. My mom is equally immobilized.

Thank God for Dee. "We think he might be having a stroke. He can move, but he hasn't spoken since it happened about a half hour ago. Or a heart attack, maybe. His chest seems to be hurting."

"Why didn't you call the squad?"

"We live on a ranch. We figured we could get here quicker."

"Always better to call the squad," the person says.

"Then we'd have waited longer for them to get to us." Dee shakes her head. "Just take care of him. Please."

Dennis is rushed back, and Mom goes with him.

Finally, I let myself breathe.

Dennis will get the care he needs here. I just hope it's enough. My mom can't lose her husband two days after their wedding. She just can't.

Dee leads me to a chair in the waiting area. "Come on. Sit. All we can do now is wait."

"This was a celebration," I say, more to myself than to Dee.

"I know. I'm so sorry, Ash."

"My mom is happier than I've ever seen her. She deserves happiness. More than anyone else, she deserves happiness."

Dee smiles weakly but says nothing. What is there to say?

The atmosphere in the ER waiting room is dull gray.

Until Dale rushes in.

I stand abruptly and run to him, right into his arms, so hard I nearly knock my giant of a husband off his feet.

"Hey." He kisses the top of my head. "Tell me what's going on."

I can't speak. I'm numb. I simply crush my head to him and shake it. He edges me slowly over to where Dee is sitting.

"We don't know anything yet," Dee says.

"Stroke?" Dale asks.

"That's what Aunt Mel thinks, but they just went back a little while ago. We don't know anything."

A nurse comes out then. "Miss White?"

I finally remove my head from Dale's shoulder. "That's me, I guess." Or Mrs. Steel. Whatever. I've been Mrs. Steel for only two days.

"Your mother asked me to fill you in," she says. "Mr. James is showing signs of a stroke, but we need to do some testing to get a firm diagnosis. In the meantime, he's been given an injection of recombinant tissue plasminogen activator."

"English, please," Dale says.

"And you are . . . ?"

"Her husband."

"Of course. It's a treatment that dissolves the clot and increases blood flow to the brain. If it's administered within three hours of a stroke, it significantly improves the chances of recovery."

I let out a sigh of relief. "It's only been an hour or so. I think." Time has kind of suspended itself.

"You did the right thing by getting him here so quickly," she says. "Though it would have been better to call an emergency vehicle."

"We were in a rural area," I say, repeating what Dee said when we got here.

"Still, that's the best—"

"They got him here," Dale interrupts. "And in record time. Is now really the best time to lecture my wife when her stepfather is in serious condition?"

The nurse cocks her head and regards Dale. "You look familiar to me. Have we met?"

"I don't think so."

"I'm sure we ha— You're Dale Steel. From Steel Vineyards."

Dale nods.

"Oh, God. I'm so sorry. I didn't mean to be rude."

"Because I'm Dale Steel? You're rude to others?"

The nurse reddens. "I have to get back. Again, I'm sorry. You did the right thing." She scurries off.

"How did she know you?"

"I have no idea. From the news, maybe. The fire. Plus, I was just here when my birth father died."

"Right. Amazing, though," I say.

"What?"

"How she treated us differently once she found out who you were."

"Stupid, is more like it."

"I'll take what I can get. She's going to go back there and tell them who you are, and they'll push Dennis to the top of the list."

"He's a possible stroke case. If he's not already at the top of the list, there's something wrong with this hospital." Dale turns to Dee. "You can go ahead home. I've got the truck, and I'll stay with Ashley."

Dee nods. "Okay. Call if you need anything, and keep us posted, please."

"We will," Dale says. "I'll walk you out. Will you be okay for a few minutes?" he says to me.

I simply nod. After the nurse thing, I'm done talking for a while.

CHAPTER THIRTY-SEVEN

Dale

A little over a week ago, I was sitting in a different waiting room at this very hospital.

When my father had a heart attack.

A few days later, he summoned me back here to make a confession.

A confession that he'd sold my brother and me to his criminal uncle for five thousand dollars.

I've kept that confession locked inside me. No one knows. Not yet. I vowed never to tell my brother. Why fuck up his life? He's happy, and I don't want to destroy that.

I should talk to Aunt Mel.

I should, but already I know I won't.

Right now, Ashley needs me whole, and if I start bringing all my shit out, I'll be far from whole.

And it hits me.

Why I married Ashley so quickly and with so little thought.

She keeps me whole.

Oh, I love her. I love her more than I ever thought possible.

But I didn't marry her for the love I feel for her or the love she feels for me.

I married her for stability. For her to be my rock. I'd

already allowed my emotion to rise to the surface, and my love for her, so far, has tamped down the horror inside me.

I can't lose her.

So I married her.

She sits, now, leaning against me in silence, her eyes sunken and sad. She cried a little. Not a lot. More for her mother than for the man she just met.

I married her to be a rock for me. That was unfair of me, and I need to rectify it, but this isn't the time.

No, this is the time for me to step up.

I will be a rock for her at this moment.

And then...

After her new stepfather is, hopefully, out of danger, I have some thinking to do.

I haven't been fair to her.

I married her for the wrong reasons.

I can't depend on her to keep my emotions at bay. She's not a miracle worker. I will burst eventually, and I can't have her anywhere near me when that happens.

I'll never be truly free, and she deserves so much better.

Willow appears in front of us, seemingly out of nowhere.

How much time has passed? I'm not sure. Time has been in a warp field lately.

Her eyes are red and puffy, her face lined where tears have flowed. Ashley disentangles herself from me and stands to embrace her mother.

They hug for a while until Willow breaks it. "I have to get back to Dennis," she says. "I wanted to let you know they're admitting him. We got the MRI results. It's an ischemic stroke in one of the frontal lobes. He seems to understand, but he can't speak."

"Mom, I'm so sorry."

"He's so young..."

"I know. He'll recover. I know he will."

She nods. "The doctor seems to think he has a good chance of recovery. But we just don't know yet."

"I'm not leaving," Ashley says.

"Yes, you are," Willow tells her. "You're newly married, and you need to be with your husband. I'm fine here."

"We'll be glad to put you up at a nice hotel," I say.

"That's kind of you," Willow says, "but I'm not leaving Dennis's side."

"All right, but the offer stands. Just call us." I grab Ashley's hand. "Let's go home. You need a good night's sleep."

"I can't leave my mother."

"Dale's right, sweetie," Willow says. "Please. Go. I'll keep you both posted."

Ashley finally relents.

We drive home.

She's asleep before we get there.

* * *

Ashley's still asleep when Penny wakes me at eight a.m. My eyes pop open. Is it really this late? We didn't get home from the hospital until well after midnight, but I usually wake naturally by six.

I rise to take care of Penny, and then I start a pot of coffee, when my phone buzzes.

Hmm. Not a number I recognize.

"Dale Steel."

"Mr. Steel, good morning. This is Jason Ramsey from

Delta County Fire Protection."

I clear my throat. "Good morning. What can I do for you?"

"We've completed our investigation of the fire that destroyed part of your property, and you're the contact we have listed on file."

"Strange. It should be my father or uncle, since it's technically their property."

"Do you want me to call someone else?"

"No, I can relay the information."

"We've determined the cause of the fire."

"Lightning?" I ask.

"That's what we thought at first, but a few things weren't adding up, so the investigation went further. Looks like a hiker left a campfire burning."

My stomach drops. "A hiker?"

No need to freak. The fire had already started by the time I left my campsite after the second night. It wasn't me.

"Yes, sir. About a mile off Hopkins trail."

My stomach drops again. I was hiking Hopkins trail. And I moved off the trail to camp the first night.

The *first* night . . .

Yes, I built a fire.

Yes, I knew the fire danger, but I'm careful. Always careful.

I've been camping in these mountains for twenty years.

Always fucking careful.

"You there?" he says.

I gulp. "Yes. I'm here."

"Apparently a hiker or camper or someone left some embers. It was probably an accident, but there's no doubt. That's how the fire began."

"Do you have the exact location?" I ask robotically, not

FREED

sure if I actually want to know.

"I can give you GPS coordinates. Sure."

I say nothing.

"Mr. Steel? You want those coordinates?"

"Text them to me please." Again in robot tone.

"Will do."

"Are charges being filed?"

"I doubt it. I'm sure there were lots of campers in the area. How would we narrow it down? Besides, these things are usually accidental."

"Yes," I echo. "Accidental. No one wants to burn down a forest."

"Not usually, and there's nothing to be done now."

"Thank you for the information. I'll relay it to my family."

"Thank you. Have a good day, Mr. Steel. And we're all very sorry for the damage to your property."

I end the call, and within a minute, my phone dings with a text.

Cellular service is spotty in the mountains, especially off the established trails. Still, I keep as accurate a record as I can when I'm out alone. Just in case I have to tell someone where to find me. I may not have the exact coordinates of where I was the night before the fire began, but I'll find something close in my record.

I pull up the text from Ramsey.

It doesn't really matter what the coordinates say. I was in that area at that time, and during that time, I saw no one else. Not a one.

I was alone.

Which was what I wanted at the time.

I don't need to read the text to find out what I already know.

That fire . . . That fire that destroyed my Syrah vines.
It was started by a camper.
By *me*.

CHAPTER THIRTY-EIGHT

Ashley

I wake to the buzzing of my phone on the night table.

What time is it? It's light outside, but I have no idea. I grab the phone without looking to see who it is. "Hello?" I say frantically.

"Ashley."

My mother. Her voice is . . . colorless.

This is not a good sign.

"Mom," I say. "How's Dennis?"

"I can't believe it."

"What? What happened?" My heart beats ridiculously fast.

"He's . . . gone, Ash. He . . . didn't make it."

"Wait, wait, wait . . ." Her words make no sense. Again the words disassemble into colored letters above me. Then the color dissipates into a dull gray.

"It was a stroke, but they caught it early. They . . ."

"What?" I say into the phone.

"Something about his heart. The stroke. I don't know, exactly."

"Mom, my God. His heart? I don't understand."

"A heart attack. At his age. A stroke. At his age. He's in such good shape."

Her words are colorless still. Without expression. She's in shock. Numb.

"How?" I ask. "How did this happen?"

Already I know the question is moot. My mother is in shock. She won't be able to answer me.

"Mom, I'll be right there, okay? I just need to get some clothes on."

"Okay, Ashley. Thank you."

"Just stay at the hospital. You shouldn't be alone. I'll be right there." I stumble out of bed and trip over my evening bag from last night. I fall to the floor, banging my knee. "Ow!" Pain shoots through me, but I don't care. I pull on the first comfortable clothes I find. Jeans and a sweatshirt. Sneakers and socks.

"Dale!" I scream as I leave the bedroom. "Dale, where are you?"

No response. I hurry to the kitchen and let Penny in. I feed her a small portion of kibble, in case Dale didn't feed her earlier, and refresh her water.

"I've got to go, girl," I say, petting her head. "I hate leaving you alone so much, but I have to get to the hospital. Where's your daddy?"

I pet her again and head out quickly to the car I borrowed from the Steels. I plug the hospital address into my map app and go.

★ ★ ★

"We're running tests," the doctor tells me as I stand next to my mother in the hospital chapel. "But from what I can tell so far, Dennis's blood pressure was extremely high, and so was his cholesterol."

"He never said anything about that," Mom says absently.

"He most likely didn't know. There's no record in his insurance database of him having a physical in the last ten years, or seeing a doctor for any reason. Not unusual for a healthy man of thirty-three. Hypertension and high cholesterol are usually asymptomatic."

"Did that cause the stroke?" I ask.

"No one knows the exact cause of a stroke," the doctor says, "but Dennis's extreme hypertension was probably a factor."

"And the heart attack?" I ask.

"Same. He was high-risk except for his age. The stroke put pressure on the body and led to the heart attack. We tried to revive him, but we couldn't."

"Did you try the paddles?" I ask.

"Yes, ma'am, we tried everything."

My mother's pallor is gray. Everything in the hospital is gray. My insides are gray.

How I wish Dale were here.

I haven't called him or texted him. I just got in the car and headed straight to the hospital. I send a quick text.

"Mrs. James," the doctor says, "you'll need to fill out some paperwork."

"Can't that wait?" I ask.

"I'm afraid not. We need to know what you want us to do with the body, and—"

My mother sways, and I steady her.

"Is all this really necessary right now?" I ask again.

"I wish it weren't," the doctor says. "But we do have protocol."

"I'll take care of this, Mom," I say.

My mom falls into a chair. "Thank you, sweetheart."

"I'm afraid we need his next of kin," the doctor says, "and that's your mother, not you."

"Can I at least come with her?"

"Of course."

We follow the doctor back to a hospital room.

A body lies covered on the bed.

My mother grabs my arm.

"It's okay," I tell her.

But it isn't. It's not okay at all.

The body . . .

It's Dennis . . .

Young and robust Dennis.

Nausea claws at me.

Strong. Must be strong for Mom.

Where's Dale?

Why hasn't he called? Texted?

I need you, Dale. I need you.

I glance through a mountain of paperwork reduced to a tablet. Page after page. Click after click.

"Sign here, Mom."

Absently, she signs.

"What do you want to do? Bury? Cremate?"

"I . . . don't know. We never talked about this stuff. He's so young."

The fact that my mom used the present tense isn't lost on me. In her mind, he's not gone yet. She's still in shock and will be for some time.

"Cremation would be best," I say. "Is that okay, Mom?"

"Yes, yes. I suppose so."

"I'll make all the arrangements. Does Dennis have any family?"

"I don't know. A mother, I think."

"Have you met her?"

"Yes. A couple times. They aren't close."

My mother isn't making a lot of sense. I'm hesitant to cremate a body without her actual consent, but I'm not sure what to do.

"How long can the . . . body stay here?" I ask the doctor.

"As soon as someone from the morgue gets here, it'll be moved down there. Once you decide on which funeral home to go with, we'll contact them, and they'll come and take care of things. I'm here because I need to know whether you want to donate his organs."

"Mom?" I ask.

"I don't know."

"He was a young man. His organs could help many people."

My mom hiccups into a sob. "I don't know . . ."

"Please, Mom," I say. "Let him help people who need it."

"All right."

"Thank you, Mrs. James," the doctor says. "I'll send someone in with the paperwork."

"More paperwork?" Mom says.

"It'll be over soon." I rub her shoulders.

"Just when I found . . ." She trails off, her voice no longer colorless. It's gray now, as I imagine Dennis's body is underneath that white sheet.

"I'll leave you two alone to say your goodbyes," the doctor says.

Goodbye? I barely knew the man. I wish I had something to say to offer my mother some comfort, but try as I might, nothing comes to me.

"Would you like some time alone?" I ask my mom.

"I should do that," she says. "Yes, I should do that."

"All right. I'll be right outside in the hallway." The idea of leaving my mother alone with a dead body freaks me out more than a little, but I close the door behind me and stand in the sterile hallway. A nurse in green scrubs walks by. Then a doctor in a white coat.

Phones buzz at the station.

A patient walks by with a walker. Isn't this the stroke ward? Or the cardiac wing? Why does that patient need a walker?

Why am I thinking about—

My phone buzzes.

Dale! Finally!

"Hey," I say into the phone.

"I just got your text, baby," he says. "What's going on?"

I sigh. I couldn't tell him someone died in a text. I said only I was heading back to the hospital for an emergency.

"He's gone," I say.

A pause. Then, "What?"

I sigh again. "Dennis. He had a heart attack. Apparently he's had high blood pressure and high cholesterol for years and didn't know it."

"And that led to the stroke?"

I feel nothing. Words exit my mouth without thought or feeling. "And the heart attack. Yeah."

Another pause. Then, "I'm two years older than he was. I can't wrap my head around this."

"Join the club. I want to comfort my mother, but I don't even know him. Shit. I mean, I *didn't* even know him. Heck, she barely knew him."

"I'm on my way."

"I'm so sorry, Dale."

"For what?"

Indeed, for what? I'm not sure why I said that, except, "Our life together isn't starting out on the greatest foot."

Silence.

I guess that means he agrees with me. I was hoping he wouldn't.

His silence looms, almost like a premonition.

And I find myself frightened.

"Dale...?"

"Yeah?"

"There's nothing you can do here. We'll be coming home. I'd like... I'd like my mom to stay with us for a few days."

"Of course. Whatever you need. Whatever she needs."

"Thank you."

"What are the plans for . . . well, for a funeral or whatever?"

"I have no idea. Mom says they never talked about that stuff. Why would they, at their ages?"

"I can have one of our assistants take care of it."

An anvil seems to slide off my shoulders. "Could you? That would be amazing."

"Does she want cremation or burial?"

God, that question again. "I don't know. She agreed to cremation, but I'm not sure she knew what she was saying. She's donating his organs. They have to get to that quickly, and then he'll be in the morgue until we make the arrangements."

"Got it. You take care of your mom. I'll take care of the rest."

"Thank you so much. I love you."

"I love you too."

I end the call, but something niggles at the back of my neck.

I'm not sure what it is, until it dawns on me.

Dale's voice.

It was colorless.

CHAPTER THIRTY-NINE

Dale

I should go.

Go to the hospital. Be with my wife.

Get out of my own head for a damned minute.

But she's on her way home. With her mother.

And I'm a fucked-up mess, as usual.

How the hell do I live with the fact that I may have destroyed my vines?

Do I even tell Ryan? The rest of the family?

I married Ashley. I married her for the fucking wrong reason, and now... How do I end it?

How do I do what's right for the woman I love when she's going through her own crisis?

And her mother...

God, her mother...

A bride and a widow in less than a week.

How does shit like this happen?

I'm trapped in one of those movies where just when you think something can't get any worse, it does.

It so does.

I need to finish the conversation with my father that we started last night.

Started at the celebration of two marriages...

HELEN HARDT

One of which no longer exists.

He's probably in the orchards or at the office building. I text him quickly.

At the office. What do you need?

What *don't* I need? What a question, and I have no idea how to answer.

Finally, I type in a reply.

Never mind. I'll talk to you later.

I've been driving around since the phone call from the fire marshal this morning. Driving around and thinking, trying not to think, and then thinking some more.

About what to do about my fucked-up life.

I need to free Ashley, but that will have to wait now.

Wait until she and her mother have healed from this most recent development.

I chuckle out loud. Development? Did I really just think of a man's death in those terms?

God, I'm so fucked up.

I liked Dennis. He seemed like a good guy. Young, strong, robust. Just goes to show you that you never know what's going on inside a body.

We Steels are always on top of our health. Having a doctor in the family assures that. Physicals and lab work every year, no matter what. It's saved us on more than one occasion. Aunt Ruby had a small cancerous breast lump a couple of years ago. It was caught so early that she made a complete recovery with no chemo or mastectomy, just a lumpectomy and radiation.

Ava and Gina have already started getting yearly mammograms even though they're in their twenties. Uncle Bryce had a cancerous mole removed last year. Again, caught early with no ramifications. Dad and Uncle Joe are both on blood pressure meds.

We Steels take care of ourselves.

If only I could heal the mess in my head.

Aunt Mel did her best.

The problem? I wasn't completely honest with her. Hell, I'm not completely honest with myself most of the time.

I could be that way when I kept all my emotions at bay.

But now?

I *will* erupt. It's only a matter of when.

Staying married to Ashley can no longer help me. Not now.

I have to free her.

And in freeing her, I have to accept that I'll *never* be free.

★ ★ ★

A few hours later, Ashley and her mother arrive at my place.

After Willow is settled in one of the guest rooms, Ashley turns to me. "I want to work."

"What?"

"I'm an intern here. I want to work."

I get what she's doing. She's using work to avoid dealing with life. I'm an expert at that. I've often wondered if I'd be as successful as I am without my issues. They give me something to escape from.

"Ashley..."

"I'm not kidding, Dale."

"Your mother needs you here."

"But I—"

"Besides, it's after four. The workday is nearly over."

"I don't care. Just give me something—anything—to do. I need to think about something other than this."

"Okay," I relent. "We'll go to the office. I have to tell Uncle Ry what's going on, anyway. But are you sure you want to leave your mother here alone? She really does need you."

She opens her mouth and then closes it. "I don't know. I just... Fuck, Dale. I don't know."

"I know, baby."

And I do. Maybe not exactly what she's going through, but I get it.

Then, before I can think anything further, she grabs two fistfuls of my hair and pulls my face to hers, kissing me.

I don't even think about denying her. I can't. I'll always hunger for Ashley, and what she needs right now is an escape.

I'll be that escape. I'll give her all she needs because the day will come when I have to free her.

That day isn't today.

I lift her in my arms and carry her to the bedroom. Then I break the kiss. "Your mom..."

"She's a grown-up," is all Ashley says before ripping the two halves of my shirt apart. Buttons go flying, pinging against the walls. "Please. I need you."

She pushes me onto the bed and pulls my boots and socks off my feet. Then she kneels between my legs and unbuckles my belt.

Seconds later, my cock is free from its confinement, and her sweet, hot mouth is on me. She sucks me hard, and already my balls are tightening, scrunching.

She's still wearing her clothes, and all I can think of is her naked body on top of me, riding me into the sunset.

God, she gives good head. So good I almost feel like I'm buried in her sweet pussy.

"Fuck," I growl.

If she doesn't stop...

If I don't get inside her...

If...

I grab the back of her head, yanking her off my cock. "Get undressed," I say through clenched teeth. "Now."

Her clothes fly onto the floor, and then she's naked, her beautiful body gleaming, her nipples turgid, her breasts rosy.

My whole body throbs in time with my cock.

"Turn around," I say. "I want to see that ass."

She obeys, and I gawk at the beauty before me. The ass I was inside on our wedding night. Only days in the past, yet months seem to have come and gone since then.

That night.

That night when I felt so free.

The night I truly thought I could do this. Could be with her forever.

I see now that can never be, but she needs me. Needs me to escape. And I'll grant her wish.

If only things were different.

If only I could be what she deserves.

I spread her ass cheeks and slide my tongue over her puckered hole.

She shivers. "Feels good," she croons, almost musically.

I want to take my time with her. Love her. Soothe her. Give her the escape, the need to experience the basest thing in life.

But my cock is so fucking hard.

I turn her around quickly and pull her onto my lap. Right onto my hard cock.

"Fuck," I growl as she encases me.

Her pink nipples are hard and level with my lips. "Ride me," I command, and then I grab a nipple between my teeth.

She squeals at the bite I give her.

Which spurs me on further.

She rises and then sinks again onto my erection, and with each stroke of her velvet pussy, I come closer to climax.

I bite her nipple again while I grab the other and give it a good pinch.

She squeals once more and then moans.

And I understand.

She craves the pain. The sharp pain that morphs into pleasure.

It's a healing salve.

Sure, it's temporary, but it's no less real.

She continues fucking me, and I hold still on the bed, letting her control the pace and the depth.

And she does. She goes deep, sitting on me and holding herself there for a few seconds, relishing in the fullness, until she moves upward once more, teasing the head of my cock with her slick pussy lips.

Still, I work her nipples, giving one breast a slap while I suck and bite the other.

With my free hand, I touch her clit, work her juices around it.

She'll come soon, and when she does, I'm going to shoot my load into her with the force of a hurricane.

A tropical hurricane.

But just as I'm about to erupt inside her, she pulls off me and stands.

"Baby?" I say.

"I need you."

"I need you too. Get back on and—"

"No." She shakes her head vehemently. "I mean, I need to

feel, Dale. Make me *feel*."

I thought that was what I was doing. I widen my eyes in question.

She lies down on the bed, face down. "Please. I need to feel something other than pleasure. I need the pain."

I bit her nipples. Was that not enough? I've spanked her before. Perhaps that's what she needs. The idea always turns me on—that gorgeous ass, pink from my hand.

I bring my palm down on her. *Slap!*

"More," she says into the pillow. "Please. *More.*"

I spank her again. Again. Three, four, five times.

"More," she says, her voice muffled against the fluff of the pillow. "Please, Dale. *More.*"

I spank her sweet bottom again, again, again . . . until my palm is stinging.

And still, her voice . . .

"More, Dale. Please. More."

I slap her again.

Again.

Again.

Again.

She finally cries out, her sweet voice still muffled.

I stop.

Let her rest.

Smooth my fingers over the bright-pink globes of her ass.

A moment passes. Then—

"*More.*"

My cock is hot and throbbing, my palm nearly numb from spanking her.

I can't. As much as I love spanking her beautiful ass, I can't inflict any more pain on her.

Not now.

Not when I'm going to inflict emotional pain within days.

"Ashley..."

"More, Dale. *Please.*"

Instead, I slide my body over hers, my cock nudging between her legs. I lie there, bracing myself so I don't give her the full weight of my body. I simply cover her body with mine.

"Enough, Ashley," I say softly. "Enough."

"No," she cries into the pillow. "Not enough. *Never* enough."

Never enough.

She's punishing herself for something. But what has she done? Not a bit of this is her fault.

"Baby," I say, "stop. Just stop."

Then the tears come. The racking sobs that I've never seen except from my little brother. After...

I've never cried that way myself. Never allowed it.

But now, as I see the woman I love sobbing, I feel more than I've ever felt. More even than when my brother sobbed in my arms after a brutal rape and beating.

Even more than...

God, no. No. Not yet. Can't go there. Not while Ashley needs me whole.

Whole? What a fucking laugh.

I'll never be whole.

But for now... This moment...

"I can't hit you anymore, baby," I say. "I'll hurt you."

"I need it."

"You're already red as a beet. I can't."

"Please. I want to feel, Dale. *Please.*"

"I'll make you feel, then." I flip her over, and though my

FREED

instinct is to shove my hard dick inside her, I spread her legs and bend my head between them.

She's wet. So wet. The spanking she wanted for pain gave her pleasure as well. But as much as I love spanking her, I know when enough is enough.

Better than anyone, *I know*.

For I was forced to endure much more than enough, and I'll never hurt Ashley. Not Ashley or anyone.

I won't give her any more pain, but I'll give her so much pleasure that it will become pain.

Climax after climax after climax, until she's begging me to stop.

I begin with ferocious strokes of my tongue around her clit while I slide two fingers easily into her wetness.

She's usually coming within a minute of this treatment, but she lies there as if her body is in some kind of dormant state.

"Baby...?"

"Can't," she says. "Don't want to feel good."

"But you said—"

"No. I said I want to *feel*. Not to feel *good*."

But the spanking clearly made her feel good. Her wetness proves that.

What does she want?

What does she desire?

"I won't hurt you anymore," I say with conviction. "I can't."

"I need it."

"You don't. I love you, and you've had enough."

Her eyes narrow. "Who are *you* to say I've had enough?"

I don't have to think how to answer. My reply is automatic.

"I'm your husband." At least for the time being.

She opens her eyes then, sniffling. Her gorgeous face is streaked with the tears she's shed.

"I'm sorry, Dale."

"For what?"

"For asking you to hurt me. It's not fair."

"Pain for pleasure is one thing," I say. "Pain for pain is another, and I won't do that to you."

"I know. I'm sorry."

"No need to be sorry. Now lie back. I'm not done with you."

CHAPTER FORTY

Ashley

He eats me ferociously.

And though it's difficult, I break down the barrier in my head and let myself feel good.

One climax morphs into two, into three, into four...

Pleasure. Pure pleasure, and I let go.

I grab Dale's head, pull on his long hair, push him closer to my pussy, to my core, and I come again.

After several more orgasms, I let go of his hair. "Enough," I say. "Can't take any more."

"One more," he growls between my legs. "Give me one more."

"Can't."

"You can." He slides his tongue over my clit and massages my G-spot with his fingers.

And I erupt once more.

This one is the culmination of all the others. It's explosive. It's transformational. It's full of love.

While I'm still in the dreamy haze of the high, Dale crawls over me and thrusts into me.

He fucks me hard and fast, and when he releases, I close my eyes and feel every spurt of his cock inside me, so sensitive is my pussy.

When he rolls over, I close my eyes.

I close my eyes and allow myself not to think.

★ ★ ★

Darla brings food over for our dinner, promising to take care of meals while we take care of the funeral arrangements for Dennis. Dale, of course, has offered to pay for everything, which my mother balks at, but then she relents after I tell her it's one less thing for her to worry about right now.

Three days pass in a haze, and then my mother and I drive back to LA in Dennis's RV. An urn containing Dennis's remains sits in the back. My mother hasn't planned any memorial service yet, but she insisted on going back to LA. That's where her friends are, where Dennis's friends are, and I understand.

Dale stays in Colorado to keep an eye on the old-vine Syrah, which is fermenting. Though I wish he were with me, I understand, and so does Mom. Once a memorial is planned, he'll fly out.

"I don't know what to do next," Mom says, once we're at her small apartment in LA.

"Take a breath," I tell her. "Then you and I will set up a memorial."

"Dennis's mother," she says. "She wants to make the arrangements."

"Let her, if you want to."

"I'm thinking about it."

"Mom, it's okay. You were married for less than three days. Let his mom take care of it. Whatever she wants. We'll pay for it."

"I shouldn't let you."

"You already told Dale yes. It can be as simple or as elaborate as you or she wants. Money doesn't matter."

She shakes her head. "Those aren't words I know."

"For this, they are. Let it be. For once, you don't have to consider money."

"I've spent my entire life watching every nickel and dime. This seems..."

"Seems what? Dennis was a pastry chef. Between you and him, you weren't going to have to..."

Shit. Why did I say that?

Mom still hasn't cried. I'm getting worried about her.

"Yes, he had plenty of money," she says, "and I've managed to put a few dollars away over the years."

I nod. I'm not sure what to say.

"We had so little time," she says wistfully.

"I know. It's not fair."

"No. But at least you can be happy, Ashley. That's all I've ever wanted."

"Mom, you deserve to be happy too."

"I used to think so. Especially after I met Dennis. Seems the universe has other plans, though."

"You can't think that way. You're a young woman. You can still—"

"No," she says flatly. "I'm done. I had a shitty childhood, and then of course the way you came into the world..." She widens her eyes. "But I never blamed you for that, Ashley. Never. Not once."

"I know you didn't, Mom."

God, my mother deserves so much more than she's gotten so far out of this life.

"You can move to Colorado," I say off the cuff. "Snow

Creek has an adorable little salon. Or you could start your own."

"This is my home," she says. "I have an established clientele. I don't want to start over, Ashley."

"You can live with us until you get set up. You don't have to worry about money, Mom. Not ever. Not anymore."

"I'm not living off my rich daughter."

"You wouldn't be. We'd just be helping out until—"

"No," she says adamantly. "Absolutely not. This is my home."

"All right." I relent. "What can I do for you?"

"Call a friend," she says. "You've been gone almost a month. Go have some fun."

"I'm not leaving you alone."

"Sweetie, I want to be alone. It's okay. I need to deal with this in my own way in my own home. Please."

I nod. I get it. It'll be nice to see some friends anyway. I scoff slightly. I've really fucked up the whole internship thing. After my commitment, too. I know they never really needed me, and Dale said I could take as much time as I need in LA with my mom. I'm supposed to call him as soon as the arrangements are made. He'll fly out to attend the service.

I told him he didn't have to, but he insisted.

My wonderful Dale.

I quickly text my friend Mariah, and she responds.

You're back? Want to hit the beach?

Beach sounds heavenly.

The beach in early October. I truly have missed LA. It's a balmy eighty in the forecast. No rubbing my arms during what Dale calls an "Indian summer."

I sigh. Colorado is my home now. Not LA.

Still, I can enjoy some time on the sand.

I'll see who else can meet us there. How about in two hours?

I text a thumbs-up to my friend, and then I unpack my bikini.

★ ★ ★

Our favorite beach is privately run, with a bar and everything. Mariah's uncle is a member of the club, and he lets her and her friends use his membership.

Funny. I used to think Mariah's uncle was rich. He's a B-movie producer, worth a couple million.

As a Steel, I'm worth a couple billion. Well, not me personally, but the company.

Unreal.

"Ash, what the hell is that?" Mariah's eyes turn into circles.

My engagement ring and wedding band.

Funny that I haven't told any of my friends in LA that Dale and I tied the knot.

"Oh. I'm married." My voice sounds more nonchalant than I mean it to.

"To who, the Prince of Wales?" She grabs my hand and stares down at the rock.

"To Dale Steel."

"Of *the* Steels?"

I nod, my cheeks warming even in the LA heat.

"My God, when did this happen? And why didn't you tell us?"

"Life has been…" I shake my head. "Honestly, it all happened so fast. I've only known him a few weeks. We did it on the spur of the moment in Vegas with my mom and her…

HELEN HARDT

And then ... Oh, God ...”

“What is it, Ash?”

The whole story pours out of me in clipped sentences. Dale. Me. Mom. Dennis.

“You poor thing!” my friend Lauren gushes.

“Except she's married to a master winemaker who's richer than God,” my friend Catherine adds.

“Still ...” This from Mary Beth.

“Let's get you a drink.” Mariah leads me to the bar.

It's only noon, but I don't balk. A drink may take the edge off.

I breathe in. The last time I was here at the beach club, I ended up fucking one of the bartenders.

“What can I get— Hey, baby!”

Fuck. Of course. *This* bartender.

“Hey, Regan,” I say.

Regan's still as sexy as ever. Blond, blue-eyed, tanned with a surfer bod. Of course, he *is* a surfing champ.

“Haven't seen you around in a while, Ashley,” he says.

“I've been doing an internship in Colorado.”

“Oh? For your wine thing?”

Wine thing? Did I actually tell him a little about myself? “Yeah, my wine thing.”

“Good to have you back. I get off at three.” He lifts his eyebrows and smiles slyly.

I flick my left hand at him. “Can't.”

“Is that what I think it is?”

“Yup. I'm an old married lady now. No more fun in the sun.”

“Bummer. What can I get you, then?”

“Sex on the beach.”

He smiles. "My pleasure."

"The *drink*, Regan."

"Of course. I don't mess with married women." He smiles again. "Not usually anyway. I could make an exception for a tigress like you."

"The drink," I repeat.

"Make that two," Mariah pipes in.

"Sex on the beach?" He lifts his eyebrows again.

"Absolutely." Mariah smiles flirtatiously.

Yeah, I know what she'll be doing after three.

I take my drink from Regan, head to our cabana, and grab my towel.

Sun, here I come.

CHAPTER FORTY-ONE

Dale

"I'm flying out in the morning," I tell Mom and Dad over breakfast the next day, while Darla bustles around the kitchen. "The service is tomorrow afternoon."

"Is there anything we can do?" Dad asks. "Should we go?"

"No, you hardly knew him. Ashley doesn't expect any of you to be there."

"Still, she's your wife," Mom says.

"She is, and if the service were here, I'm sure she'd appreciate the effort, but she and I talked. No one expects any of my family there, especially since we're still dealing with the aftermath of the fire."

God, the fire. I'm still harboring that secret.

Strong. Stay strong for Ashley. Get her through this thing with her mom, and then you can fall apart. Not before.

"When will you be home?" Mom asks.

"I fly back the next day. I have to keep watch over the Syrah. It's a very crucial time."

"What about Ashley?" Dad asks.

"I guess I assumed she'd fly back with me. I got her a ticket."

"She may want to spend some additional time with her mother."

I didn't think of that. "Then we'll change the ticket. No big deal."

"Sounds like a plan." Dad stands. "I've got to get to the orchard. Love you." He kisses Mom's lips.

"Love you too."

Cute. My parents almost never leave a room without professing their love for each other.

Is it just habit? Or do they really feel it after all these years?

"I need to ask your opinion on something," Mom says.

"Sure. What's up?"

She sighs. "Mary gave her notice yesterday."

Mary is the Snow Creek assistant city attorney. "Oh? She's been with you for … Forever, I guess."

"Yeah. So I'm going to need a new assistant city attorney."

"Sorry, I don't have a license to practice law." I force a smile.

She smiles back. "I'm talking about your brother. Do you think he'd be interested in the job?"

"Donny? Mom, he's on a partnership track at a major Denver firm. I don't think he'll give that up."

"Even for his mother?"

"Mom…"

"I want someone I can trust. Mary is brilliant, and so is Donny."

"Do you really need the best legal mind for Snow Creek?"

Mom huffs. "I do, Dale. Being the city attorney for a small town may seem boring to you, but I take it seriously. I don't settle for second best."

"Hey, no sweat," I say. "I didn't mean anything by it."

"Yeah, you did."

Fuck. This is a classic conversation with Mom. She takes everything I say the wrong way. I want to give her what she wants—closeness to me—but we don't relate. We never have.

She and Donny, though—that's different. They're über close. Which is maybe why this isn't the best idea.

"Are you sure working together would be good for both of you?"

"Why wouldn't it?"

Oh, maybe because you're too close. Maybe he wouldn't like taking orders from his mother. Maybe he's thirty-two years old and is done doing what his mommy wants.

"I don't know. Just a thought."

I can't say any of this to her. No matter how diplomatic I am—which isn't my strong suit anyway—she'll take it all the wrong way.

"Do you think he'd be good at it?"

"Donny'd be good at any job. He's kicked ass everywhere he's worked since he started clerking during law school."

She nods. "Which is why I want him. He's the best."

Which means he can do a lot better than assistant city attorney in a Podunk town.

"It'd be a huge pay cut for him," I say.

"Since when does your brother—or any of you—need to worry about money?"

I don't reply.

"Plus, I won't work forever," she continues. "I'm fifty-one years old, and I'll retire in five or ten years. Fifteen, at most, and then the job will be his."

I can't see my mother retiring until she leaves this earth, but I keep that to myself.

"Yeah. Sure, Mom."

"So it's a good idea. Right?"

Hell, no, it's a shitty idea. "Sure, Mom. Good idea."

"I'll call him from the office and offer him the position. No interview necessary. That'll be a first." She kisses the top of my head. "Love you, honey. Have a good day." She whisks out of the kitchen through the garage.

Should I warn my brother her call is coming? Yeah, I should. I make a quick call, but it goes to his voicemail. He must be in a meeting. "Hey. Fair warning. Mom's going to call you in a half hour and ask you to take the assistant city attorney job in Snow Creek. Mary's leaving. I figured this might give you a chance to come up with a valid excuse. I'll talk to you when I'm back from LA. Ciao."

Good enough.

Now to the winery. To my Syrah.

While I try not to think about why we have only half the amount is because of me.

CHAPTER FORTY-TWO

Ashley

Dale insisted on taking a cab from the airport. I was more than happy to pick him up, but he didn't want me braving the LA traffic. My husband is quite the gentleman.

I melt into his arms when he arrives at Mom's place.

"Hey." He kisses the top of my head. "How's she doing?"

"She's grieving, finally," I tell him.

Mom finally traded in her numb exterior for uncontrollable sobbing. She's out now. One of her salon friends is giving her a facial and massage gratis. I hope it calms her down.

I doubt it, though.

"I booked us at the Beverly Hills Hotel," Dale says. "You need some pampering tonight."

"It sounds lovely, but I shouldn't leave her alone. Not right after the funeral."

"Which is why I booked her a small suite as well. She needs some TLC."

"You're wonderful," I say, "but she'd probably rather be here."

"No problem. She has a choice. It's there if she wants it. And if you want to stay here, of course I understand."

"Trust me. I want to be with you. I want to go home with you tomorrow."

He nods. "You're already on my flight, but it can be changed if she needs you."

I nod against his chest, relishing in his warmth. His strength. "You're the best."

He kisses the top of my head again.

Then I lead him to the couch where I've been sleeping. "My mom will be gone for another hour," I say temptingly.

"Say no more." He bends me over the couch and slaps my ass right through my shorts.

Already I'm hot for him. Hot and ready and so needy.

I hate being this needy, but my mother has zapped me of all my energy. I need a fresh infusion of Dale.

Within seconds, he's stripped me of my shorts and panties, and then he's inside me, as I lean over the couch, letting the friction of the upholstery jolt my clit with spark after spark after spark.

"Yes!" I cry out. "Fuck, yes!"

He thrusts harder and harder, and I revel in being taken, being fucked.

His hand comes down on my ass cheek when he pulls out, and the tingle shoots through me as he slices through my barrier once more.

The pain. The pleasure. The ultimate escape.

I jerk into a climax, and I rise, rise, rise . . . out of this place and out of this grief.

So good, so very—

The front door opens.

A gasp.

From my mother or me, I'm not sure.

"Christ!" Dale pulls out, turns, and then *oofs* as he zips himself up. Luckily our backs were to the door, though Mom probably got a good peek at Dale's very fine ass.

I grab the afghan from the back of the couch and wrap it around my waist.

"God, I'm so sorry," Mom says.

"You were supposed to be gone another hour," I say, trying not to sound angry.

"I just... I couldn't get into the massage, so we stopped after the facial. I guess I should have called."

"Don't be silly," Dale says, his cheeks red. "This is your home. We should have been more... discreet."

Being any more discreet would have put us in Mom's bedroom, and just no. I can't have sex in my mother's bed. Sure, I've had sex in public places, but I have to draw the line somewhere.

"Please don't make a joke about a candy wrapper," I say.

I expect my mother to chuckle. It's been our joke since that fateful day when she saw the used condom on my bedroom floor at our old place.

She doesn't, though. I haven't heard her laugh since Dennis died. Understandable.

Dale lifts his eyebrows, his cheeks still red.

"Private joke," is all I say, wishing for all the world that a hole will open up and swallow me.

"We should get some lunch," Dale says. "What's this In-N-Out Burger I've heard so much about?"

"You'll hate it," I say.

"Why do you say that?"

"Because I doubt they source their beef from Steel Acres."

He smiles. Sort of. He's really embarrassed. "I'm not a beef snob."

I swat his arm lightly. "Are too."

"Okay. I admit it. A beef snob."

"And a wine snob," I add.

"That goes without saying. Willow, care to join us?"

"Yeah, Mom. You should." She hasn't eaten more than a crust of bread since we got home.

"No, thank you. I'm not hungry."

I bite my lower lip and plead at Dale with my eyes.

He lifts his eyebrows.

I plead with my eyes again.

Finally, he says, "We both really want you to come."

She sighs. "I just can't. I need to rest before the service."

"We'll bring you a burger." Maybe that'll get her to eat. She loves In-N-Out Burger.

"Sure, whatever," she says before heading to her bedroom.

"I'm worried about her," I say to Dale.

"She'll be okay. She just needs time."

"I know. I should stay here for a while."

"I understand."

"But I don't want to, Dale. I want to come home. With you."

He goes rigid for a moment.

"What's wrong?" I ask.

"Nothing. If you need to stay, then stay. I understand. Family first."

"But you're my family too."

Again, the tension flows off him in waves.

What's going on?

I can't give it thought right now. I must get through this service for my mother's sake.

I'll worry about Dale later.

An ominous feeling drapes over me.

★ ★ ★

After a service for a man I hardly knew and an awkward meeting of his mother and various other relatives, Dale and I head to dinner at the restaurant where Dennis worked as the pastry chef. Mom finally relents and joins us. Dennis's family all had a gathering and didn't invite either of us. Bitchy of them, but Mom doesn't seem to care.

"Mr. Steel," the maître d' says, "we're honored to have you here."

"My wife was Dennis's daughter-in-law. We're so sorry for the loss."

"Thank you. He was a wonderful chef. Follow me, please."

After we're situated at our table and Dale has ordered a bottle of wine, I turn to Mom.

"You held up great today."

She sighs. "I did my share of weeping."

"That's normal, Mom. He was your husband."

"For less than a week."

"That doesn't mean you loved him any less. I swear, his family is a piece of work, huh?"

Mom nods. "They are, but I honestly don't care one way or the other."

"Did Dennis leave a will?"

She shakes her head.

"Then you're his next of kin."

"I suppose so."

"Did you already consolidate your accounts?"

"No, not yet. We were going to take care of all that once we got back to LA."

God, what a mess.

"I can have an estate attorney get in touch with you," Dale says. "To help you sort it all out."

Mom smiles. Sort of. "That would be kind of you, Dale. Thank you."

"Our counsel will know someone in LA. I'll take care of it first thing in the morning."

Mom nods. "I hope his mother doesn't try anything."

"She can't," Dale says. "If Dennis died intestate, you're his next of kin. It all goes to you."

"I don't even want it."

"You're entitled to it," I say.

"He didn't have a lot. His salary was good, but you know as well as I do, Ashley, that living here is expensive."

"Did he own a home?" I ask.

She nods. "We were going to put it on the market. He wasn't sure he'd have a job after the buyout of this place was complete, so we figured we'd sell and go RVing for a while. I was so looking forward to getting out of California and seeing the country."

You can still do that. The words are on the tip of my tongue, but I hold them back. She can't. She can't travel the country alone in an RV. It's not safe.

"The attorney will be able to find all his assets and get them through probate," Dale says. "It takes some time."

"All I have is time," Mom says.

"Mom," I say, determined to put her needs before my own, "I'm going to stay with you for a while. Help you get through this."

"Don't be silly, Ashley. You're a newlywed. Your place is with Dale. I'm fine."

"You're not fine. You've hardly eaten in days."

"I ate the burger you brought me."

True, she did. Thank God. "Still..."

She shakes her head with conviction. "Absolutely not. Just because I was cheated out of my honeymoon doesn't mean you should be."

Huh. Honeymoon. I haven't given a honeymoon a thought, and judging by the look of surprise on Dale's face, neither has he.

"Don't tell me you haven't planned a honeymoon," Mom says.

"Well ... no. We've been a little busy," I say.

"Harvest time," Dale says absently. "And some of the wine is already fermenting."

"Right. There's no way Dale could leave the ranch for more than a day or two at a time. That's why he's going back tomorrow."

"Right." Mom nods.

But I wonder at Dale's countenance. Does he even *want* a honeymoon?

What's going on?

I make my final decision then. My mother's a grown woman. Dale will get her an attorney to sort out Dennis's estate.

And I'm going home.

Home with my husband.

I love him, and he loves me. I don't question that.

But still...

I fear for our young marriage.

CHAPTER FORTY-THREE

Dale

I hold Ashley's hand on the plane ride home. We're seated alone in first class, and Ashley turns down the flight attendant's offer of a drink.

So do I.

I don't drink in the morning. In fact, I rarely drink before six p.m.

"Hey," Ashley says. "Are we okay?"

Fuck, what a loaded question.

She's fine. Ashley herself is more than fine. I, on the other hand, am a fucked-up mess.

I married this woman for the wrong reasons.

I stare down at her fingers interlaced with mine, the diamond-and-garnet ring sparkling in the overhead light. The bauble was made for her. For my Ashley.

God, what was I thinking?

Marrying her in Las Vegas? I've never been one to act on impulse, and that was pure impulse. No two ways about it. Now I have to break *her* heart as well as my own.

I should have held back. I should have never fallen in love.

Why? Why did I let my guard down?

Why did I open my heart?

Why did I allow emotion to rule me?

Emotion ...

Emotion sucks.

Good or bad, it leads only to heartache.

I've been holding myself together.

But after that phone call from the fire marshal ...

How much longer can I steel myself?

I did. For Ashley. To get her through this.

But it's done now. Sure, her mother will grieve still. Ashley will grieve for her mother's pain.

But it's done. Over and done.

And I have to end things.

I have to tell Ashley our marriage was a mistake.

She'll say I don't love her.

She'll be wrong.

I *do* love her.

And that's why I'm going to let her go.

She must be free of the shackles marriage to me will bind her with for a lifetime.

As for me?

I'll never be free.

★ ★ ★

You'll never be free.

The words of our captors, after they beat my little brother, leaving marks on marks on marks on his young flesh.

You'll never be free.

He sobs in my arms, and I rub his back, taking care to avoid any tender areas. The way I remember our mom rubbing our backs to give comfort when something upset us.

Something like Vance Moreno, the school bully, who made

fun of Donny for carrying empty egg cartons to school for an art project.

Or something like the teacher calling me out for never raising my hand to answer a question even though I always knew the answer.

Those things seem so trivial now.

Why would something so stupid upset me? Upset Donny?

Still, Mom was always there. Always ready with a hug, a kiss, an "I love you."

Where is she now?

Is she looking for us?

Does she care?

"It hurts, Dale." Donny is no longer sobbing.

We both stop crying after a while.

"I tried," I say to him. "I tried to get them to take me instead."

His head lies on my shoulder.

He says nothing.

CHAPTER FORTY-FOUR

Ashley

I work with Ryan at the winery the day after we get back.

Dale isn't here. He's on a business trip to Grand Junction. I wanted to go with him, but he said no, that I was needed here.

I'm not needed here. Ryan and his staff have everything under control. I keep a close eye on Dale's Syrah, as he asked me, measuring Ph and alcohol content.

I feel good that he trusts me with his wine.

"Ryan?" I ask.

"Yeah?"

"Can you tell me anything about Dale's childhood?"

He flattens his lips into a straight line and pauses for a minute. Then, "He grew up here. It was idyllic. Talon and Jade are good parents. You're Diana's friend. You know that."

"Nice try at a pivot," I say. "You know what I'm asking."

Ryan sighs. "No, I don't."

"Let me be specific, then. Do you know *anything* about Dale's childhood before he came here? Before Talon and Jade adopted him?"

"What has he told you?"

"Nothing."

His eyebrows nearly jump off his forehead.

"Does that surprise you?" I ask.

"He married you."

"He did, but it was quick. Very spur of the moment."

"Obviously." He rakes his fingers through his silver-streaked dark hair. His cognac-colored eyes seem to look through me.

"Please," I say. "I'm worried about him. About *us*."

"Dale isn't the kind to do something he doesn't want to do, Ashley. If he married you, it was because he wanted to."

"I don't doubt that."

"Then why are you asking me questions about his past?"

"Because I love him. I want to know everything about him."

Ryan sighs. "I can't say anything. It's not my place. You need to ask Dale."

"I've tried."

"I'm sure you have."

"Would Talon tell me? Jade?"

"Jade probably wouldn't. Talon… I don't know. He's probably your best shot, but I wager he'd protect Dale."

This time my eyebrows shoot up. "Protect Dale? From *what*?"

"Fuck." Ryan inhales.

"You can't leave me hanging here. What's wrong? What's wrong with Dale?"

"Nothing's wrong with Dale."

"What happened to him? What happened before he came here?"

"Fuck," Ryan says again. Then he pulls his phone out of his pocket, makes a call, and presses it to his ear. "Tal? We need to talk. Can you meet Ashley and me at your office?" *Pause.* "Yeah, you're right. Maybe it's time." *Pause.* "See you in a few."

Maybe it's time? Time for what?

"Come on," Ryan says. "Let me get Jack to finish up what I was doing. I'll be with you in a minute."

I shiver, rubbing my arms to ease the nervous chill. Ryan returns in a few minutes, and we drive over to the office building. We take the elevator in silence to the fourth floor, where all the Steel siblings have their corner offices. We walk, still in silence, to what I presume is Talon's.

Ryan knocks. "It's me, Tal."

"Come in," Talon calls.

Ryan pushes the door open, and I walk in. He closes it and clicks the lock in place.

The lock?

What the hell?

"Hi, Ashley," Talon says. "Please, have a seat."

I swallow audibly as I sit. I say nothing.

That numbness?

It's back with a vengeance. A bomb is about to be dropped, and I don't want to feel anything when it happens.

"Jade and I have talked about whether to tell you what I'm about to tell you, Ashley," Talon says. "We agreed not to, unless..."

I clear my throat. "Unless what?"

"Unless you asked."

"I see." I rub my arms once more. Odd that I'm numb and still shivering.

"It's fitting that Ryan is here, as well," Talon continues.

"Why is that?" I cock my head, still numb.

"Because I was there," Ryan says.

I lift one eyebrow. "You were there ... when?"

"When we found Dale and Donny."

"Wait … What?"

"It's a long story," Talon says. "Ruby had been kidnapped—"

"What?" I stand abruptly.

"Sit down," Ryan says. "Like Talon said, it's a long story. Did Dale ever tell you that Ruby used to be a cop?"

Had he? "I don't know. Maybe. Or Dee did. She told me something about every member of the family that first night, but I'm not sure I recall everything. It sounds vaguely familiar."

"Ruby was a detective when we met," Ryan says. "She quit the force before we got married."

"Why?"

"Because they wouldn't give her a leave of absence to investigate her father."

Again, "What?" I'm not sure my eyes have ever been open quite so wide. I'm so not following. What does any of this have to do with Dale?

"Ruby's father had her kidnapped, and Ryan and I went off to find her. But before we found her, we found Dale and Donny."

Chills skitter along my spine and up my neck. "Where? Where did you find them?"

"On a private island in the Caribbean. They'd been…" Talon clears his throat.

"I'll do it, Tal."

Talon nods. "Thank you."

Ryan continues, "Dale and Donny were also kidnapped."

I pick up my jaw long enough to say, "By whom?"

"By a child trafficking ring that Ruby's father worked for. They'd been locked up for over two months when we found them."

Child trafficking ring. The Steel Foundation. Mental

illness and child trafficking. I'm seriously going to be sick. My bowels clench.

"Locked up?" My stomach rises to my throat.

"Yes," Ryan says. "They were kidnapped, trained with torture—all kinds of torture—and meant to be sold overseas to a master."

I retch.

Literally retch on the carpet in Talon's office. I don't even try to hold it back. It wouldn't work anyway.

Luckily nothing comes up.

Ryan's arm goes around me. "Easy, Ashley. Let it out."

I retch again. This time a little comes up. I want to ask questions.

I want to bury my head in the sand.

I want to puke my entire body up until I'm inside out.

I want to hide inside myself until everything's okay again.

Except everything will never be okay again.

Not ever again.

"Dale and Donny..." I finally say between heaves.

"Dale and Donny," Talon says, "were held. Were hurt. Were..."

"Easy, Tal." Ryan's voice.

This must be hard for Talon. For both of them. To know what two little boys went through at strangers' hands.

A throat clears. "I'm okay." Talon's voice.

"We don't know exactly what the boys went through," Ryan says.

"Only their therapists know," Talon continues. "Jade and I know some, but Dale, especially, wasn't overly talkative during therapy."

I swallow down a heave and look up. A toxic color of

brownish yellow permeates their voices.

Talon's face is stark white. Not an easy feat for a naturally tan man with ruddiness in his cheeks most of the time.

Ryan doesn't look a lot better.

How do I deal with this? Any of this? Suddenly being conceived by a rapist and living in tent city in San Francisco seems like just another day in the park.

And Dale . . .

Dale will be angry at me. At Talon and Ryan for telling me.

Dale will be angry.

But I can't keep this from him. He has to know that I know.

He'll be able to see right through me anyway.

"This is important," Talon is saying.

"What? Yes, of course it is."

"I mean," he says, "it's important that you understand. That you be there for him. He should have told you before he married you. He should have . . ."

Talon continues speaking, but the words mesh together in a dark-gray hue, like a thunderhead ready to explode in the sky.

All gray.

All gray . . . and gray is the worst color of all.

Sounds are only gray when . . .

When . . . there's no hope.

CHAPTER FORTY-FIVE

Dale

I unlock the door to Floyd Jolly's home.

It's a rental, and the landlord gave me a key to go in and haul his shit out. I've hired a company to meet me here in a couple of hours, but first . . .

First, as much as it pains me, I need to look around. Need to try to understand why a man would do such a heinous thing to two innocent children.

Two innocent children he'd fathered, no less.

Too much.

Too much all at once.

Ashley catapulted into my life, awakening the dormant emotion within me, threatening to unbury something I never let myself think about. Slowly it's creeping to the surface. Floyd's confession brought it closer, and the fire marshal's call . . .

So much I've fucked up.

I'll never be free.

I don't deserve to be free.

The house is a mess.

"*Meow!*" a cat squalls.

Floyd's cat. What was its name? Puzzles? Poozles?

It must be starving. Though there's probably a surplus of

rats in this mess of a home.

"Here, kitty," I say. "Come here. You hungry?"

I head into the kitchen. The cat bowl is empty, of course. God knows when she was last fed. I'm not a cat person, but I sure don't want to see an animal starve. I quickly find the cat food and fill up the bowl. What about water? Do cats drink water? On TV, they always seem to be drinking milk. I grab a bowl out of a cupboard and fill it with water, setting it next to the food. Then I open the refrigerator. Sure enough, a carton of milk sits on the top shelf. I pull it out, open it, and—

"Gyahhh!"

Rotten. Smells like sour milk, literally.

"Sorry, kitty. No milk today. You'll have to make do with water."

For God's sake. I'm talking to a cat.

I leave the kitchen, and within a few seconds, the cat scurries past me and starts chowing down.

Yeah, she's hungry. I'll have to take her to a shelter. Damn.

I walk around the house, searching.

For what? I'm not sure. Just some tiny clue about who this man was. This man from whom I got half my DNA.

Does he have any photos? Any books? Anything that might tell me something about how a man can father two boys, abandon them, and then sell them into slavery for five grand?

His furniture is tattered brocade, and his kitchen table is a card table. The sour milk in the fridge is joined only by some pimento loaf and a box of baking soda. A loaf of molded bread sits on the counter, along with what's left of a case of cheap beer.

That's it.

That's what my birth father had in his house when my real father, Talon Steel, came and offered him the chance for rehab.

Did he really go into rehab and just leave his cat here unattended?

Really?

If possible, the man just disgusted me more. I can't abide abuse to animals. Like children, they can't protect themselves from human cruelty.

How I know that better than most.

But I can't take Floyd's cat home with me. I just can't. Not because I'm not a cat person. No. I could deal if it were just that.

It's because I'd think of the bastard—and what Donny and I went through because of him—every time I looked at the cat.

I can't put myself through that. The cat deserves better.

I sigh. I hate shelters, but I have no choice. Ava likes cats, but then I'd see the damned thing anytime I visited her.

No. No choice. But maybe I could at least find a home for her. The idea of a shelter makes me want to vomit.

And I already want to vomit big time just being in this house.

I walk around briskly, opening and shutting drawers, looking for something—anything—to make me see that Floyd Jolly was slightly human.

I find nothing.

The man abandoned his cat.

Of course, that was nothing after abandoning two sons.

All I find is a tattered book of poems. A turned-down page marks a poem by Robert Frost.

Two roads diverged in a yellow wood,
And sorry I could not travel both
And be one traveler, long I stood
And looked down one as far as I could
To where it bent in the undergrowth;

Then took the other, as just as fair,
And having perhaps the better claim,
Because it was grassy and wanted wear;
Though as for that the passing there
Had worn them really about the same,

And both that morning equally lay
In leaves no step had trodden black.
Oh, I kept the first for another day!
Yet knowing how way leads on to way,
I doubted if I should ever come back.

I shall be telling this with a sigh
Somewhere ages and ages hence:
Two roads diverged in a wood, and I—
I took the one less traveled by,
And that has made all the difference.

The words are slightly familiar. I probably read this poem in high school or something. Who knows?

I can't help a laughing scoff.

Why would my father mark *this* poem of all things?

He took a path that led him here.

Maybe he was lamenting not taking the higher road? Not abandoning his sons and then forsaking them altogether?

"Yeah, right," I say aloud and then slam the book shut and throw it onto the old couch.

The doorbell rings.

The junk haulers. Good.

"Come on in," I tell them. "Take it all."

"Got it." He shoves a tablet under my nose. "Sign here."

I sign quickly and turn to look around the room once more. My gaze zeroes in on the book of poems lying on the couch. I walk over and grab it. The cat, its belly now full, whisks around my legs.

"Hey." One of the haulers leans down to stroke her head. "She looks a little skinny."

"The guy who lived here abandoned her for a week. I just fed her."

"You taking her with you?"

"To a shelter, unfortunately. You want her?"

"My wife'll kill me if I bring home another stray. Then again, she hates shelters."

"Tell you what." I pull out my wallet. "I've got three hundred dollars. It's yours if you give her a good home."

"What's her name?"

"Puzzles, I think."

He scoffs.

"Hey, I didn't name her."

He strokes her head again. "Your new name is Bella." He waves the money away. "Keep it."

"Please." I push it into his palm. "It would make me feel better to know she's going to a good home. Use it for cat food."

"All right. You're a good guy."

"Thanks," I say.

He's wrong, though. I'm not a good guy.

I'm fucked up.

And I'll never be free.

CHAPTER FORTY-SIX

Ashley

"Ashley."

The voice comes from somewhere above me. I'm not sure where. It's a voice I know.

But I can't see or hear anything through the gray.

All the gray.

"Ashley. Come on, honey."

The voice again.

It's not Dale's voice. No, it belongs to his father.

"Ashley."

"Was it a mistake?" another voice asks.

This one I also know. It's Dale's uncle. It's Ryan's voice.

"She has the right to know." Talon again.

Finally I make out their figures through the gray haze.

My stomach is clenched.

My heart is breaking.

Breaking for what my husband and his brother went through.

Breaking into shards of glass . . .

"Ashley." Talon again.

"I'm here."

"It's okay." Talon? Or Ryan. I'm not sure.

"How?" I demand. "How is any of this okay?"

"It was a long time ago," Talon says.

"You don't get over something like this," I say, more to myself than to either of them.

"It's always with you," Talon says, "but Dale is strong."

Talon speaks with a tone of authority. As if he knows. Well, he knows his son better than I do, I suppose. Which in itself is a travesty. I'm married to him. I committed to a lifetime with him.

And I don't know him.

I don't know him at all.

So much about him makes more sense now, though. Why he's such a loner. Why small things set him off sometimes.

Why he's so secretive . . .

"What do I say to him?" I ask, my voice monotone.

"Nothing," Talon says.

"I can't keep this from him. He has to know that I know."

"You'll know when the time is right," Talon says.

"Will I?" I shake my head.

"You will. Or he will. He *will* tell you, Ashley. It's just a matter of when."

"The time would have been before he married me."

"In a perfect world, yes," Talon agrees, "but this isn't a perfect world, and Dale isn't a perfect man."

"He's close," I say.

"Spoken like a woman in love." Ryan smiles.

"I *am* in love. You must believe me. I know it hasn't been long, but—"

"You don't have to reassure us," Talon says. "We Steels have a history of falling fast and falling hard."

"What can I do?" I ask. "I want to help him. I want to . . ."

What? I want to what?

"You want to free him," Talon says. "I understand. But you can't. Only Dale can free himself."

"I can't even imagine what he goes through."

They're both silent.

"It was a long time ago," Talon finally says, "but you're right. Some things stay with you."

"How will he ever be free?"

"Being free isn't a matter of forgetting," Talon replies. "It's a matter of dealing with something that never goes away. You're helping him, Ashley. More than you know."

"I don't feel like I'm doing anything at all."

"You've brought feelings out in him that his mother and I thought might never surface," Talon says. "For that, we're very grateful to you."

I nod. I have no idea what else to say.

Silence reigns for what seems like an hour but is only about five minutes.

"I need to see Dale," I finally say. "When will he be back from his business trip?"

Ryan sighs. "He's not on a business trip, Ashley."

"Where is he, then?"

"He went to his birth father's home. To dispose of his belongings."

I widen my eyes. "I could have gone with him. Made it easier on him."

"This is something he had to do alone," Talon says.

"What about Donny? Shouldn't he be involved?"

"Donny went back to Denver while you were in LA. He's needed at his firm. He asked Dale to take care of it, and Dale agreed."

I nod. "Of course Dale agreed. He's still taking care of Donny."

Talon smiles. "You understand him more than you realize."

"Oh, God…" The nausea returns with a vengeance. "He… Donny…"

"Yes," Talon says. "Both of them, and yes, Dale did what he could to protect his little brother."

"Oh, God…" I say again.

"He's a good man," Talon says. "A strong man, with good values and a wonderful heart. He deserves happiness, and with you, Jade and I think he'll finally find it."

"That's a lot of pressure on me," I can't help saying.

"Don't think of it that way."

"I didn't mean it in a bad way. I love him. I want to devote my life to him. I just hope I'm enough."

"You are. Believe that."

I regard Dale's father—the man who, by Dale's assessment, knows him better than anyone else.

I have to trust that he knows what's best for his son.

And if he says it's me, I need to believe it.

I love him so, so much, and I don't doubt his love for me.

I just hope it's enough to break him free of the cuffs he still holds himself in.

Until he's willing to free himself, I'm afraid of what he may do.

CHAPTER FORTY-SEVEN

Dale

The dive bar that doesn't even have a name sits in a seedy area of Grand Junction. Dad opens the door for me, and I walk in.

"Talon Steel!" an old barkeep says. "It's been a while."

"Too long," Dad says. "Meet my son Dale. He's twenty-one today."

"And you brought him here?" The barkeep guffaws.

"Nowhere else I'd bring him." He sits down on a barstool and nods to me to sit next to him.

"Nice to meet you," the bartender says. "I'm Luke."

"The usual," Dad says. "Two."

"You got it." Luke slides two drinks in front of us.

Dad raises his glass. "To my firstborn."

I grab mine and clink it to his. Then I take a drink—

My eyes tear as what can only be battery acid burns my throat. "What the hell is this?" I gasp.

"You were expecting Peach Street?"

"Maybe not here, but I sure wasn't expecting this rotgut."

"You get used to it," Dad says. "In fact, you learn to like it on occasion."

I grew up with the finer things—for the last eleven years anyway, and before that, I never tasted alcohol. I'm used to good wine and spirits, which this brown stuff definitely is not.

"What occasion might that be?" I ask. "Surely not my twenty-first birthday."

"You wouldn't think so, would you?" Dad takes another sip of the crap and then exhales harshly. "It takes a bit, but there's a strange beauty in the causticity of it."

I chuckle and shake my head. "My first legal drink, and you bring me here?"

"Yes, your first legal drink, the minute you're entitled to it."

I shake my head again. Dad's always marched to the beat of his own drummer, just like I do. But I don't get what he's doing here. I raise my eyebrows in question.

"I learned a lot about myself in this place," he says. "Met a man named Mike, who in some ways I think might have been my guardian angel."

I scoff at him. "I don't believe in guardian angels."

"I can understand why you don't, given what you went through when you were young."

"It's not that, though you raise a good point. I just don't believe in any of that stuff."

"Fair point. I didn't either, for my own reasons. I was older than you. Thirty-five. I remember because I'd just met your mother."

★ ★ ★

Funny. At the time, I didn't know Dad had been through something similar. How could he possibly believe in guardian angels either?

Aren't parents supposed to protect their children? If my own father sold me off like chattel, how the hell could I believe in guardian angels?

My *own* father.

The words strike a chord in my head. In my heart.

My own father.

Floyd Jolly may have sold Donny and me, but my *own* father, Talon Steel, rescued us.

I sit here at the old dive bar, nursing the same rotgut that scorched my throat over a decade ago, waiting for my guardian angel. Someone to tell me I can live with everything. That Ashley and I can make it. That the past doesn't matter.

I imagine some old-timer named Mike or Deke or Harold or Earl sidling up to the bar, letting me buy him a drink and imparting some wisdom that will change my life.

Instead, a young woman ambles up to me. "Hey, handsome."

"Hey."

"Buy a girl a drink?"

She's dressed in a denim miniskirt and a faux-fur jacket. She's attractive enough, brunette with brown eyes, and gold hoops dangle from her earlobes. It's her lipstick that gives her away. It's bright red, and it doesn't work on her.

"Not interested," I say.

"A hundred bucks, and I'll do anything you want."

I signal the barkeep. "Get the lady what she wants."

"Now you're talking." Her voice is husky. She must be a smoker. "I'll have a vodka tonic, Newly."

Newly slides her drink over.

"You got a place to go?" she asks.

"Still not interested." I flash my left hand at her.

She guffaws. "You think I care if you're married?"

"You may not"—I clear my throat—"but I do. Enjoy the drink." I throw some bills on the counter and walk out.

No guardian angel. No wisdom.

Only rotgut whiskey and now a headache.

★ ★ ★

"Hey, girl." I fluff Penny's head, and she sniffs my legs for several minutes. Smelling the cat, no doubt. I'm oddly happy about finding a home for Floyd's cat, despite the throbbing in my temples.

I did a good thing, finding the kitty a home.

I wish it made me feel better about what I'm going to do now.

It doesn't.

I let Penny out, drink a glass of water, and let her back in for the night. Then I walk to the bedroom.

Ashley is asleep on my side of the bed, her head cuddled in the fluffy pillow. Her hair is fanned out like a yellow curtain, and her cheeks are the lightest pink. Penny curls up on her bed in the corner, turns around twice, and settles in with a happy groan.

I want to wake Ashley.

Wake her and finally make love to her the way she deserves. I've had good intentions before—to do it slowly, sweetly—and I've never been able to slow down enough to lavish the attention on her that she deserves.

I want to. I want to so badly.

Especially because . . .

Tomorrow . . .

Tomorrow, she'll hate me after I say what needs to be said.

But she's sleeping so soundly, like an angel.

I can't disturb such peaceful innocence. Not when I'm

about to shatter it tomorrow.

I head to the bathroom to brush my teeth and wash up, and then I remove my clothes and put on a pair of lounge pants.

I tiptoe to the other side of the bed and get in. I try not to disturb her, but—

"Mmm... Hey, you." She snuggles into my shoulder.

"Shh. Go back to sleep."

"I love you," she says. "I love you so much. Nothing you can ever say or do will change that."

Where's this coming from?

I have no idea, but it's only going to make tomorrow harder.

Hell, nothing can make it harder than it already is.

It's going to break my heart and hers.

"Love me," she says softly.

"I do. I love you."

"Mmm. Not what I mean. Make love to me."

My dick responds abruptly.

Maybe I can.

I'll do it this time. Make love to her the way I've dreamed of. The way she deserves.

I get rid of my pants quickly and efficiently. Ashley's already naked, so no worries there. I climb on top of her, grab both her wrists and secure her arms above her head. I hold her there, bracing my own weight so I don't crush her.

Then I kiss her.

I begin slowly, ignoring my throbbing dick. I lick her lips, first the top and then the bottom, sucking its plumpness between my teeth. Then I ease my tongue between her lips, swirling it around her silky mouth.

She responds, kissing me back, and though my instinct

is to deepen the kiss, it's the middle of the night, and I'm determined to go slowly.

To relish this last moment with her.

For tomorrow . . .

But I won't think about that now. No. This is me loving my wife. God, my wife.

What was I think—

No. This time I deepen the kiss. I need to keep thoughts at bay. I want to feel, only feel. I want her to feel, only feel.

I want to make this something she'll remember always.

I leave her lips then and trail kisses over her perfect jawline, across her cheek to her earlobe. I suck the lobe into my mouth and tug.

She groans.

God, her flesh is like silk against my lips and tongue.

So soft and supple.

How can I—

No.

I slide downward, then, over her chest and to her breasts, where I lick one hard nipple. Her hips rise, and my cock tightens further.

She spreads her legs. An offering. She wants me to slide inside her. So tempting, but I suck on her nipple instead, eliciting sweet moans of satisfaction from her. What color are they? To me, they're a soft pink, but that's only my imagination. She actually sees color in sounds.

She's so wonderful.

"Mmm," she says softly. "Inside me. Please."

I let her nipple drop from my lips with a soft pop.

Her plea strikes my heart. My soul.

And my cock is more than willing. I nudge my cockhead

over her folds and then enter her, determined to go slowly.

Once I hit balls deep, my body shudders, quivers, as if all of me, not just my dick, is gloved within her heat.

I wrap my arms around her and pull us both onto our sides, still joined. I look down between our bodies, at my dick submarined inside her. I pull out slowly, gritting my teeth so I don't go too fast. I watch myself emerge and then bury again inside her warmth.

God, it's beautiful, our bodies coming together.

Then I meet her gaze. "Open your eyes, Ashley."

She obeys, and our gazes meet.

"Look at me," I say. "Look at me as I make love to you slowly. Never take your eyes from mine."

Her blue eyes sparkle, even in the darkness of our bedroom in the dead of night.

So much love is reflected back at me.

So much . . .

"Look at me," I say again, "and see how much I love you."

"Your eyes," she replies. "They're playing that joyful music. The green music, Dale. So beautiful."

"Together, we are music, Ashley. The most beautiful tune ever written."

I slide in and out, going slowly as well as I can.

But soon, I no longer have the control. I need her, and I go faster, savoring every ridge inside her pussy. Every touch of her flesh to mine. Every look from her gorgeous baby blues as I thrust harder, harder, harder . . .

"I love you, Ashley. Always. I'll always love you."

"I love you too." Her words come out on a moaning sigh. "Always."

I hear the truth in her words, but she doesn't hear the truth in mine.

For though the words are far from a lie, they're also something else.

They're goodbye.

CHAPTER FORTY-EIGHT

Ashley

I wake with a smile on my face, the sun streaming in through the east window in Dale's—*our*—bedroom. I reach for my husband but find his side of the bed empty.

Of course he's gone. It's late. I should have been up hours ago. He's no doubt at the winery, checking on his old-vine Syrah. Timing is critical.

Except...

The horror that Talon and Ryan revealed rises to my surface. Last night was so beautiful between Dale and me. I let myself forget, for those few timeless moments, what he's been through. What must haunt him every day of his life.

I breathe in deeply. I'll think about that tomorrow.

Penny must be outside. Otherwise she'd be in here rousing me out of bed. I rise, don a robe, and walk to the kitchen. I'm parched, but a tall glass of OJ will take care of that. After letting a tail-wagging Penny in through the French doors, I gulp down some juice and call Mom. Maybe it'll get my mind off Dale's past.

"Hey, honey," she says.

"Just checking in. How are you doing?"

"One day at a time. I talked to the attorney Dale set me up with. She thinks we can get through probate fairly quickly, even without a will, since I have a valid marriage certificate. As long as Dennis's mother doesn't contest it."

"Why would she?"

"I have no idea." Mom sighs. "I don't even know the woman."

Of course she doesn't. Mom and Dennis eloped without telling anyone after dating for six months. Dennis's mother could be a sweetheart or a shrew. After her behavior at the funeral, I'm thinking shrew. Still, Mom has the upper hand.

"You'll get through it," I say.

"I suppose so." Her tone is wistful.

"Just say the word, and I'll be right there."

"I know that, honey, but your place is with your new husband."

"Mom, I—" I stop abruptly.

Dale walks into the kitchen. Strange. I didn't hear him come in. Penny whisks around his ankles. He leans down and pets her absently.

Then he meets my gaze.

I swallow. Something's wrong.

"Mom, I have to go. I'll call you back, okay?"

"Is anything wrong?"

"Everything's fine." I end the call.

Everything's fine.

I just lied to my mother.

It's written all over Dale's face.

Everything is most assuredly *not* fine.

I inhale. Stand tall, though my husband dwarfs me.

His hair is a mass of blond surrounding his perfectly sculpted face. His green eyes pierce me with coldness. No longer do they play the jubilant songs. No, the green is menacing. It's an eerie solo violin, playing a melody of hell.

I chill all over and rub my upper arms. It does no good. This chill soaks me to my soul.

I'm not scared, exactly, though I do feel fear. Dale looks ominous, as if he's just seen something terrifying, as if he's ready to stand up to destruction.

As if he's a storm rioting in for one purpose, though I don't yet know what the purpose is. To put out a fire? To start a fire?

To create? Or to destroy?

A chilling breeze swirls through me. It's my imagination, I know, but it's so real. So cold and real.

I say nothing, just let his eyes pierce two freezing holes in my flesh.

Finally, he speaks.

"We need to talk."

I hold back a gasp. His voice.

It's no longer that gorgeous Syrah red that I love.

It's darker. Nearing pure black in its opacity.

Where is my beautiful husband? Where is the terrified child he must have been? I see neither in the man before me.

We need to talk. Has anything good ever come from those four words?

I say nothing. I don't move. I stand, as if those chills have actually frozen me.

And I wait.

CHAPTER FORTY-NINE

Dale

My heart is breaking, but I steel myself. I have to do this for Ashley's own good.

I have to, before that carefully constructed wall comes crashing down, and I destroy her.

"Ashley," I say.

She inhales. "What?"

"This isn't easy."

"Spit it out, Dale. We both know it's bad. Just get it over with before I throw up orange juice all over your kitchen."

She's so strong, my Ashley. She'll get through this. She'll hurt at first, but she'll be okay. She has her mother. They'll be in basically the same situation. They can comfort each other.

"I can't do this," I finally say, nearly choking on the words.

"Do what?"

"This." I gesture around the kitchen and then to her. "This. Us."

"Dale, I—"

I shake my head. "No. I know everything you're going to say. That we love each other. That love is enough. It's not, Ashley. It's not."

She bites her lip. I expect tears, but she holds them back. I wish I had her control.

"We got married in Las Vegas," I say, trying my level best to sound like I don't care.

"So? It's still valid."

"I know that, but we can get it annulled pretty easily. Vegas weddings are often annulled because people get into them in a drunken stupor."

"Neither of us was in a drunken stupor, Dale."

"Ashley, don't make this harder than it is."

"Harder? This is *hard* for you?"

"Of course it's hard for me. I never wanted to hurt you."

She crumbles then, right into my arms, her cheek against my chest. "I know what happened, babe. I know everything."

My arms go numb. "You know . . . what, exactly?"

She pulls away, meets my gaze. "Your Dad. Ryan. They told me . . ."

Anger wells in me. I move backward. I can't be near Ashley right now. I can't. Because I'm ready to burst, and I can't burst on her.

"Dale . . ." Her lips tremble, and her voice cracks.

"If they told you what I think they did," I say through a clenched jaw, "then you know why I can't be with you."

"No." She gulps. "I love you, and you love me. The past doesn't matter."

I rake my fingers through my hair and stare at the ceiling. "How the hell can you say that?"

"Because—"

"You don't know the half of it."

"It doesn't matter. It—"

"It *does* matter, Ashley. It matters because I can't be what you want me to be. I *can't*."

"I never wanted you to be anything other than who you

are," she says timidly.

"You say that. You may even believe it. But there are things inside me. Things I can't control. And I don't want you anywhere near me when they come out."

She doesn't reply, but her eyes... Her beautiful blue eyes... They regard me with love and sympathy... and something else.

Something else...

Fear. She's scared. Just what I don't want.

Just why this has to end.

But the fear in her eyes gives way to indignance as she whips her hands to her hips and advances on me. "I call bullshit."

I don't raise my voice. "It's not bullshit."

"It's bullshit. You could have figured all this out a week ago, before we got married."

She's not wrong. "I always knew, Ashley. But I wanted you so much. I wanted to believe I could be happy."

"You *can* be."

"You don't understand."

"Because you don't let me, Dale. You don't let me in."

I shake my head, wanting to pull out my hair strand by strand. This is nuts. What made me think I could ever do this? That I could ever have a normal marriage? That I could ever be this happy for more than a few days?

"I don't let you in for your own good."

"If you love me, you won't do this."

"Because I love you is why I *have* to do this. Why can't you see that?"

"No," she says. "You won't. You won't hurt someone you love."

Oh, how wrong she is. I have hurt the person I love most. Twenty-five years ago, I did just that. I forsook my little brother, and as God is my witness, I won't do that to Ashley.

I pull myself together as best I can. "My mind's made up. I'll contact my lawyer and get the papers moving for an annulment."

"And if I don't sign?"

"Then I'll get it anyway. No one can force me to stay married to you."

She goes white then, and her lips turn downward.

I've never seen this look on her face, and it takes me a minute to assess it.

It's defeat.

She looks defeated.

Ashley has never looked that way before. She's always indignant. Always ready to fight. Always bursting with courage.

Not at this moment, though.

"I'll take care of you," I say. "All the money you and your mom will ever need."

"I don't want your money," she says, her voice expressionless. "I never wanted it. I'll pack my things."

Good. She'll pack. I'll get her a room in town and make arrangements for her travel home to LA.

She heads to the bedroom.

I walk to the family room and plunk down into my recliner. Penny jumps into my lap and licks my face.

"Not now, girl."

My dog means well, but I don't want her comfort. I don't deserve her comfort.

I don't deserve anyone's comfort.

★ ★ ★

It starts like any other day. We awake on the cold concrete floor, huddled together for warmth. I take a piss in the bucket in the corner. No one has changed it in a few days, but I got used to the smell long ago.

What choice do I have?

A few minutes later, the door opens. Breakfast, of course. It's usually bread and water, but today—

"You." The masked man points to Donny. "Come with me."

I place myself between my brother and the man. "No. Take me. Whatever you do, you do it to me. Not him."

"Sorry, big brother." The man sneers. "Not today. Today we have something special planned."

"No!" I shout. "Donny, go sit in the corner."

"I'm taking the little one." The man punches the side of my head.

My legs give way, and I end up on the cold floor.

"Dale, no!" Donny cries.

I turn to him. "Shut up! Just sit there and don't say another fucking word!"

His eyes widen when I say "fucking." Yeah, I've heard it enough from the pigs who torture us. I mean it, too.

The masked man stalks toward Donny, but I lunge into him as hard as I can. He lets out an oof *when I slam into his chest. Without thinking, I plunge my teeth into his upper arm as hard as I can.*

"You little fucker!" The man swats me across the face and then kicks me away from him.

Not to be deterred, I get up and ram into him once more.

He grabs me by the shoulders. "You little shit. Fine. You want it? You got it."

He pushes me out the door and then locks Donny in.

"You'll be sorry, little fucker. Really sorry."

But I'm not.

Donny's safe in the room, at least as far as I know.

They've never removed us from the room before. I have no idea what kind of horror awaits me.

But it's okay.

Because it'll happen to me and not to Donny.

I succeeded.

That's all that matters.

Whatever lies ahead, I'll suffer through it.

As long as I keep my little brother as safe as possible.

Two masked men throw me into another concrete-floored room, which is even colder than what I'm used to.

"You like to protect your brother," one man says in a low voice. "We can respect that. Right?"

"Sure enough." This one has a higher-pitched voice. "And we can also make you wish you hadn't." He laughs maniacally, like one of the deviant clowns in horror movies.

I swallow and wrap my arms around my knees. What can they do to me that they haven't already?

Too soon, that question is answered.

CHAPTER FIFTY

Ashley

I pack.

I leave.

I text Brock.

He drives me into town.

He wants to talk. I stay silent.

He drops me at the hotel, where I thank him and tell him to go home.

He wheels my bag to my room, and then he does what I ask. He leaves.

And I cry.

CHAPTER FIFTY-ONE

Dale

She's gone.

She left over an hour ago.

And I'm on my third Peach Street. I'm angry and disgusted and brokenhearted. What were Dad and Uncle Ry thinking? My past is mine. Fucking *mine*. Not theirs. They had no right to tell Ashley.

I throw my empty low-ball glass against the wall. The crash sends shards of clear glass flying. Fuck Peach Street. I don't deserve fine bourbon. I want that rotgut at the dive in Grand Junction. My gaze falls on the book of poetry from my birth father's place. I pick up the book and send it flying after the glass.

"Fuck!" I roar.

Images. Sounds. Voices. Hot breath. Searing pain. Torturous humiliation. My determination—sheer willpower—and then . . .

Finally the thoughts come rioting into my mind.

That last time . . . The time I don't think about . . .

The time they broke me.

★ ★ ★

"Had enough yet?" Higher Voice rams into me with a broom handle.

They've both raped me before. I'm used to it. Numb to it, even. I can escape in my head, think about going home. About escaping.

But today is different.

Today it's a broom handle.

I squeeze my eyes shut, grit my teeth. Determined. Determined to take everything they gave.

Determined, because it saves my little brother. Can't last forever. Can't last forever.

Finally it's over, and I open my eyes slightly. It's covered in blood. My blood.

I close my eyes once more.

They'll leave me alone now. What more can they do?

They've beaten me, whipped me, raped me.

What else is there?

"He's strong, the little fucker," Low Voice says.

"Even the strongest can be broken," replies High Voice.

Though I'm determined not to cry out, I can't help it when a whip comes down on my cheek.

"There you go," High Voice says, invisible slime oozing from his tone. "Made you scream."

I press my lips together. I won't scream again. I will not.

The leather whip comes down on my cheek once more. Will I have a scar? So far, they've been careful not to scar us—at least not where anyone can see. Don't care. Donny's safe.

High Voice pries my lips apart. I know what's coming, and I hate it. Can't breathe when they do that. I always vomit afterward, but there's nothing in my stomach today. I get ready. Ready for him to shove himself into my mouth, but instead—

He grabs my tongue and slices into it with a sharp blade.

I cry out again, but it sounds like a muffled "waaagghh"

because he's still holding my tongue.

"You don't really need this, do you, bitch?" High Voice says. "The more room in there, the better."

Blood from the cut dribbles out of my mouth. Oddly, my tongue doesn't hurt any worse than if I'd bitten it myself. I try to breathe, but he's holding on to my tongue, and I choke, coughing and sputtering, and then—

I retch. Bile burns my throat, and High Voice lets go of my tongue. He boxes my ear for good measure.

"Back on your knees, little bitch," Low Voice says. "We've got a surprise for you."

I don't move. I never do. I learned long ago that they eventually move me where they want me. I won't be a willing participant in this. Not ever.

Strong hands grip my hips, and soon I'm back in the position they wanted. I'm sore, but I've been sore since that first time. They can go and go and go, but eventually the pain can't hurt any more than it already does. Right now I'm glad I still have a tongue.

They can shove something else in there. It won't hurt any worse at this point. Doesn't matter anyway. I'm ready to die. Donny and I made the pact. If a gun were within reach, I'd grab it and end this torment.

Except I won't. I know that as soon as the thought crosses my mind.

Because then they'll turn on Donny.

Only Donny has an out from the pact. I never will, as long as my brother lives. I'll die protecting him.

I brace myself for the intrusion that will inevitably come.

I wait.

And wait.

I hear a door open, and a whoosh of warmer air blows over me. I relish in it for the few seconds I feel it.

Since the lukewarm shower that first day, warmth is a luxury Donny and I have been denied.

It's gone too soon, of course, and then I suck in a breath as something cold and spiky trails over my tender back.

They're going to beat me again.

I suck in what little breath I can, trying to ready myself for something I'll never be ready for.

But the blow doesn't come.

Instead—

"No!" I cry.

Something tears into the already sore flesh inside me.

My insides are being ripped apart. I'll never heal from this. Never be whole again.

"Made you scream, bitch!" Low Voice squeals. "Little bitch, that's what you are. You'll always be someone's little bitch."

I scream again and again. "Stop! Please! It hurts! Mommy, where are you! They're hurting me!"

"Take it, bitch," High Voice says. "Take it all."

Needles, broken glass, sharp talons… They're all inside me, scraping out my insides and letting them bleed onto the cold concrete floor.

Take it. Take it. Take it.

"Break, you little bitch! Give in!"

The words fly around me as they continue to torture me with the object I still haven't seen. Don't want to see.

Until—

"Stop!" I finally cry out. "No more. No more."

"More," Low Voice says. "More until you break."

I'm already broken. I'll never heal from this. Has to stop.

No more. No more.

Tears fall down my cheeks. My nose runs, snot flowing onto the concrete floor.

Can't. Can't be strong anymore. Need it to stop. Stop. Stop.

"Please," I cry. "No more. Do it to someone else! Anyone else!"

"To your little brother?" *The pain continues, cutting through every part of me.*

No. Won't say it. Won't say it. Won't . . .

"Yes! Just stop! Please!"

And finally, it stops.

★ ★ ★

"Dale!"

I'm curled into a fetal position, lying among the broken glass, clutching my birth father's book.

It's out.

My deepest, darkest, dirtiest secret.

I threw my little brother to the wolves when I couldn't take the torture anymore.

I broke.

And I'll never be whole again.

So long this secret had lain dormant inside me, but now . . .

Now I *feel*.

I feel, and my self-hatred is more torment than anything those evil psychopaths did to me.

I deserve nothing good.

Nothing.

And that's what I'll get.

"Dale!"

The voice. I know it.

It's my father.

My father, who helped me escape the torture.

Days passed—I don't know how many. They dragged Donny away, and all I did was sit in a corner and imagine what horrific acts they were doing to his little body.

Because I told them to.

"Dale!"

I open my eyes. Talon Steel stands above me.

Talon Steel—the man who rescued my brother and me and made us his sons.

My savior. The savior I couldn't be to my brother.

The heinous picture I've kept buried inside for so long. It's out. I knew the day would come. I tried to fight it off for Ashley, but she awakened too much inside me.

And now I'll pay the ultimate price.

"Dale! Get up!"

I squeeze my eyes shut. I'm not getting up. Not for anyone. Not for Dad. Not for Donny. Not even for Ashley.

It's over. *I'm* over.

"God damn it, Dale, pick your fucking ass up!"

Strong arms grip my shoulders and haul me out of the family room and down the hall to my library. He forces me into a burgundy velvet wingback chair by the window. The library? This chair? Why not my office? Why not leave me in the family room?

"For Christ's sake! This is enough, Dale. God damned enough."

"I can't do it, Dad. I can't."

"You're going to sit there, and you're going to tell me everything that's going on inside that head of yours."

"You won't understand."

"Damn it, Dale. I'm the only one who *will*."

CHAPTER FIFTY-TWO

Ashley

I'm lying on the lumpy hotel bed when someone knocks softly at the door.

Go away.

The rapping becomes louder.

"Go away." Out loud this time.

"Ashley, it's Jade. Let me in. Please."

Dale's mother. As much as I love her—as much as I need someone to talk to—I can't. Not to her. I say nothing.

She knocks again. "Please, Ashley."

I sigh. I'm all cried out. I can't even imagine what I look like. Don't care anyway. She may pull the Steel card and pay off the maid to let her in with the pass key. I'm only postponing the inevitable. I rise and open the door.

Jade stands in the hallway, looking lawyerly in a light-gray suit and black pumps. She must have come straight from her office. "May I come in?"

"Nothing stopping you," I reply sarcastically. Then, "I'm sorry. This isn't your fault. I shouldn't take it out on you."

Jade sighs and sits down on the bed. "Perhaps it is my fault. I tried to be the best mother I could to Dale. I tried so hard. Maybe too hard at times. I never could get through to him the way I did the other three."

"It's still not your fault," I say.

"Talon told you," she says matter-of-factly. "He and I were hoping Dale would open up, especially after the two of you got married."

"I wish he had. It doesn't change anything for me. I still love him."

"Of course you do. I never thought otherwise."

I plunk down next to her on the bed. This tiny room doesn't have a decent chair.

"We did everything we could," Jade says. "And Talon . . ."

"Yeah?"

"Talon, he understands the boys better than . . ."

I hear what she's not saying, and I hear it in a hazy cloud of gray. Talon knows. Talon truly knows. And if possible, I feel even sicker.

I open my mouth, but she gestures for me to stop.

"It's okay. I'm not going to go into any detail. I'm going to say simply this. Please come home. Please don't give up on my son."

"I didn't, Jade. He gave up on *me*."

"He hasn't. I know he hasn't. He's given up on himself."

I scoff softly. "How is that any different?"

"Because he loves you. He loves you so much, Ashley, and I've never seen him quite as alive as he is with you. Ryan says the same thing. As much as Dale loves those vineyards, as much as he loves making wine, none of it put the spark in his beautiful eyes like you did."

A spark of warmth tries to take flame in my heart, but I stop it. I can't go there. I can't risk the hurt again. I won't survive it.

"I'm sorry," I say. "It's over."

"Please. He needs you."

"Whether you're right or wrong doesn't make a difference," I say. "In his own mind, he can't do this, and until that changes, nothing will."

Jade doesn't reply. Instead, "Why don't I take you into Grand Junction? We'll book a spa day tomorrow, both of us. We can get Bree to play hooky and join us. It'll be a Steel girls' day."

I gulp. "I'm not a Steel girl."

"You are. You always will be." She smiles and places her palm over my hand.

Except saying something doesn't make it true. And the best facial in the world won't cure my swollen, red eyes. I shake my head slowly.

She nods. "Okay. What, then? What can I do for you, Ashley?"

Nothing.

She can't do anything.

"It is what it is, Jade," I say. "And we both have to accept it."

CHAPTER FIFTY-THREE

Dale

"Why?" I ask Dad. "Why in here?"

"You're holding a book," he says. "The library seems appropriate."

I unclench my hand from the mass market paperback book of poems.

Dad takes it from me. "What is this?"

"Nothing." I turn away.

"You were holding on to it for dear life, so it's something." Dad opens the book to the turned-down page. "Hmm. Frost, huh? I didn't know you read poetry, Dale."

"I don't."

"Then why—"

"It belonged to my father, okay? It's the only thing I took from his house."

Dad eyes me. Is that a hint of sadness in his gaze? Regret? "I see. I'm glad you have something to remember him by."

I scoff, images coming to me in vivid color—so real I feel that if I reached forward, I'd touch something solid. "I don't want to remember the bastard."

"Oh?"

"Throw the book out."

"This is a great poem," Dad says. "One that obviously

meant something to him."

"I couldn't care less."

"If that were true, you'd have left the book."

He's right. Logical and right, and I know it. I say nothing. Silence looms for a few minutes, until—

"How can I help you, son?" Dad asks.

"You told Ashley."

He doesn't ask what he told her. He knows. He knows exactly what I mean. "I did. I take responsibility for that, and I have no regrets."

"It wasn't your place."

"You're right. I still have no regrets." Then, again, "How can I help you?"

"You can't help me. No one can."

He sighs, heads to the small bar where a crystal decanter of bourbon sits, and pours himself a glass. "Want one?"

I shake my head.

"Probably just as well. You've obviously already had a few." He brings his drink back and takes a second sip as he pulls up an ottoman and sits across from me. "You know what? You're right, Dale. You're right. No one can help you, and there's a simple reason for that."

"Yeah? I'm all ears."

"Because you won't *let* anyone help you."

"Bull, Dad. I let *you* help me. You got me therapy. You got me—"

"For fuck's sake, Dale. I'm not talking about all those years ago. I'm talking about *now*. You carry the goddamned world on your shoulders, and I should know, because I used to do the same thing."

"You didn't—" I stop abruptly.

"I didn't what?"

I swallow, wishing now that I had some bourbon to coat my throat with its spicy warmth. I face my father.

He's old now. Still a full head of thick hair but sprinkled with gray. Crow's feet crinkle around his eyes. Lines from his dimples draw an intersection down his cheeks. He's still vibrant, though. He's calm, but his fiery brown eyes tell the true story. He's angry with me.

Angry, and he has no reason to be. I'm not hurting him.

I'm hurting Ashley.

And myself.

And it dawns on me. *That's* why he's angry. Sure, he doesn't want to see Ashley hurt, but even more so, he doesn't want *me* to hurt.

He doesn't know the truth. He doesn't know about the phone call from the fire marshal. But even that isn't the biggest thing I've hidden from him.

He doesn't know about that horrible day. The day they broke me.

And I smile. Not a happy smile, but a smile because I've just discovered a universal truth, and there's a certain constancy—even beauty—to it.

When you hit rock bottom, there's nowhere to go but up. So I basically have nowhere to go. Period.

It pours out of me, then. From my mouth and in my voice, though in some ways it seems to come from somewhere far away.

I confess.

I confess all the truths of my life to my father. It flows out of me like lava hiccupping out of an active volcano. All of it. Every last bit. The fire. My birth father's confession. Even the day they broke me.

Tears run down my cheeks, though I don't sob. I speak. I speak in actual words what I've never told another soul. What I've let eat away at me for the last twenty-five years. What I was sure would never surface.

Until Ashley awakened me.

I tell him everything.

And I wait for him to disavow me.

For what seems like days, I wait, sitting in the uncomfortable wingback upholstered in burgundy velvet. The color of Syrah. Of my voice.

Finally—

"You have two choices." Dad's voice.

"I have *no* choice," I say.

Ashley's words haunt me. *You do, Dale. You always have a choice.*

I grab a tissue off the table next to me and blow my nose. "It doesn't go away."

"You're right." Dad nods. "That's not what I was talking about."

"What the fuck, then, Dad? I've hit bottom. I've fucked everything up. What the hell is my choice?"

Dad pauses a moment, rubbing his forehead. "I once had to make a similar choice, Dale."

He still hasn't told me what the choice is. "You didn't lose your orchard."

"No, I didn't. Not that autumn, anyway. I'm not talking about losing half the Syrah. I'm not talking about what your father—your birth father—did to you. I'm not even talking about what you think you did to your brother."

"What I *think* I did? Are you kidding?"

"You were a child yourself, Dale. They were hurting you. Violating you. You held out longer than anyone else would have."

"I'll never forgive myself."

"I understand," he says, "but you must. You must, or you'll never be free."

"I don't deserve to be free."

Dad smiles then. He fucking smiles! And my fists curl. I swear to God I'm about to punch my father in the jaw.

"Easy," he says. "Let me tell you a story."

Is he going to finish what he began the night of the reception? Before Dennis had the stroke and everything went to shit?

"First, by telling you this," he says, "I don't want you to think I'm belittling your situation. Our situations are different. They have some similarities, but I admit several things make yours harder. I know how much the Syrah means to you, son."

"Do you?" I shake my head.

"Of course I do. How could I not? Do you think I didn't seek solace of my own?"

"You joined the military, Dad. You served your country, and while I admire that greatly, it's hardly seeking solace."

He lets out a scoffing chuckle. "I didn't join the military to serve my country."

I widen my eyes. "Why, then?"

"Dale, I joined the military so I'd get sent to Iraq, and I did."

"I know. And you were a hero."

He scoffs again. "Was I? I saved some lives. Lives I wouldn't have saved if I'd been trying to save my own ass."

My heart nearly stops. "You mean..."

"That's exactly what I mean. I went to Iraq to die, son. I didn't think I was coming back."

I go numb. Numb and sick. What if . . . ? What if my father *hadn't* come back from Iraq? He wouldn't have been there to save Donny and me. We would have died as someone's property. Sold into slavery for others' pleasure, and once we were too old, we'd have either been killed or abandoned.

Diana and Brianna would have never been born.

And Mom . . . . They never would have met.

I clear my throat. "But you came back."

"I did. I got a hero's welcome. I turned down national recognition because I wasn't a hero, Dale. I went back in to get killed. While I was there, I saved a few lives."

"Six, Dad. You saved *six* lives."

He smiles. "So I did."

"Those six people sure think you're a hero. Donny and I think you're a hero. If you had died in Iraq, no one would have rescued us."

He nods. "That's true. For many reasons, I'm very glad I didn't die in Iraq."

"I am too."

"My point is, I had just as hard of a time dealing with what I'd been through as you're having."

"Well, your father didn't start the process."

Dad sighs. "As a matter of fact, Dale, he did."

I stare at my father. His countenance is serious. He means what he says. I open my mouth to ask for an explanation, but only silence emerges.

I have no idea what to say to him.

"Your mother and I, along with the rest of the family, decided to keep our history buried as best we could," Dad says.

"We wanted to protect you. Protect your brother, sisters, and cousins. I wonder now if maybe it was the wrong decision, given what you and Donny went through. At the time, though, we thought it best, and if there's one lesson I've learned during my long life, it's never to second-guess yourself. It only leads to heartache because you can't change the past anyway."

I nod. The what-if game. I'm pretty familiar with it.

"At any rate, the decision was made then, and nothing can change it. I don't talk a lot about my parents, and now you're probably beginning to understand why. It's a long and complicated story, but suffice it to say that my father played a significant role in my abduction and abuse."

"Yeah? I'm sorry about that, Dad. I really am. But did he sell you for five thousand dollars?"

Dad shakes his head. "No. He paid to have it done. And he didn't pay five thousand. He paid five *million*."

My jaw drops.

"Like I said," he continues, "it's a long and complicated story. He didn't realize he was paying to have me abducted and tortured, but that's what ultimately happened."

I shake my head, ready to puke. "I can't hear this."

"I understand. I don't like thinking about it. But I can't change it. And this is where your choice comes in, son."

I scoff. "What choice is that again?"

"There *is* a choice, and it's an important one."

"I'm listening."

"You sent Ashley away."

"Of course I did. She shouldn't have to deal with any of this shit."

"But you love her, and she loves you."

"What's that got to do with anything?"

"She makes you happy."

"Dad, nothing can make me happy now."

He smiles again, and again I want to punch him in the nose.

"Dale," he says, "you have to live with this no matter what. What your birth father did to you and Donny. With the results of the fire. What *you* did. All of that is yours to live with."

"I fucking know that!" I tug at my hair. "See? No fucking choice."

"But there is," Dad says calmly. "It's like the poem says. You can choose which road to take."

"My father and that damned poem!"

"He marked it for a reason—a reason we can only surmise. But you found it. Let it speak to you. Think about which choice to make now."

"Neither changes what I've been through."

"You're absolutely right, Dale," Dad says. "You have to live with all of it. That's not part of the choice. Your choice is—do you want to live with it *with* Ashley? Or *without* her?"

CHAPTER FIFTY-FOUR

Ashley

The next morning, I force myself out of bed. I didn't sleep. I seriously don't know if I'll ever sleep again.

I'm going home to LA.

Home to my mother. We can commiserate together. We're both basically in the same situation—the end of a short relationship with men we loved. Except her man didn't leave her by choice.

No. I can't cry about this anymore. I just can't.

I traipse into the small bathroom.

Ugh. I'm unrecognizable. My eyes are still bloodshot and swollen, my nose nearly raw from crying and blowing it into the sandpaper tissues this hotel provides.

I can't stay here. I have to go as soon as I can make arrangements. I need a car. Or a plane ticket and a trip to the airport. A plane ticket will be easier. I take a quick shower and then fire up my laptop. The sooner I can escape Colorado, the better. I'll call a cab to take me to the airport. It'll cost a ton, but I have a credit card.

I've stopped caring, anyway.

I'll go home. Finish school. Get my degree. Get a job.

I'll go through life the way I always thought I would.

Except now it's no longer enough.

I inhale deeply. Doesn't matter. It is what it is. The words I said to Jade yesterday.

It is what it is.

The travel site opens on my computer, I plug in my destination, and hit search.

I jerk when someone knocks on the door.

Housekeeping, most likely. "I'm still here. Please come back later," I yell.

The knock comes again. Then again, much louder this time. My God, the maid here must be a linebacker.

I get up and pull the door open. "I said I'm st—"

My heart thumps wildly.

Dale.

He stands on the other side of the door, looking worse than I do, if that's even possible. His gorgeous green eyes are bloodshot, and his hair… Well, the only time I've seen it worse was after the fire.

"Ashley…"

Oh, God. That voice. That Syrah-coated voice that makes me tremble.

Why? Why has he come here to torment me?

"Why are you here?" I ask in a clipped voice.

His gaze drops to my left hand. "You're still wearing them."

My wedding band and engagement ring. I couldn't bear to take them off. Now I wish I had… until I notice he's still wearing his band as well.

He strides inside the small room then, owning it as usual. He owns every room he walks into. That's just who he is. Dale—so strong and masculine and brilliant and full of vigor—and he's the only one who can't see it.

He holds a small paperback and a bottle of wine. Château

Lascombes. His favorite. He opens the book. "Read this."
"What for?"
"Please. Just read it."
I take it from him with a huff.

Two roads diverged in a yellow wood,
And sorry I could not travel both
And be one traveler, long I stood
And looked down one as far as I could
To where it bent in the undergrowth;

Then took the other, as just as fair,
And having perhaps the better claim,
Because it was grassy and wanted wear;
Though as for that the passing there
Had worn them really about the same,

And both that morning equally lay
In leaves no step had trodden black.
Oh, I kept the first for another day!
Yet knowing how way leads on to way,
I doubted if I should ever come back.

I shall be telling this with a sigh
Somewhere ages and ages hence:
Two roads diverged in a wood, and I—
I took the one less traveled by,
And that has made all the difference.

"Robert Frost," I say.
"Yes."
"I've read it before."
"Does it speak to you?" he asks.

I close the book and hand it back to him. "Robert Frost wrote beautiful stuff. It speaks to everyone. What is this about? Because if you're here to break my heart again—"

"No, Ashley." He reaches toward me, his hand trembling, as if he wants to touch me but fears my reaction. As well he should. "I'm here to tell you the truth. I'm here to beg your forgiveness. I'm here to share my favorite Bordeaux with you. Only you. I'm here to... I'm here to take a road I didn't think I could ever take."

He opens the bottle of wine, grabs two glasses from the table in the room, pours, and hands one to me. I take a sip. It's delicious, but that's all I can contemplate, because Dale begins to speak.

He speaks earnestly.

And I listen.

I listen to the man I love tell me his innermost secrets. I watch him cry. His red-wine voice morphs into silver sadness.

He lets go. He opens up. He tells me things he thinks will turn me away from him forever.

Instead, I turn toward him, my heart breaking for the lost little boy inside.

And I hold him.

EPILOGUE

Dale

Freed.

Finally.

Ashley is home, and we're going to make this work. Yes, it will take work. My past won't disappear. Not ever. Like Dad said, I have to live with it. That's not part of the choice. The choice is how I live with it—which road I choose to take.

I'm seeing Aunt Mel again to help sort everything out. The big question is whether I need to tell Donny what happened those last few days of our captivity. I waver on that. I want to tell him, to be honest with him, but he's happy. I don't want to destroy that.

Ashley made arrangements to finish her coursework online. By May, she'll be a true doctor of wine! Where she goes from there is up to her. She has my full support, whether she wants to use her knowledge at the Steel Winery or live her dream to become a sommelier at a fine restaurant in Grand Junction.

Willow is moving to Colorado. She'll be here by Thanksgiving for the big party for Uncle Ryan and Aunt Ruby. She'll stay with us until she finds a place of her own. Ashley has already found a place in town for her to open a salon. She's starting over in a new place, and Ashley couldn't be happier.

And Donny...

Donny's moving back home.

He accepted Mom's offer to become the assistant city attorney for Snow Creek. Yes, my little brother gave up a partnership track at a top Denver firm to come home. I can't help wondering if Callie Pike had anything to do with that decision. They were cozy the night of the reception.

The old-vine Syrah has finished fermenting. Now the aging begins. It's going to be an amazing vintage, and even though it should have been twice the amount, I'm living with it and my part in the tragedy. There's no way to know if my campfire truly started the fire. I've accepted that it most likely didn't, as I'm always very careful, and I remember being extra careful both mornings.

But I'll never know for sure, and I have to accept that.

Part of being free means I have to accept those things in my life that I can't change. It's not easy, but it's doable.

I'm doing it.

I'm at my office now, answering a few emails before I head to the winery to check on the Syrah and other wines, when my phone dings with a text.

Brendan Murphy?

Why is he texting me?

Dale, we need to talk. Important. Tonight at my place. Bring Donny.

AUTHOR'S NOTE

"The Road Not Taken" by Robert Frost
is in the public domain.

CONTINUE THE STEEL BROTHERS SAGA
WITH BOOK NINETEEN

MESSAGE FROM HELEN HARDT

Dear Reader,

Thank you for reading *Freed*. If you want to find out about my current backlist and future releases, please like my Facebook page and join my mailing list. I often do giveaways. If you're a fan and would like to join my street team to help spread the word about my books, please see the web addresses below. I regularly do awesome giveaways for my street team members.

If you enjoyed the story, please take the time to leave a review on a site like Amazon or Goodreads. I welcome all feedback. I wish you all the best!

Helen

Facebook
Facebook.com/HelenHardt

Newsletter
HelenHardt.com/SignUp

Street Team
Facebook.com/Groups/HardtAndSoul

ALSO BY HELEN HARDT

The Steel Brothers Saga:
Craving
Obsession
Possession
Melt
Burn
Surrender
Shattered
Twisted
Unraveled
Breathless
Ravenous
Insatiable
Fate
Legacy
Descent
Awakened
Cherished
Freed
Spark
Flame
Blaze

Blood Bond Saga:
Unchained
Unhinged
Undaunted
Unmasked
Undefeated

Misadventures Series:
Misadventures with a Rock Star
Misadventures of a Good Wife (with Meredith Wild)

The Temptation Saga:
Tempting Dusty
Teasing Annie
Taking Catie
Taming Angelina
Treasuring Amber
Trusting Sydney
Tantalizing Maria

The Sex and the Season Series:
Lily and the Duke
Rose in Bloom
Lady Alexandra's Lover
Sophie's Voice

Daughters of the Prairie:
The Outlaw's Angel
Lessons of the Heart
Song of the Raven

Cougar Chronicles:
The Cowboy and the Cougar
Calendar Boy

Anthologies Collection:
Destination Desire
Her Two Lovers

ACKNOWLEDGMENTS

This was another tough one to write. Whenever I put my characters through the wringer, I feel everything with them. Both Dale and Ashley went through a lot in *Freed*, but they managed to find happiness in the end. I hope you enjoyed reading about their journey.

Huge thanks to the always brilliant team at Waterhouse Press: Jennifer Becker, Audrey Bobak, Haley Boudreaux, Keli Jo Chen, Yvonne Ellis, Jesse Kench, Robyn Lee, Jon Mac, Amber Maxwell, Dave McInerney, Michele Hamner Moore, Chrissie Saunders, Scott Saunders, Kurt Vachon, and Meredith Wild.

Thanks also to the women and men of Hardt and Soul. Your endless and unwavering support keeps me going.

To my family and friends, thank you for your encouragement. Special shout out to Dean—aka Mr. Hardt—and our amazing sons, Eric and Grant.

Thank you most of all to my readers. Without you, none of this would be possible.

To all of you who feared the Steel Brothers Saga was ending with *Freed*...it isn't! *Spark* is next up. Who will it be about? Wait and see...

ABOUT THE AUTHOR

#1 *New York Times*, #1 *USA Today*, and #1 *Wall Street Journal* bestselling author Helen Hardt's passion for the written word began with the books her mother read to her at bedtime. She wrote her first story at age six and hasn't stopped since. In addition to being an award-winning author of romantic fiction, she's a mother, an attorney, a black belt in Taekwondo, a grammar geek, an appreciator of fine red wine, and a lover of Ben and Jerry's ice cream. She writes from her home in Colorado, where she lives with her family. Helen loves to hear from readers.

Visit her at HelenHardt.com